Project Return Fire

by Antony Davies & Joe Dinicola

ISBN: 151717371X
ISBN-13: 978-1517173715

Novels By Antony Davies
writing as "A. D. Davies"

Adam Park Thrillers:
The Dead and the Missing

Alicia Friend Investigations:
His First His Second
In Black In White

Standalone:
Three Years Dead
Return Fire – *co-authored with Joe Dinicola*
Rite of Justice

For Joe's Pop Pop and Antony's Granddad, both of whom fought for their countries to secure the freedoms we enjoy today.

Prologue

General Santarelli's driver wrenched the wheel to the right and yanked the handbrake, fishtailing the tiny Soviet box car into a controlled skid, dropped the handle and accelerated into the boulevard. Traffic was heavy and the Kremlin gleamed in the middle distance, its light shining on the street, slick with rain, yet their speed increased. The driver made tiny adjustments, weaving in and out of chugging cars, vans spewing black smoke, and even a limo. The wing mirror on the general's side shattered in a hail of noise and plastic. He hoped the limo came off worse.

He had always hated Moscow. It reminded him of Seattle in the springtime. Only colder. And on many nights, like this one, a damned sight more dangerous.

'Sir,' the driver said. 'Can I ask now why I was pulled from deep cover?'

The general turned his head and body, knowing his appearance gave folks the willies when they first met him—his broad shoulders, his scarred cheek, his hard eyes. He said, 'Keep driving.'

The driver looked at him. 'Sir, it's just that … I took over a year to establish that identity—'

'Son, you want a good lesson for your career prospects? Then remember this: when a general speaks, you listen. Clear?'

'Clear, sir.'

'Now...' He calmly pointed out the windshield.

A wall of brake lights greeted them. No way through. At the same speed, the driver jumped the curb, smashing the undercarriage on the sidewalk in a shower of sparks. If anything important fell off this rust-bucket, the general would have to run. He hated running more than he hated Seattle in the spring. He would make the driver run too, even though the former-undercover agent was only really needed to corroborate the evidence the general obtained. Santarelli's word would be good enough to hit pause on World War Three.

Still, as the Muscovites leapt out of the way and the horn blared (well, *peeped* enthusiastically), he couldn't help but wonder if they would make it in time.

And he was right to wonder. Almost a thousand miles from Moscow, in a chamber deep below the Arctic tundra, two men in Soviet military uniforms read a printed message. Up top, both knew the land blew sub-zero winds against an insulated silo. Both knew what the contents of that silo could do to the world. And both knew they were the final stage of a process that began with a coded order, verified in triplicate, then relayed to the computer. In turn, this state-of-the-art equipment sent a signal to the printer in their panel, and as lights flashed, its carriage whirred and fired ink onto paper, informing the pair that they were about to kill a million or more people.

They took a second or two to absorb what they were being asked to do. But only a second.

Then they moved, repeating sequences rehearsed a hundred times before, switching between controls, as slick and precise as chefs in any upscale Manhattan restaurant. Finally, they came to a halt, one hand each on a key, the insertion points too far for even the largest lone man to reach. They nodded to one another in time.

3...

2...

1...

And, in unison, both turned their keys.

Immediately, enormous clanks and creaks sounded throughout the base, as the gears and hinges on the great silo above prepared to open, and heat up the Cold War to boiling point.

Five hundred yards from the Kremlin, a mailbox exploded as a tiny white Yugo smashed through it. Vehicles at the intersection blared their horns and hammered their brakes, while the little car weaved through the melee.

Inside, General Santarelli pried his fingers from the dashboard and pretended he didn't notice the smirk on his driver's face.

He said, 'Down the side.'

'You don't want to go in the front?'

'No. The way we're going, they'll blow us to pieces before we get within shouting distance. I need to show them I know their secrets.'

'To threaten them?'

'To prove I'm their friend.'

The driver followed the general's directions, up a narrow one-way street the wrong way, more wing mirrors sacrificed to their greater cause. This close to the Kremlin, though, security was still tight, and when they veered into the final road skirting the edge of the Soviet Union's most famous building, they would go no further.

Soldiers patrolled the wall, despite there being no obvious way in, and when the general's hurried transport sped toward them, guns came up, bolts racked, but still the car kept going. The scale of the military presence was only to be expected, of course. You don't leave anything to chance when your leader is meeting with the President of the United States.

The first of three Soviet troops opened fire, the bullet spider webbing the windshield high on the driver's side.

'Stop,' the general said.

The driver pressed his foot to the brake and the car screeched to a halt.

General Santarelli opened his door and hung his empty hands outside. Then he stepped out, the guards yelling at him to stay where he was, to get on the ground, but when he stood fully, faced the captain coming towards him with a sidearm drawn, the soldiers emitted an audible collective breath.

The willies.

While the driver copied him move for move, the general spoke loudly in Russian. 'You know who I am?'

The captain said, 'I think so, yes.'

'And I know that right in that recess is a door that accesses the old catacombs. Those lead to several places, not least the room in which President Reagan is meeting with Mr. Gorbachev.'

'How...?'

'Because I reviewed the security for this visit. I have evidence that separatists have faked the launch sequence of a nuclear missile, and—'

The captain held his gun more firmly. 'I cannot let you in.'

'You know me,' the general said. 'You have seen me here, with your KGB generals. I am who I say I am.'

'But—'

'Damn it, Captain! I need to speak with Mr. Gorbachev now!'

History would record what happened next as a routine training exercise. The official account would never be anything more than a footnote in a normal day in the Soviet military. But a handful of people would always know. The two men who launched the missile would remember that, as they watched the sun-bright tail of the most lethal payload ever created, they placed phone calls to their wives and told them to flee to the countryside, to take their children as far from cities and military bases as they could get. They had to leave now, before the roads choked to a standstill with others like them.

The abort order came midway through one of those calls.

Both men beamed widely and fumbled their keys, their hands shaking even more than when they launched. The keys went in. Their countdown was faster this time, and when the authorization clicked together, both reached for the button at once. They pressed it, one hand over the other, and although they didn't hear the crack and boom of the missile's body breaking up mid-flight, they saw the blip fade from their radar.

After, they sat in their chairs, called their wives again, and told them to stand down. Everything was going to be okay. The world was not ending after all.

1

The University of Oxford, United Kingdom, 2015

The audience in the Grand Hall applauded. A full house, as usual. On stage, General Anthony Santarelli took a bow. A shallow bow. He wasn't really able to bend over properly these days. Pushing ninety, that sort of maneuver was never easy. He waved his book, *Inventing the Right Stuff,* but from the wings, stage-right, Jonathan Santarelli couldn't understand the point of releasing it now. The old coot was way beyond retirement and way wealthier than any human being needed to be, but he clung to past glories as most people clutch their last pennies of the month.

Adjusting the Sig-Sauer P226 under his suit jacket, Jonathan absently said, '*I need to speak with Mr. Gorbachev now. Gimme a break.*'

Over the applause, Chase's voice came through the subvocal earpiece. 'You didn't like the speech, Santa?'

Santa. One of the more annoying bequeathments from his grandfather. Elite units in the Army were too fond of these nicknames, or 'handles' as they were known. *Santa* was the general's handle throughout his career, only dropping it when he reached officer class, but when Jonathan Santarelli enlisted and snatched the opportunity to join the US Rangers' top squad, well, it came back. And haunted him for the past three years. Taking the name of a soldier as decorated as Anthony Sr. would always draw comparisons. Even though

Jonathan was only twenty-four, he was still expected to be some sort of commander, a natural leader, like ... well, like the man spilling bullshit all over the stage.

'It was well-presented,' Santa told Chase. 'But you didn't have to listen to it change over the years.'

'No? This story changed?'

'The sparks on the undercarriage is new. He added the mailbox last Christmas.'

'Well, shit, I liked this one. Sounds kick-ass.'

The general commenced another anecdote from this 'sensational' autobiography, another secret operation declassified thanks to the wonders of time passing. This snippet of history concerned his first meeting with a young whippersnapper by the name of Neil Armstrong.

Santa caught Chase's eye from across the stage on the opposite wing, and mimed blowing his own brains out.

'Give the old man a break,' Chase said. 'He can add what he likes. He's a motherfuckin' hero.'

The 'motherfuckin' hero' finished his speech to the usual sycophantic applause and, despite his inability to bow without creaking, he exited stage-right with rock-star-style waving and a skip in his step that made Santa hope he inherited the old man's genes, if nothing else. Because that was the thing that caused Santa to reconsider his military career most often—the expectation that came with it. Perhaps his dad got it right in shunning the general's profession, a life that shunted him from one temporary home to the next. In that respect, he reminded Santa on a regular basis that he was lucky to have grown up in a single, very nice, house, attended one school, and kept all his friends throughout his academic career. He suspected it was partly his dad's repetitive demands for gratitude that helped sell the Army to him.

Of his grandpa's great skills, he had exactly two areas of true expertise: first, he was a master of military planning, of both the physical logistics in battle and the political implications of such actions, earning him the ear of the top brass and at least three presidents; second, he could play the markets like a banjo. While Santa's dad delved into this latter world, Santa opted for the former. Sitting on your ass making more cash than you'll ever need made Santa's gut ache, while travelling the world *kicking* ass and helping the needy lightened his step and clenched his fist in pride. Okay, it was the kicking of asses and venturing beyond his mom and dad's suburban Utopia that first appealed to Santa when he enrolled at eighteen, but now, eight years into his career, combat was wearing on him. If he never fired another shot in anger he would not object. The sooner he could get out of here and take what he'd learned into the private and charitable sector, the happier he'd be. For more than one reason.

Chase said, 'So come on, man, you don't think this shit happened?'

'I don't know,' Santa said. 'If someone else would come forward and confirm his version of events. The driver, maybe. Anyone.' He sighed. 'I don't care if he exaggerates, just knowing a bit of it is true...'

The general's voice: 'Hey, Jonnie, how'd I do?'

Santa stood face-to-face with the general.

A squirrelly publicist appeared from under General Santarelli's elbow and said, 'That was great. You looked ... great out there.'

Santa said, 'Ah, who cares?'

'Pardon?' The general tilted his head. 'What did you say?'

Santa indicated his ear.

Anthony Sr. dismissed his publicist with a flick of his hand and said, 'It's okay, Jonnie. Consider yourself on a break. Speak freely. What's the problem?'

Santa removed the sub-vocal mic from his ear, cutting him off from his team. He said, 'Fine, Grandpa. Every time you tell these stories, they get more sensational, more wild. More ... cinematic. Sparks now?'

General Santarelli smiled and bowed his head toward his shoes before returning to Santa. 'So I add a little ... flavor now and again. Shoot me.'

'Yeah.'

The old man pulled his suit tight and adjusted his stance so he could hold himself as tall as his slight hunch would allow. 'Anything else before you're back on duty?'

'No, sir,' Santa said. 'Except ... happy birthday, Grandpa.'

Santa found himself drawn into an embrace, a strength he always found impressive in a man the general's age and, as usual, the hug broke with a firm slap on the back. The general gave a brief laugh, then rejoined his publicist to talk about the next stop on his tour—a shop called Waterstones in Birmingham, which Santa understood to be a chain much like Barnes and Noble back home.

He re-inserted the sub-vocal unit in his ear canal and said, 'Package is heading for transport.'

'No problemo,' came the soft southern voice of Thompson. 'Cakewalk.'

2

On the edge of Switzerland, close to the French border, the Juras Mountain range lies silent under a full moon, the whistle of wind the only sound. In a valley untouched in decades, an alpine forest spreads to where rock grows sheer from the ground, a snow-dusted face towering over the trees, and odd clusters of vegetation amongst the evergreen shrubs. Deer roam freely here, rabbits creating clouds of white as they kick up the powder in rituals involving mating or perhaps territorial disputes.

But early this evening, a low rumble breaks through the peace. Rabbits scuttle for cover, and deer hold stock still until the initial shaking eases, then they bolt uphill as fast as they can, some primitive hangover in the genes urging them that seeking the high ground means a greater chance of survival.

Then the whole area shudders.

Trees dance.

The mountain itself shakes.

Boulders plummet from above, slamming into rocks at its base. As they hit, many break into smaller chunks, bouncing and crashing into the forest, felling trees, gouging bushes from the frozen soil.

As suddenly as it started, the quake ceases. The land's shimmering side to side steadies, and the trees themselves seem to breathe a sigh of relief.

And yet, in the sheer grey wall, beyond a smashed section of boulder that has lain untouched for almost a century, a rusty line extends from the ground, upwards for seven feet, and splits left at the sort of right-angle not found anywhere in nature; *the frame of a door.*

A metal door. A metal door under enormous stress from the undulating plates pushing from below against solid mass of rock above.

Then the frame itself creaks and groans, until ... it cracks open.

A hiss sounds, decades-old air escaping. And, perhaps, something else too.

High above this mountain, the untouched landscape appears pure. Hundreds of miles away, the lights of civilization blink on and off, as the Europeans get on with their lives. Many of them will have felt this quake, minor though it was. No leveled cities, no tsunamis.

Still, no matter how minor, some nations take an interest in all natural phenomena. Those nations put satellites into orbit, and those satellites, like the one christened 'Eagle Eye 3' by those who launched her, they observe those regions with more than one lens.

Eagle Eye 3, for example, possesses the sort of lens that detects shifts in the earth, and another that searches for stricken vehicles and crumbled buildings, just in case humans find themselves in need of immediate assistance. It also utilizes a camera watching for certain frequencies and for unusual spectral anomalies. And when one of these spectral anomalies blinks to life in a place where no spectral anomaly has occurred before, Eagle Eye 3 alerts someone.

Sembach US Military Base, Germany

Within Sembach's listening station, the graveyard shift was just commencing when the signal from Eagle Eye 3 flashed red on the International Alert Monitor. Because this shift was actually the least desirable on base, anything that broke the monotony of observing Russia test her neighbors' borders, but never do anything to necessitate US intervention, was welcomed with all six troops vying to investigate. Okay, so it would probably be a false alarm, but that didn't mean the opportunity to wake the colonel was something to sniff at.

The shift commander printed the readout and placed it in a folder along with the schematics of Eagle Eye 3 itself, so anyone analyzing it could see where the potential glitches may lie, plus a copy of the standard operating procedures in the event such alerts proved correct.

The folder slapped into the hand of the ensign who won the impromptu rock-paper-scissor tournament, and he spent five minutes in the bathroom sharpening his look and slicking down his hair. Then he slipped the reports under his arm and marched toward Colonel Johnson's living quarters.

However, Col. Johnson himself met the ensign on the edge of Runway 2, the shift commander having phoned ahead, depriving the ensign of a lengthy chewing out, and therefore speeding his return to the dead zone of international monitoring. He placed the folder in Johnson's hand and waited while the sixty-year-old veteran read it. He flipped to the Eagle Eye 3 section but spent less than thirty seconds on the detail.

He handed the paperwork back and fished a cellphone from inside his jacket, found the number he needed, and held it to his ear.

He said, 'Who do we have in Europe for critical incident recon?' He listened to a reply. 'No, sir, we need to investigate ASAP. Code Z.'

3

The two Humvees cut through the English countryside at under thirty miles per hour. These lanes were designed for horse-and-cart, and Santa didn't like the closed-in nature of those dry stone walls, the tight turns making for excellent ambush points. He'd have preferred a helicopter to recon ahead, but the general insisted he remain low key. He even screwed up his nose at the Humvees, but at least they were armored.

The two vehicles pulled in through General Santarelli's front gate and crunched up a driveway to the sort of house more akin to the meeting of Mr. D'Arcy and Jane Austin, a sentiment Santa said out loud without meaning to.

In back with Chase, the general said, 'Jane Austin is the author. Mr. D'Arcy is one of the characters. It's unlikely they ever met.'

Santa checked in with Thompson, Mac, and Dang who'd driven on ahead. 'We clear?'

'Clear,' came Thompson's reply.

Up the thousand-yard driveway, Santa parked outside the main entrance to the ten-bedroom house. Thompson was already waiting, while the youngest member of the crew, a Cuban-American kid they called 'Dang,' hopped out and held his submachine gun in the air like he was posing for a movie still. Santa occasionally had trouble remembering

Dang's real name—a common problem when groups like Alpha Team used handles more often than not. 'Dang' came from the kid's surname, which was, literally, 'Danger,' but no one knew if he'd altered it legally or if was born with it.

Dang said, 'Clear, sir.'

Without Santa's order, the general stepped out, Chase spilling after him.

'Wait there,' Santa said. 'I haven't—'

The old man held up his wrist, checking his watch. 'And … three … two … one … you're all off the clock. Feel free to help yourselves to my beer.'

All but Santa managed to smile. He said, 'Dang, clear the house.'

'All of it?' Dang said.

'You and Mac. Where is he?'

The far-side Humvee door opened and the hulking figure of Jim 'Mac' McLaughlin heaved himself out. The man had muscles like basketballs, but moved smoothly.

He said, 'Come on, Santa, the general said we're off the clock.'

'Yeah,' Dang said. 'The place is under surveillance twenty-four-seven.'

'Behave,' Santa said. 'Or you'll be pulling double-duty instead of heading to that geek-fest on Saturday.'

Dang forced the military mien back into his walk and headed for the front door, muttering, 'Trek's mainstream now, you know. Thanks to JJ.'

He and Mac entered using the keys issued to all members of the team, and Santa pressed his finger to his ear, an unnecessary gesture, but since the general now stood next to him, he hoped it might deflect the need for conversation.

The older man said, 'Still think you're not a leader? Not

many folks countermand a general's order to relax and open some cold ones.'

Santa lowered his arm. 'Not many people have a grandfather like you. With your reputation.'

'You think that's why I'm pushing you? Because it isn't. When I was your age——'

'I'm not *you*, though. No matter how much people in this Army want me to be.' Santa pressed his lips together to prevent saying any more. He was still addressing a four-star general. Then he figured, *fuck it*, and said, '*I'll* be the one who decides if I stay on or pension out. When I'm your age, I'll probably be on a beach somewhere a damned sight hotter than Emily Brontë's country.'

'Emily Brontë is further north. Everywhere's warmer than the north of England.'

'Even Moscow?'

Before the general could reply, Dang emerged from the house in a hurry.

Santa said, 'Report.'

'Intruders,' Dang said.

Chase and Thompson dropped into firing crouches, while Santa gripped the general's arm and ushered him to the Humvee.

The house door opened and Mac stepped out carrying a princess-pretty girl in a cute-as-apple-pie dress. She waved frantically. 'Daddy!'

Santa said, 'Lily?'

Mac set her down and as Thompson and Chase reset their guns to safe-mode, the little girl ran across the drive, arrowing straight for Santa. Dang ran alongside her, simulating a race of sorts, but she gave him a happy shove and the soldier performed a somersault to the side, pretending to fall, which drew laughter but did not slow her down. Seven years old, and as beautiful as the day he first laid eyes on her, Santa scooped his daughter into his arms and gave her a much-practiced daddy-cuddle.

He said, 'What are you *doing* here?'

'That would be me.'

Another 'intruder' sauntered over. A career military man, his hair speckled a wise grey, Sergeant-Major Vince Jacobs shook hands with Santa. Although convention was to not salute an officer out of uniform, Santa did so anyway, which Jacobs returned and said, 'At ease. And don't worry, I swept the house.'

Lily beamed, released Santa from her cuddle. 'Greatpa wanted to surprise you.'

'And he did,' Santa said. He faced his grandfather, speechless.

The general said, 'Her mom's headed to a conference with Colin, so I flew her in.'

'Who's Colin?'

'Some civvie,' Lily said.

As the team chuckled, Santa said, 'Right.'

Jacobs approached General Santarelli. 'Sir. Mission accomplished.'

The general grinned, then more hand-shaking commenced. Two old pals, a friendship Santa often wished wasn't so close. Several times now, Jacobs deferred to him, when Thompson was technically Alpha Team's second in command, and although Thompson was too easy-going to make a thing of it, especially questioning the sergeant-major, Santa could tell it grated on him.

Chase lifted Lily from Santa and tickled her until she shrieked. He said, 'Hey, how's my princess? How's my princess?'

Jacobs' phone rang and he excused himself, still smiling as

he went. Santa wasn't sure who to pay attention to—his commanding officer or his little girl on the dirty floor in what was clearly a new party-dress.

'Uncle Mac!' she shouted. 'Help me!'

Mac aimed his thumb and forefinger at Chase like a gun. 'Let her go, scumbag.'

Chase raised his arms, and Lily jumped up and wrapped her legs around Mac's thigh and tickled him.

She said, 'Got you! It was all a trick.'

While Mac feigned fits of laughter, Santa found Thompson beside him, hands in his pockets.

The south-Georgian said, 'So how'd you like the nepotism of rank?'

'Like you minded sitting this one out. Anyway, I'm officially handing command of the unit back to you.' He gave a shallow bow at the end.

'You want it for another cakewalk like this, you got it.'

Lily stood triumphant over the defeated Mac, a foot on his chest and fists in the air. Jacobs stepped back in amongst them, a hand on Lily's head.

He said, 'Y'know, I was happy to extend my vacation and bring this little angel over, see how you guys were gettin' on babysittin' the general. First class, too. Real nice.'

Mac sat up, attention on the sergeant-major. All heads bowed, predicting what came next.

He said, 'Thing is, vacation's over. We got a code Z. Suit up.'

Within minutes, the team hustled inside and changed from their suits into combat-black, and reconvened by the Humvees to speed to the nearest airbase. Lily still wore her dress and Santa hugged her goodbye, only moments after hugging her 'hello.'

He said, 'You're gonna stay with Greatpa tonight. He'll look after you 'til I get back in the morning. Okay?'

'Like a sleepover?'

'Just like a sleepover.'

General Santarelli put his arm around her. 'And we'll have my birthday party tomorrow instead.'

Santa forced a smile. 'I'll even put on a suit, just like Greatpa's. Okay?'

Chase hung out the Humvee as the engine roared to life. 'Hey, Santa, hurry the fuck up.'

Lily said, 'That's a bad word.'

'It is,' Santa said. 'I'll put Uncle Chase on the naughty step when we get on the plane.'

He kissed her again on the forehead, but the general stopped him getting in the vehicle.

Out of Lily's earshot, he said, 'Jonathan...' but he almost choked on the word.

Strange. 'Going to get emotional on me, Grandpa?'

'I ever tell you how you got your name?'

'About a thousand times.'

'Oh, right. Then ... I know it's my birthday, but I was going to give you this later.' He handed Santa a combat knife in a ceremonial scabbard. 'It has special meaning to me.'

Santa *shink*ed out the blade. Still shiny, like new. He'd seen the weapon numerous times when growing up, warned never to touch it as his grandpa kept it razor sharp, even after he retired. It meant a lot to him, and Santa swallowed a lump in his throat, worried about what it might mean that he was giving it away at this precise time. He would address that in the morning. For now, he said, 'Thanks, Grandpa.'

The pair hugged in that masculine way, though Santa held him a moment longer than he normally would have. If the old general noticed, he didn't let on, just waved Santa on board, and held Lily's hand, as Alpha Team drove away in a cloud of dust.

4

Over the Juras Mountains, Switzerland

The AH-60 Black Hawk hurtled low over an alpine forest, a silhouette against the snow-covered mountain range. The same helo Alpha Team now occupied resembled an insect on Santa's satellite feed displayed on the iNav, a six-inch touchscreen device the Rangers were testing for black-ops. The brass called it a 'tactical partnering tool,' which ran on sat-phone technology rather than 4G, so as long as there was an American satellite in orbit on this side of the planet, it would never lose its signal. In live mode, it made noises and lit up; when in the field, it was silent, and the interface somehow remained clear, but utilized live-ink on a beige background to eliminate glow. Santa tried not to rely on it too much, but it was hard not to with razor-sharp imagery like the topography now feeding in.

'Recon Team Alpha, acknowledge,' Colonel Johnson said in their ears. He commanded from recon control on Sembach, monitoring their every move.

'Alpha Team online, sir,' Jacobs replied.

Watching their progress in live time helped Santa focus on the mission ahead. They were still blind on the objective, the rush to physically get them here paramount.

Lily. That's who Santa thought about all the way out to Germany, then as they scrambled to the Black Hawk, and launched into the air. At one point, Chase even pushed Santa's bottom lip back into his mouth and told him to cheer the fuck up. He saw little enough of his daughter as it was without being wrenched away from her in a foreign country.

The result of a one-night stand on Thompson's stag night to Vegas, Lily's mom was a lawyer for an entertainment firm, six years older than the newbie recruit Santa was at the time, and Santa only learned about Lily's existence thanks to her mom's badgering of the DoJ and one high-ranking Army officer out of New York. She only ever knew him as Santa, which is hard enough to pick up women with, but imagine entering the name of your newborn's father as 'Santa.' Yeah, but she did. From the moment she confirmed the pregnancy, she did not stop trying to find him. He deserved to know, she said, no matter how 'classified' his real name was. She was financially-independent, and wouldn't force Santa to have anything to do with Lily, but she sensed he was a good person, and she was determined to give him the choice. All it took for Santa to make up his mind was a single photo, presented to him in the mess by the high-ranking officer with a curt, 'Recognize that? It's yours. Call the number on the back.'

Now Lily was embedded with her Greatpa—Great Grandfather—and Santa had no idea what they'd be up to. The general seemed to swing wildly between a cast-iron dedication to duty and all-out relaxation and pleasure. He would either be going over his Ling Mai tactical victory and explaining the subtleties of command, or teaching her Beethoven on the piano. Whichever, he'd feed her too much ice cream afterward, then ask his PA to help get her into bed. He spent more time with Lily than he ever did with Santa, but that was to be expected in a man for whom leadership, and duty, trumped all else. Perhaps something in Lily softened the general. Heck, the old man even *cried* when Santa introduced the pair. The first little girl born into the family in three generations.

Santa's arm pinged. Coordinates for the drop fed into his iNav.

All six team members were strapped in, headsets on, noise-dampened against the rotors and engine. All heard everything and all were wired in.

Through their headsets, Colonel Johnson said, 'Okay, listen up. Time to introduce your passengers.'

Like Alpha Team, the man and woman were kitted out in white coveralls over PS-930 Kevlar body armor, plus helmets, throat communicators, and shoulder-cams.

Johnson said, 'Swiss and US military agreed that Army Rangers are best-equipped to handle this. However, you will notice your comms expert, Barbara Hawkson from Swiss intelligence.'

The woman carried the same weapons as the men—a short-barreled SCAR-M with retractable stock, Sig-Sauer P226 sidearm—plus a non-US-issue knife on her hip and the backpack between her legs was larger than theirs.

Mac said, 'Don't worry, Miss. You're with the greatest military force on the planet. If it turns into a hot zone the US of A'll take care a' ya.'

'I am not a kitten,' Hawks said, her English fluent, only slightly tinged with German. 'I do not require American babysitters.'

Chase smirked, and Hawks caught it. She was about to react, but Johnson went on.

'You also got yourselves a real-life physicist from CERN.'

The man was skinny, the clothes and flak-jacket a size too big, and he appeared to be unarmed, unless he was carrying something impressive in his fanny pack. He gave a little wave and in a British accent said, 'Hello. I'm Doctor Lear. Nicolas.

No, Nick. Call me Nick.' He plonked a helmet on his head, squashing his floppy well-quaffed hair. 'How cool is this?'

The pilot called back to them, '*Five minutes 'til ropes-down.*'

Jacobs stood, one hand steadying him against the turbulence, the other holding a tablet computer that brought to mind an Apple iPad, but was actually bespoke military equipment showing the satellite feed of the target area: alpine forest, mountains, snow.

He said, 'Forty square miles of nothing. Zero population. Sounds like standard recon, but I'm guessing that ain't the case.'

'Dr. Lear,' Colonel Johnson said. 'The floor is yours.'

'Great, thanks!' Dr. Lear stood to address the team, bracing himself in a mimicry of Jacobs' position. He wobbled a lot more and his helmet fell off. 'Umm ... Right, well, earlier today, we detected an earthquake, followed by a short radiation burst. It dispersed quickly, so we're sure it will be safe. But we are unable to tell exactly what it is without me ... heh, zooming-in with you fellows ... in case there's a ... bomb. Which I hope there isn't. Take these.' From his fanny pack, he removed a handful of what looked like silver cigar tubes with a button on top, and distributed them whilst gripping a strap on the roof. He said, 'Great little things. Designed them myself. I call them rad-pens. Pen. Radiation. Right? You see?'

'Whoa,' Chase said. 'Radi-fuckin'-ation?'

'Less chat,' Johnson said. 'More ears.'

'Thank you, Colonel.' Dr. Lear twisted his rad-pen. It beeped slowly. 'Like a really cool update of a Geiger counter. The more radiation, the faster it beeps. The light on top flashes if things become intolerable.'

'Intolerable?' Santa said. 'What happens then?'

Dr. Lear switched the pen the other way and it fell silent. 'Well, we run.'

The pilot called, *'Two minutes!'*

Jacobs heaved open the side door, filling the interior with wind, a thundering noise drowning out even their headsets. The team checked their equipment—night-vis goggles, iNav touch-screens on their forearms, mags, straps, bolts.

Thompson checked his precious weapon, an M2010 Enhanced Sniper Rifle which could have been mistaken for a regular rifle's skeleton, such was its pared-down appearance. He said, 'Whatever we meet down there, it'll be nice to give Delilah a night out.' He long-ago found space to etch 'Delilah' on the folding stock, but never revealed its significance. Mac once suggested it was his childhood dog, but even he couldn't be sure.

As Dang checked his own kit, he once again expressed his approval at losing the Heckler & Koch MP5s they'd been equipped with in the UK. Like the rest of the team he far preferred the new SCAR submachine guns they field-tested and passed for regular use. The MP5s were fine weapons, no doubt, and less obtrusive for civilian ops like the one that protected General Santarelli, but now they were heading into what could be a combat situation, the SCAR—like a compact, chunkier M-16—was the only choice for the discerning special forces operative. A year ago it would have been a SCAR-H, a 7.62mm beauty whose recoil was more akin to a gentle nudge, but the new 9mm SCAR-M was basically a deadly massage.

Hawks followed suit, unzipping her pack to reveal the main comms unit that would operate the sub-vocal network once they were on the ground, and keep orienting them so they would know where to meet the chopper afterward. Although they could usually rely on satellites to bounce their chat to each other, a local backup was useful, especially if they ended up underground, or penned in by a valley. Plus, it could boost the signal for exfil when the regular comms weren't sufficient.

'Hey,' Chase said to her. 'How'd those little knives work out for you in all your wars?'

Santa slapped the back of Chase's helmet. He said, 'Don't mind Chase, Miss Hawkson. He's our resident *ass*-hole.'

She continued checking her pack, a quick glance at Chase. 'First, sir, it's just Hawks. Not "Miss." I'm a sergeant. Second, ha ha, *Mister* Chase, that's very original. Small knives. Not heard that one before.'

She whipped out a large knife-grip. A combat blade *shniked* out; the biggest switchblade in the world.

Jacobs said, 'Okay, kids, recess is when I say, not before. Here.'

The sergeant-major tossed a black, brushed-metal oblong to Thompson. As soon as he caught it and checked it over, he grinned wide and bright. He said, 'Sir? This what I think it is?'

'Yup.'

Thompson met the inquisitive looks from his friends with, 'The new Hobbit scope.' It was about six inches long and three wide with two dials on the side. 'HD digital rifle sight. Four modes, all designed to allow us experts to do the job without a spotter. Oh yeah, this is a work of art, alright.'

'And,' Jacobs added, 'Alpha Team gets to field test it. Thompson, you keep your regular scopes close by in case it fritzes out, but battery should last forty-eight hours.'

'Oh, baby.' Thompson held the device close to his rifle. 'Hobbit, meet Delilah. Delilah, Hobbit.'

'Alpha Team,' Johnson said. 'This might be something. It might be nothing. But do not take any unnecessary risks. If I gotta break out the bunker-busters, it'd be best for all of us if you were clear.'

'No, sir,' Jacobs said. 'Siege warfare is *so* last century.'

'Helo will wait five clicks east. We got lucky with a couple-mile-long mountain pass that's fairly flat, and nice and wide. Exfil three minutes after you call. Clear?'

All nodded, mouths tight. No fear on display here, no sir.

Johnson came back on the air. 'One more thing. Santa, this is hopefully just a recon mission, so we're gonna hand the reins to you.'

Santa held back the real words he wanted to say, but appealed to Jacobs. 'Sir?'

Jacobs said, 'Colonel wants to see what you got.'

'The colonel does? Or my grandfather?'

'Request from a general—'

'*Retired*. Sir, you don't have to listen to him. Besides, Thompson's got seniority.'

'Nice and easy recon,' Thompson said. 'I'm cool with it.'

'Plus,' Jacobs said, 'it's, y'know, an *order*. And I guess you want your attention on your new toy.'

'Affirmative, sir.'

'And, Santa. You're in charge. No arguing.'

'Yes, sir,' Santa said, and repositioned the knife his grandpa gave him. Again, he wondered why the hell the general chose that moment, and whether he'd be returning to bad news after figuring out what they were facing here. Perhaps that was why he was pulling strings with the colonel, an obsessive wish to see his grandson fulfill his so-called potential. He was a very old man, after all.

But Santa wondered if his potential lay elsewhere. Like New York? Being a dad?

Vince Jacobs mentally assessed his team. They called the close protection detail a 'cakewalk' and referred to it as 'vacation,' but Jacobs saw to it that they were fully prepped. Indeed, the general insisted Santa lead, so while it was okay for Thompson, only one step above, to stand down temporarily, it would not have been appropriate for a sergeant major to play second fiddle. And, despite their sometimes-casual attitude, he was also fully versed in their training, and their commitment. The only person he had any concerns about was the one he just placed in charge, as nothing more than a favor to one of the biggest influences in Jacobs' career.

Not just his career. But his life.

How could Santa disrespect the general like that? His own grandfather. He was twenty-five now, not some teen with a chip on his shoulder, trying to prove his independence. Does even understand how important that man is to the world? Glasnost aside, Anthony Santarelli was like no other general he'd worked under. Not only has he had a hand in almost every important event since the turn of the century, he was well into his nineties and still kicking ass. Regardless of the tongue-in-cheek nature of his book's title, he really did 'invent the right stuff;' he put NASA on the map by crafting the first astronauts' training regimens, many of which were still in use today.

He rarely, if ever, voiced his true feelings about General Santarelli to Jonathan as the young soldier might deem it sycophantic or even dishonest, pushing the general's reputation to convince Santa of his own ability.

And he did have ability. Jacobs witnessed it plenty. The quick thinking, the decisions under fire, the sheer enjoyment he gleaned from a job well done ... Santa was the real deal. Just not quite yet.

But the general was rarely wrong. Vince Jacobs trusted in that, and he trusted the old man was not simply exerting his authority and former rank in order to further his grandson's career out of love. He trusted that the general was right about Santa, as did Colonel Johnson, and they performed this favor willingly, even though it risked diluting the importance of the mission.

That trust had to extend to the rest of Alpha Team, and see to it that they didn't let their bravado spill over into sloppy behavior. It never had to date, but there was a first time for everything.

Mac said, 'Nice and cozy, Doc?'

The biggest guy in the bird pulled the smallest one tight, strapped to his front as if prepping for a tandem skydive.

'I could do this myself,' Dr. Lear said, adjusting his groin. 'I went abseiling earlier this year in Scotland.'

'Right,' Thompson said. ''Cause this is just the same.'

'Good luck,' the colonel said, and everyone removed their headphones and switched to sub-vocal, the tiny plugs in their ear canals.

'Ten seconds!' the pilot called, and the chopper banked hard, each soldier instinctively righting themselves. The down-draft stabilized, and Santa pulled open the second hatch to a blast of freezing air that made Jacobs' mustache feel brittle on his skin. Chase and Dang positioned themselves on the edge of opposite doors, a thick line coiled by their feet. The pilot said, 'And rope.'

The pair tossed the coils outside, and with no further warnings, no countdown, they pushed off, rappelling to the ground in a single smooth movement. Thompson and Hawks followed, and then in their tandem clinch, Mac launched, and Dr. Lear's whoop of delight echoed through every earpiece.

Jacobs said, 'Not quite Scotland, huh?' When Santa didn't reply, just hooked himself to the chord, he asked, 'You okay?'

Santa gave him a firm nod. 'Why wouldn't I be?'

Jacobs pressed a tiny button in his ear, taking himself off the sub-vocal network. He suspected it wouldn't be the last time he had to do this today. Perhaps it was Lily's presence that was clouding Santa's attitude more darkly than usual. Whatever it was, he needed to come out of it. Jacobs said, 'Santa, you have to see what the general sees. What we all see.'

'Potential?'

'A lot of it?'

'Right.'

'And he's never wrong? In all the years you knew him, he never got one thing wrong?'

'Sure, a couple of times. But—'

'Then how do you know he's right about me? If I don't even want to go down the path he's pushing me, what sort of leader will it make me?'

'One like him,' Jacobs said firmly. 'Who does his duty, even when there's a personal cost.'

Santa screwed up his face in that pissed-teen way he did when he had no comeback against his grandfather.

Jacobs said, 'You said back there that I don't have to listen to him. But if there's one thing I've learned in my thirty some odd years in this United States Army, it's that when a general speaks, retired or not, you fucking listen.'

Santa bowed his head. Prepared to exit the Black Hawk.

Jacobs reconnected to the network, checked behind himself, and called, 'Clear!' and dropped out the side, leaving Santa to simmer on that for a second. Jacobs' boots crunched into the snow moments before Santa's. Their eyes locked for a moment, before the downdraft swirled the snow around them, and battered them all as the Black Hawk rose once again, dipped its nose, and sped out of sight.

The mission was now hot.

5

Sometimes, silence was worse than gunfire. Worse than shelling. To-night wasn't one of those times, though. Now, ten feet up a tree, above the rest of the team, he watched through the Hobbit scope's night-vision mode, panning from trees on the left, over rocks, to trees on the right. Nothing. The white vision of a stag grazed some distance away, ghostly in the greenscope. The battery indicated a full charge, so he would have no problems keeping this up for the duration.

He said, 'Nope, zero bad guys outside the target.'

Thompson was never one to be casual about any mission but, in this case, he was sure it was a crap-hunt. The false-positives from satellites came in a couple of times a month, and Alpha Team had scrambled on any number of them, usually convening in some dusty hole in the ground. Jihadi fuckwads found it easier to get hold of uranium than folks realized, but so far none of them had acquired anything harmful enough to create a weapon. They scavenged deplet-ed shells with traces of uranium, excited when their instruments confirmed it was *technically* radioactive, but then when they managed to gather even a tenth of what would be needed to kill a puppy, an Eagle Eye would detect such anomalies and send in the troops. Either Alpha Team, or some other lucky group.

But here, in the mountains on the French border? It was possible, he supposed. The French suffered their own prob-lems on the terrorism front, but from everything the iNav intel showed, this area had been inaccessible for decades. Roads and towns long-surrendered to nature, snow all summer long, and a *shit-ton* of snow throughout winter.

Still, no matter how unlikely, you gotta play it like there's a battalion of suicide bombers around each and every corner. He would give the scope the best workout he could, though, and report back how it performed, what could be improved, as well as the conditions in which it took place. They knew it excelled in the desert, but mountainous terrain was new for the Hobbit.

'On my six,' Santa said.

The kid checked his iNav, the concertina flap and E-ink concealing the glow from any look-outs. Doubtful the stags and rabbits would give a crap, though.

It was kinda' cute, in a way. Santa was fast-tracked from the regulars, partly thanks to his grandfather's standing, but he was also one the best soldiers Thompson had worked with. Although people often mistook Thompson's attitude for being 'laid back' or 'casual,' he was always watching, always listening, and the more he watched and listened to Santa, the more he wished the kid would go with it.

Below, the team convened behind Santa, who took point, crawling over boulders and rocks. He crested a rise, revealing what Thompson had already seen: across a five-hundred-yard plateau, the mountainside itself reached up to the stars, high above the forest. Set into the wall of grey, a steel door had cracked open at the frame in one corner.

Santa said, 'Hey, Hawks, you got a fiber optic in that Swiss Army bag?'

Whenever Jacobs gave over command to Santa, he always asked Thompson's opinion afterward, so he made a note that Santa hit the first female on the team with a pun that might be considered humor rather than strictly business. It was hard to tell on these missions because they were such cakewalks, like the close-protection detail on the general, but acting as a covert training sergeant suited Thompson nicely. That Santa felt like crap whenever he was ordered to take Thompson's place actually amused him. He was *assessing* Santa, not making way for him.

Through the scope, with Delilah's safety still on, Thompson observed Hawks equip Santa with a fiber-optic cable attached to a camera small enough to fit down someone's throat. She fiddled inside her pack, and the camera's image synced with their iNavs. Thompson allowed himself a glance at his as Santa fed the lens through the crack.

Old metal fittings, a roof of dry rock, and dust wafting in a blade of moonlight.

'No body heat,' Hawks said. 'No residuals.'

Santa said, 'Okay, Thompson, I don't think we need a bird's eye on this. Wanna join us? Keep low, though.'

About time, Thompson thought as he shinned down the tree trunk, although it sucked that he wouldn't get to try out the Hobbit's other modes. Now he was even more certain this was a nothing-mission, he could have run over at his full height without incident, but it was Santa's moment, so he played it straight and crawled over the rocks like the others.

When he reached the door, Mac had his fingers in the crack. Santa gave the 'execute' hand-gesture, and Mac strained at the fixture. He grunted. A clunk sounded and the door shifted a fraction. If Mac couldn't get it open, they'd have to rely on Dang's explosives skills, and Thompson still wasn't one hundred percent about the new kid. Someone that young shouldn't be in charge of that much C-4, but he had a cool head and Jacobs vouched for him. Thompson's concern lifted, though, as a final surge of effort from Mac opened the door, the squeal of rusted hinges about three times louder than Dang's C-4 would have been.

A combination of flashlights and laser sights danced inside, a visual confirmation of Hawks's optic.

Mac said, 'We really gotta go in there?'

'Man,' Dang said, 'I do not want a live-long-and-prosper moment.'

Chased frowned at him. 'The fuck?'

'He's referencing Star Trek Two,' Dr. Lear said. 'Mr. Spock dies of Radi-fucking-ation.'

'Huh. Thought it was Kirk who died.'

'Not that monstrosity—'

'Hey!' Santa said. 'Is your pen beeping? No. Then keep your head in the game. By the numbers.'

Thompson had gotten pretty good at concealing his smirks whenever Santa lost it with his buddies. Part of leadership was keeping your shit together when the team was dicking about. Don't let 'em see you riled.

'Yes, sir,' Chase said, with just a hint of sarcasm.

As the team prepared to enter the hole in the mountain, Jacobs pressed his finger in his ear to temporarily take himself off sub-vocal. So only Santa and Thompson heard, he said, 'Thought you didn't want to lead.'

Thompson caught the flash of annoyance from Santa, but he and Jacobs shared a solid nod so brief it almost never happened. The kid pushed it away, and took point as they all donned night-vision goggles, and stalked inside.

6

When he learned Vince Jacob's boys were in the UK gaining close-protection experience courtesy of General Santarelli's book tour, Colonel Johnson could not believe his luck. With the Eagle Eye 3 report in-hand, he figured he'd be stuck with some SEAL rejects or having to call on NATO, which he hated doing in the best of times.

But the six camera feeds attached to the shoulder of each member of Alpha Team reminded him that his neck was on the line here. He turned down NATO's Fast Reaction Force in favor of waiting an extra two hours for Vince to mobilize. Sure, the FRF remained on standby here at the base, in case the satellite picked up something new, but then the F-16s would take care of anything that posed an immediate threat.

This had to be handled properly. If it was what he feared, namely a jihadi cell in possession of unthinkable power, it needed a more precise response than what NATO could offer. Still, he had to make one concession before the Swiss agreed to allow them into their territory: the intelligence officer, Hawks. But since they flew in the egghead from CERN free of charge on the same transport, he didn't object too strongly. She was familiar with their comms systems, so why the hell not. Let the big boys handle the big stuff.

Tonight's operators at Sembach seemed eager to please, too, so instead of restricting the command station to essential personnel, he allowed one on each of the shoulder-cam monitors. That decision enabled him to display each viewpoint on the main screen at the flick of his finger, rather than dicking around with a handheld pad or hitting buttons on a console.

He ran through the routine again, to be ready for if the op became a serious hot-zone, pointing at different monitors in turn. He received the point of view of each team member as they descended the metal staircase: first Jacobs, then Santa, Chase, Mac, Dang, and Thompson. *Thompson.* The only one who couldn't be bothered with a handle. But he was a good man, a decent second in command.

Johnson worried occasionally that granting General Santarelli those favors, pushing Santa harder than the others, might have led to issues within the team, but because Thompson was usually okay with it, everyone else followed suit. Reviewing the video and audio files from their missions was one of the colonel's guilty pleasures; seeing how boys were molded into men, men into soldiers, soldiers into something a little bit more.

They reached the bottom of the staircase and took a right. The metal walkway continued through a tunnel hewn from the mountain. No one spoke. The monitors showed a hand occasionally pop into view to tap another team member on the shoulder, meaning 'proceed,' and that soldier went forward six steps, then crouched, covered, while the next overtook.

Santa's cam entered a small room off the main corridor. It found a desk and a chair, and on the desk sat a radio the size of a Buick. Analog dials, knobs, a desk-mic and a set of chunky headphones. Santa's hand wiped the brand-name.

He said, 'German. A little power, it might still work.'

'What next?' Jacobs asked.

'Move on.'

A growling boom rumbled through the array, and the team all stumbled.

Johnson leaned on his fists, trying to pick out if anyone was hurt. 'Report.'

'Earthquake,' Santa replied. 'Small one.'

'Just an aftershock, chaps,' Dr. Lear said with forced casualness. Not uncommon with civilians when surrounded by fighting men.

Chase said, 'Got a door. Twenty feet ahead.'

The cams all moved on. Johnson signaled to bring Jacobs' view up to the large screen, mainly so he could see how Santa was getting on. He'd always delivered on these minor exercises, but as soon as anything hairy showed up, Johnson would have no hesitation in ordering Vince to take back command. Perhaps he should move Santa to a less elite squad, give him a temporary leadership post that he couldn't relinquish, and that no one would recall from him in the field. It'd be a shame to get him all focused like tonight, only to let him off the hook at a moment's notice.

Santa took point again, Chase his wing man. The weak link in the team, given to distracting Santa with humor and a hot head. He heard Chase tried his luck on the stand up circuit before joining up. Maybe it was that failure that drove him so hard. But with a surname like 'Chevy' (hence his handle) it was always going to be tough in those bars and clubs. Whatever his history, whatever his shortcomings, he possessed some of the best instincts Johnson had witnessed, remained the coolest head under fire.

Jacobs held steady as the unlocked door swung open, and the cam-views wobbled forward, taking Johnson and the ops team into a cavernous room, partially illuminated by a faint glow in one corner. The infrared tech still cast the scene in eerie green, but that scant light gave everything a sharper hue. Johnson had the operators flick between the troops' views in turn.

Santa's position found Hawks, and she stopped suddenly. She'd kicked something. She angled down and almost screamed, but held herself in check.

Johnson's main screen switched to hers, revealing what lay at her feet: the mummified remains of two men; skin taut over bone, eyes dried in their sockets.

Chase came in close, and his cam found first the bodies, then Hawks's pissed-off face. He said, 'Now it's gettin' interesting.'

Mac approached two doors in the wall opposite the glow, both wooden, with a sign on each. 'Guys, is this German?'

Dr. Lear viewed them and said, 'This says "Power Supply," the other here is a … cafeteria. Hey!' He bent over and when he stood, he held a rad-pen in front of the camera. 'Who isn't taking me seriously?'

If forced to bet, Johnson would put his money on Chase. He said, 'Whoever dropped that is on latrine duty. One week. Santa, make a note.'

'Sir.' Santa's view showed him touching a piece of cloth hanging on a wall. It spanned a good ten feet, but the night-vis washed out the detail.

Then every monitor flashed in brilliant white, as if something exploded.

Johnson scanned the screens. 'Alpha Team, what's happening?'

Chase's voice came through first. 'Jesus on a *fuckin'* motorcycle.'

Then Thompson said, 'Little warning next time, Mac.'

The monitors cleared, morphing from night-vision to regular view. Santa's feed revealed Mac ambling out of the power supply room.

'That's better,' he said. 'Hate the dark.'

But it was Jacobs' feed that drew Johnson's eye. Focused on Santa, who was still holding that cloth hung over ten feet of wall, it showed the young Ranger drop the material and step back. With a red background, a white circle, and a mangled black cross in its center—a Swastika—they all stared up at worn, bullet-ridden Nazi flag.

Santa whipped off his night-vis goggles and blinked away the white spots that came with an overload of light. The first thing he made out was the rest of the team mimicking his movements, trying to get used to seeing again. The second thing was Mac ambling out of the power supply room.

He said, 'That's better. Hate the dark.'

Dang waved his goggles at the big man. 'Dammit, give us some warning next time.'

Chase said, 'Motherfucker,' over and over.

The third thing Santa discovered in the new brightness was that the piece of cloth he was holding spanned the width of one wall. But more startling was that it was a Nazi flag, streaked with black in places, like something burned nearby, and bullet holes peppered the material through to the rock behind.

Hawks said, 'Nice.'

She was referring to the two bodies at her feet: the men, clearly mummified from being sealed in a dry room for many years, wore lab coats. One held a clipboard. The other wore spectacles.

Jacobs rounded what appeared to be a strewn file cabinet and upturned table. He kicked a scattering of bullet casings.

'Okay,' Santa said. 'Looks like ... abandoned facility. Zero hostiles.'

'About time, kiddo,' Thompson said, his attention on the light source they spotted upon entry.

Relaxing a little, Santa flipped him the bird. Low down, so Johnson wouldn't see. A sideways glance from Thompson meant a wry smile in return.

'Agreed,' Jacobs said. 'Hell of a fight, though.'

Their earpieces filled with Colonel Johnson's voice: 'Thank you, Alpha Team. Sorry we cut your vacation short.'

Santa absently picked up a battered leather notebook from the only upright table. 'So what did the satellite detect?'

Dr. Lear, gazing at the window in the far corner, made a noise like 'ha.' He said, 'I'd say the glowing machine over here might be a clue.'

'That fucker just diss us?' Chase said.

Thompson joined Dr. Lear and slapped him on the back. 'Kinda startin' to like this guy.'

But Dr. Lear did not notice the compliment. He was too busy observing the room from which the light emanated, his eyes wide, mouth open a little.

As Santa made his way over, he passed Jacobs, who picked up something from the same table as the notebook. It was only upright because it was bolted to the floor. Jacobs looked at the thing in his hand and frowned, but when Santa reached the window, and kicked away the remains of a broken mug, he could not prevent his own mouth from opening like the British scientist. 'What *is* that?'

'It's the smallest one I've ever seen,' Dr. Lear said. 'But that is definitely a nuclear reactor.'

7

Santa wouldn't have recognized a nuclear reactor if it slapped him in the face, but it wasn't hard to take the doc's word for it. Beyond the thick glass, a walkway wound around a pond of water, ten or twelve holes spaced at one-foot intervals, with rods positioned above, all lit by a single orange bulb on the same wall as the viewing pane. A steel door with a window was also visible, resembling an airlock that gave access to the room.

'Mother ... fucker,' Chase said, joining them.

The whole team now gawped, including Jacobs. Dr. Lear swept his hand over the console before him, scattering freshly-dislodged rock and dust to the floor. A single light blinked red, about the size of a quarter.

Santa said, 'It's active?'

Dr. Lear's hands skittered over the knobs and dials, hovered over the handle that worked twin levers. He didn't touch anything, but he was like a kid with too many presents to open. 'It's ... similar to a TV on standby. The quake must have loosened the rock above, and the jolt of it falling sent the power surge to the core, which activated the matrix.'

Santa flicked through the notebook to see German writing, hand-jotted diagrams, and schematics. He passed it to the doc. 'This help?'

Dr. Lear skimmed through a few pages and said, 'That's not a nuclear manual,' and pocketed it.

'Nazi bunker, then,' Santa said. 'Experimenting with nuclear technology either during World War Two or just before.'

'But if they built *this*,' Dr. Lear said, 'if they had *this* technology, we should all be speaking German. Including you Yanks. Do you realize how *advanced* this is?'

Dang poked his head around the doc's arm. 'So the core turning on is what the satellite picked up.'

'At a guess,' Santa said, 'I'd say their experiments didn't give them anything usable. Berlin didn't want this falling into anyone else's hands, so ordered them all executed.'

'The bodies,' Hawks said.

'Yeah,' Thompson said, 'otherwise we'd've heard about it, right?'

'Right.' Santa checked his rad-pen. Nothing.

In their ears, Johnson said, 'I need you to secure the scene. If we picked it up, no telling what other parties did as well. We'll monitor chatter, and we'll bring another Eagle Eye over to give you a heads-up on ... unfriendly movement.'

'Sir,' Hawks said. 'Switzerland is a sovereign nation, and this is a joint operation. Our government will send experts, and I am sure a joint ... what are you doing?'

Johnson said, 'I beg your pardon, young lady?'

'Not you, sir. Dr. Lear.'

The doc spun a dial, dimming the bulb inside the reactor room.

Santa said, 'Hey, you shouldn't be doing that.'

'I am a nuclear physicist,' Dr. Lear said. 'I think I can handle seventy-year-old technology.' As punctuation, he rotated a different dial.

Static filled every earpiece, and each soldier pulled the tiny plastic mold from their ear canals. A soft 'whumpf' sounded and dust filled the air, wafting from the inlet beside what appeared to be an airlock. Jacobs yanked Dr. Lear backwards, and spun the dial back to zero.

'Touch that again,' Jacobs said, 'I will personally shoot you in the elbow. Got that?'

Lear nodded rapidly. 'Got it. Yes. Loud and clear.'

With the sub-vocal comms back in, Johnson was barking for info. 'Alpha Team, this is command, do you—'

'Copy, sir,' Santa said. 'Got a surge here.'

'Your monitors went dark too,' Johnson said. 'Now fall back, and secure the perimeter.'

'Yes, sir.'

Thompson tapped Santa on the shoulder and drew his attention to the inlet carved into the rock. What seemed like a natural formation was actually an alcove containing a door. The burst of dust was the seal breaking on a round entrance the size and heft of a bank vault. And now a second viewing window became apparent, completely blacked out, but obviously looked into the hidden room.

'Sir,' Santa said. 'We have another room to clear. Stand by.'

The team convened by Santa and Thompson. Dang was first to activate his laser sight, but one by one they all flicked theirs on, the normally-invisible beams a series of straight lines through the airborne dust.

Santa secured his SCAR-M tight to his side, and drew his sidearm; better in close-quarters if anything dangerous lingered, although he doubted some Nazi who'd survived down here for the past seventy-some years would pose much of a problem. He pressed his back against the wall, and advanced foot over foot, while Chase glided to the opposite wall. Santa reached the vault door, and slipped his fingers into the crack where it opened. Not taking any chances, even on the sub-vocal network, he gestured that he was about to open it.

Chase signaled that he was ready. Thompson held back with Jacobs, sending Mac and Dang forward in crouches, their beams landing on the door at angles that wouldn't carve Santa to mincemeat in any crossfire.

Santa counted down with his fist.

1...

2...

3...

He pulled the door open. It swung smoothly but slowly, a hydraulic mechanism taking over. More dust, more sheets of gravelly debris shifted, its unintentional camouflage dropping away with every inch. When it was halfway open, a light flickered on inside, and Santa hugged the wall, his Sig-Sauer pointed at the interior. Before opening fully, the door stopped with a hiss, about three-quarters.

Santa entered the doorframe, Chase right up beside him. The room was circular, a dozen or so spotlights lining the ceiling. Santa stepped inside what was clearly an empty chamber, gun still up, aimed ahead as he explored. It was cold and smelled strongly of copper. The floor was tiled ceramic, the metallic walls crusted with green.

'Heavily-oxidized copper,' Dr. Lear said from the doorway. 'Wow, this is ... I don't know what this is.'

By the time he made a full circuit, Chase and Dr. Lear were with him, while Dang and Mac guarded the doorway. The doc crawled on his hands and knees, examining the join between floor and wall,

'A groove,' he said. 'On a round floor. It kind of suggests the floor should rotate.'

'Cool,' Chase said. 'A Nazi disco.'

Dr. Lear stood up quickly, finding something fascinating embedded in the ceiling: a dull crystal the size of a man's fist.

Mac said, 'Maybe it's for executing Jews.'

'No,' Santa said. 'Too elaborate. Most Jews were killed by firing squad. Far more than in gas chambers or... whatever this is.'

In his ear, Hawks said, 'You like the History Channel, sir? We get it in Switzerland too—'

'My grandpa. He enjoys talking about the war. I like to listen. Well, I used to.'

'Grandfather? Wait. Santarelli? Are you related to the famous general?'

Jesus, gimme a break. Can't even come to Europe without him following me.

Santa said, 'Let's wrap it up.'

'No,' Dr. Lear said. 'A few more minutes. This is too brilliant to walk away from.'

'No more minutes. Move it now.'

'Look at this.' Dr. Lear fished the notebook from his pocket. Showed several pages of gobbledygook to Santa, flashing them to the others. 'Outside, I didn't think it was possible, I didn't think even the Nazis could be serious about this.'

'Skip the bullshit,' Chase said. 'What *is* this thing?'

'They were actually trying to build...' Dr. Lear chuckled at the daft notion. 'A time machine.'

Santa holstered his firearm with a sigh. The rest of the squad turned from Dr. Lear. Santa said, 'Time to go.'

A second aftershock then rumbled to life. Everyone staggered.

'Shit!' cried Hawks, and ran into view in the chamber's alcove.

Dust and debris clouded around the team, billowing in through the vault-like door. Dr. Lear dashed to the viewing window and beckoned Santa over. Dislodged rock crumbled onto the panel, and now more lights flashed on. Santa set himself to run, to give the evac order, but the remainder of the team found shelter inside the chamber.

'That's nasty,' Mac said, dusting himself off.

As the quaking eased, metal screeched, and something hydraulic hissed.

Santa shouted, 'Out now!'

The crackling voice of Johnson demanded updates, but then static filled their ears, giving them pause. The chamber door swung towards them. Mac pushed against it, slowing the effort, and everyone else piled in behind. It was no use.

The huge metal door closed, sealing them inside.

And something hummed.

Above them, the dull crystal glowed a fiery yellow.

Dr. Lear said, 'Oh ... wow.'

Then a spark.

'Wow?' Thompson said. 'Hopin' that ain't an understatement.'

The wall shifted.

'Oh,' Hawks said.

They all stepped away, and the wall all around them turned.

'Not good,' Dang said.

The crystal pulsed, and gave off more sparks.

'On me,' Santa ordered. 'Stay close. Get ready.'

'For what?' Mac said.

'Unknown,' Jacobs said. 'Just be ready.'

The team gathered together, nowhere to run. Each face remained firm, all eyes roving, searching for that gap, that one way out, but the electricity crackled overhead, reaching out of the spinning wall, expanding all around them, surrounding them with lightning.

'Mother ... *fucker!*' Chase yelled.

Finally, like a concussion grenade going off, everything exploded, and then went black.

8

Mac was first to recover. His eyes opened to see the team unconscious, their limbs at odd angles from whatever the fuck blew them over. Still lying in position, he made a mental inventory of his own body: he wiggled his toes, clenched both fists, touched his balls. Yep, all the essentials appeared intact. He pushed himself up onto his knees. As if someone filled his head with water, he pitched gently.

Don't puke.

Don't puke.

Don't puke.

He didn't puke. The dizziness passed, and he found his feet with a groan. Normally, he'd check on the CO first, and in this case he was unsure if it was still Santa, or if the assault meant Jacobs had taken back control. The last Mac knew, Santa was running things, so although he never really understood this notion of placing the youngster in charge when Thompson outranked him, he went with the current chain of command.

He shook Santa. Tapped his cheek as gently as could. Then a bit rougher, and Santa opened his eyes. He sat up with a start. 'AHH! What happened?'

His shout stirred the rest of Alpha Team. Mac figured the grenade or whatever must have been a weak one, his larger mass allowing him a faster recovery. The others moaned almost as one, but they were all in one piece, which counted as a win in itself.

As with Mac, the fug cleared for Santa within a few seconds. He gazed around, and for the first time, Mac noticed it too: the whole chamber was clean, a perfect copper shine, the crystal in the roof a dull stone.

Chase said, 'One mean fuckin' cleaning system.'

Mac helped Dr. Lear to his feet. 'Still brilliant, Doc?'

The floppy-haired Brit blinked rapidly. 'Less so than before.'

Jacobs unholstered his Sig, aimed at the door that was all the way open. He said, 'Least we ain't trapped anymore.'

One at a time, Alpha Team followed Jacobs out. On full alert, Mac raised his SCAR to eye level, and jammed the stock in his shoulder. From the moment he wrenched open the old door in the mountainside, he expected no resistance at the bunker, and his hunch seemed correct at first. But now, after the ambush inside that machine, he would take no chances. At least the lights were still on.

With no need to vocalize the movement, Mac covered the left, while at his other shoulder, Thompson took the right. Ahead of them, Santa and Chase did the same, Jacobs on point, with Dang bringing up the rear, Hawks and the doc falling in between.

Jacobs said, 'Recon control, copy?'

But sub-vocal was dead. No static, no whistles or that weird bubbling noise it sometimes made. But dead. Silent.

All sighted down their weapons, sweeping the room. It was all different, put back together by unknown bad guys. Question for Mac was, *who*? Who would attack them, then leave them to roam around the damned place?

It was Santa who noticed the weirdest stuff first, though. It was Santa who froze in place and lowered his weapon with his eyes wide. He said, 'Guys.'

One by one they drew their attention to him. Jacobs gave him a frown, but when he realized the whole team was focused on something, he looked up at the wall too: where previously hung the tattered, hole-ridden swastika, now—in pristine condition—a bright red flag covered the wall. It was so clear, so ... *new.*

As a single unit, they all snapped back into combat mode. A tight circle, facing out. Even the chick, Hawks, found a knee, her gun aimed out, slotting in like she'd been with the group forever.

The whole lab was now clean, bright, working: lights and dials on the control panel, the miniature nuclear reactor was lit in blue, not orange. Not a speck of dust anywhere. The main table was well-organized with charts, a map, and schematics, with the cabinets positioned neatly against the walls. No corpses, mummified or otherwise.

Chase said, 'Where'd the dead fuckers go?'

'Someone musta' moved 'em,' said Thompson.

Dang tutted, shook his head. 'Is it so hard to believe—'

'Okay, full sweep,' Santa said. 'By the numbers.'

As the others moved, Mac headed toward the room labeled 'cafeteria' in German. But before he got halfway over the floor, voices sounded on the other side of the door.

Mac said, 'Santa, hold on.'

They all listened. Muffled laughter. Casual, happy. Not the noises of jihadis or euro-trash terror freaks. Not the noise of anyone who'd fucked over a team of US Special Forces.

Mac backed up into the alcove where the chamber was set, and Santa pointed at other cover points—the control panel, the table, the wall by the flag.

All spread out.

Trained their weapons on the cafeteria.

The handle turned.

And someone inside opened the door.

9

Santa's previous mission into a war zone was on the border of Pakistan and Afghanistan. His patrol received intel about a Taliban commander running a cell from a tailor's shop in a village with under a hundred residents, none of whom looked like they could afford a bespoke meal, let alone a bespoke suit. The standoff that followed lasted four hours, and ended with the seventy-year-old fanatic opening the front door and 'surrendering,' wrapped in a suicide vest. He charged. Santa shot the man in the head. The dead man's switch fell from his hand, and as the soldiers and villagers all jumped for cover, some flaw in the vest's design saved them, as the delay between release and the signal reaching the detonator lagged by about three seconds. That was all they needed to find cover.

And now, like then, he summoned an image of Lily, of her in that party dress in front of his grandpa's ridiculously-huge house, so if he was to bite it here, in some hidden laboratory, his final thoughts would be of her.

The cafeteria door opened fully. The balding man who stepped out wore a lab coat and glasses, carried a coffee, chatting over his shoulder in German. Two more scientists followed, the bearded one offering a half-pint of whatever passed for whiskey out here, but baldy and the young one declined. Beardy took a quick swig, and pocketed it.

All three wandered over to the reactor window. Didn't even see scattered members of Alpha Team in their improvised foxholes. Crouched by the scientists' feet, Dang aimed up from behind the chamber's console. The scientists gazed upon the reactor, the young one making notes as the older two dictated readings.

Jacobs signaled to Santa and Mac. Santa stashed his SCAR-M and drew his sidearm. Aimed it at the newcomers. Mac mirrored him the other side.

Santa said, 'Hey.'

The scientists turned to Santa. Baldy froze mid sip. The others backed up to the wall, hands in the air. Dang stood up, gun in Baldy's face, making him drop the cup. It smashed on the floor, and Baldy joined his pals. All three jabbered in German.

Beardy shut his eyes tight, pulling away from Dang. '*Nicht schießen! Nicht schießen!*'

Baldy held himself in a calmer manner. His eyes roamed from Alpha Team's weapons, to the touchscreen tech, to the helmets. He said, 'Willkommen! Ich bin Dr. Uhrmacher. Dies sind meine Kollegen—'

Dr. Lear stepped forward, his weight on his heel, arms out to the side. Santa didn't see where he hid, but guessed the British physicist was pretty much crapping himself. He held up a hand to the German doc and moved closer to Santa and said, 'He's called Dr. Uhrmacher. He ... bids you welcome.'

Uhrmacher spoke more German, slowly this time.

'He suggests it is strange for you. Wants to know how far you've come.'

Alpha Team were stones. Guns steady. Santa opened his white coverall and pulled a tag on his chest that released a Velcro flag—the Stars and Stripes.

Uhrmacher said, 'Americans?' He pointed excitedly at the exit. 'Die wachen werden bald wieder.'

Chase smirked. 'I think he needs to go potty.'

Santa pulled Uhrmacher from the wall; pushed him toward Lear. 'Talk to him.'

'It is okay,' Uhrmacher said. 'I speak your language. Do we lose? Please tell me we lose.'

Chase said, 'What in the world of fuck is he babbling about?'

Uhrmacher appealed to Dr. Lear for a translation.

Lear said, 'The American requests that you to elaborate.'

Thompson hustled forward, Sig-Sauer still at eye level. 'Which means "tell us what's goin' on".'

'You must know,' Uhrmacher said, 'if you came through the tunnel.'

The stone-like soldiers shifted slightly.

'Tunnel?' Santa said. 'What tunnel?'

Dang's gun-arm wavered slightly. Relaxing for a second, but he soon snapped back. He said, 'It's a tunnel through *time*. A *wormhole*.'

'Bullshit,' Chase said.

Jacobs circled Uhrmacher. 'How the hell is that even possible?'

'The crystal.' The German scientist pointed into the copper chamber. 'There. With the right amount of electricity, it can do … incredible things.'

Jacobs fiddled with something in his pocket. Maybe whatever he picked up earlier.

'Gentlemen. The date is the first of May, nineteen forty-five.' Dr. Uhrmacher spread his hands. Light reflected off the top of his head and his glasses. He somehow willed his grin wider, jigged his hands as if waiting for applause.

Thompson said, 'What a load of horseshit.'

'Yeah,' Mac said. 'They're tryin' to mess with our heads.'

Dang faced away from his task, lowered his weapon like a

noob. 'There is so much we don't know about this universe. It *has* to be possible. I mean, look at the way they left the chamber unoccupied. That's got be so they don't meet their older selves coming through the—'

'Dang,' Santa said, 'get your head straight. Cover the prisoners.'

The youngster returned his aim to the two other scientists against the wall, but Dr. Lear said, 'Actually, theoretically, Dang is correct.'

Dang nodded sagely.

Jacobs said, 'Well, screw theoretically. *Literally* cuff these guys.'

Dr. Lear and Dang seemed caught in wonder for a moment, but disinterested expressions from the team snapped them back.

Santa said, 'Okay, let's head topside, leave the magic bank vault alone. See if we can get comms back up—'

'Santa?' Jacobs said.

'Sir?'

Jacobs holstered his sidearm and placed a hand on Santa's shoulder. 'Whatever this is, I think we can all agree, it ain't recon no more. I gotta take back command.'

While Chase, Mac and Dang cuffed the scientists with snap-ties, Santa told himself he was not disappointed. He never wanted the responsibility anyway. This was the way it should be, after all.

This was the way it should be.

10

Outside the bunker, Alpha Team emerged into daylight, cold biting at their faces, and the sun low in an impossibly-blue sky. The scent of fresh grass and sap hung in the air, and the rocks surrounding the clearing seemed smoother than last night. The open space sloped downward to where trees had been cut out, thinning the wider area to make an approach more difficult. But more concerning to them, the snow had melted, clinging only to the higher peaks spanning the horizon.

'Jeez,' Mac said, 'how long were we out?'

As Alpha Team stripped off their white coveralls to reveal their black ops gear, Hawks worked her comms pack, and Santa tried not to feel too jealous at her green camo fatigues. They expected to be in and out of alpine terrain, so had not required anything but their urban operational gear under their whites.

From the pack, only static replied.

Jacobs said, 'Helo musta' followed orders.'

Hawks slapped the transmitter. 'I cannot raise control either.'

'Tried 'em on the radio?' Chase asked.

'No,' she said. 'I am only a communications specialist. I didn't think of that.'

Mac pointed at his ear. 'We're talkin' to each other.'

'Your sub-vocal network operates through my pack. When the battery goes, you hear nothing.'

Jacobs said, 'Did you hear *that*?'

'Yeah,' Mac said. 'I told you, I can hear—'

'He doesn't mean that.' Santa cocked his head. He'd heard something too. 'He means Bigfoot.'

All listened. Down, through the trees, rustling carried up on the light wind. Voices. Too low to catch.

Chase said, 'That way.'

Jacobs checked the three Germans were secure: cable ties binding their hands, no cellphones, no weapons. He said, 'Dr. Lear, you stay close. Dang, Hawks, I want you to keep an eye on these guys. Clear?'

'Yes, sir,' Dang said.

'Sir,' Hawks said.

Santa put all his concerns about Hawks away for now. She was falling in with the team, and following orders. They couldn't ask for more from her. Even though she clearly didn't like Americans coming in and showing them how it's done. With that in mind, Santa took point with Jacobs, while Mac, Chase, and Thompson fanned out through the trees either side. The four docs, shepherded by Dang and Hawks, brought up the rear.

As they advanced, they took more care on the few patches of crisp snow, pushing branches aside and letting them back gradually. In a few seconds, the voices grew louder, and Jacobs held up a fist. *Silent mode.*

Thompson reached Jacobs, tapped his shoulder. Jacobs stepped to the right and aimed from behind a tree. Still unsighted, Santa moved behind Thompson. Touched his shoulder. Thompson branched left, and the team repeated the process, one at a time, spreading out, observing, unwilling to burst onto whatever was unfolding yards beyond the tree line.

At a signal from Jacobs, Dang joined them. Hawks held

back, clearly unhappy, but remained alert at the rear with the prisoners and Dr. Lear.

The team swept forward again in increments, this time widening their arc, until, finally, they found a second clearing. This one was occupied, and it took Santa five or six seconds to process what he was seeing.

11

Twelve men in Nazi uniforms shoved eight others in US Army fatigues toward a rock formation that reared out of the ground like a giant, fossilized tooth. Two final men in Nazi dress-up costumes, this time officers, joined them. The one who appeared to be in charge was blond and tall, and probably blue-eyed; a Nazi poster-boy.

The American GIs were filthy, tired, and unarmed, a mix of youth and the fairly young, with only one grizzled-looking veteran among them. The sergeant stood up, puffed out his chest.

He said, 'Sergeant Montgomery Brown, US Army. Number—'

'I do not care what your name is,' the blond officer said. 'Tell me your mission, Sergeant.'

'Not a chance.'

The Nazi cosplayers hustled the other GIs to their knees. To a man, they each bore the air of defeat, utterly out of hope.

The officer in charge said, 'Look around. We have no POW facilities. Not even a hole in the ground in which to keep you.'

'Then why're we even havin' this conversation?'

'Hm. Good point. READY!'

The Nazis lined up—a firing squad.

Sgt. Brown nodded a firm, manly nod at the youngest GI, a skinny kid in his late teens, probably never even started shaving properly yet. But the sarge's courage allowed the kid to gain some grit.

The officer said, 'AIM!'

The guns racked. The Nazis raised them to their shoulders.

Then a voice: 'Hey, how do you say "Freeze, Mother-fuckers" in German?'

The blond officer turned first to find Chase holding a submachine gun on him, laser sight painting a green dot on his uniform.

Then the rest of Alpha Team streamed out of the trees, precisely covering the row of Nazis and two officers. While the squad of troopers froze in place, the Nazi commander tried to brush the dot from his chest. When it was clear he could not, he barely shrugged. Took it in his stride.

The GIs watched in silence.

Jacobs said, 'Guns down.'

'Senken sie ihre waffen,' said the officer in command. '*Im moment.*'

The Nazi men obeyed their leader, and placed their weapons gently in front of them and stepped back.

'Okay,' Jacobs said. 'Talk.'

'I am *Hauptsturmführer* Karl Eisenberg. Or "captain" if you prefer. These are my Brandenburgers. You are trespassing on private land.'

Mac pointed at the troopers. 'What the heck is a Brandenburger?'

'Hitler's elite forces,' Santa said.

Eisenberg appraised Alpha Team with curiosity rather than fear. 'Where exactly did you come from?'

'Where did we come from?' Chase said. 'The United States of none-of-your-fuckin'-concern.'

Jacobs said, 'Okay, what's gonna happen here is, you're gonna let those boys go, then you're gonna explain exactly what it is you assholes are doin' runnin' around dressed like that.'

'Hey,' Thompson said, 'we got us a joker in class.'

One Nazi had slipped a handgun into play—a Luger. He aimed right at the young, scrawny GI, angled so no one from Alpha Team could draw a clear bead.

Eisenberg barked in German, his tensed body leaving no doubt that he was pissed at his subordinate. The rebel replied in quick-fire German, virtually spitting the final word: '*Pflicht.*' Santa's language skills weren't great, and with the doc at a safe distance, he had to rely on the few words he learned from the general, one of which was 'pflicht.' It translated, broadly-speaking, as 'duty.'

The rebel Nazi was doing his *duty.* He stepped forward, gun steady.

The American youngster closed his eyes tight. His buddy did too, cringed, awaiting the inevitable. He's dead...

But while Santa was listening, observing, translating that one word, he fell back. As the conversation between the commander and grunt played out, he snuck around the perimeter, behind the tooth-like rock. With the rebel's finger tightening, Santa stepped out, grasped the Nazi's wrist, cricked his elbow, and pointed the Luger back in his face. The twist and grip forced the finger tighter around the trigger. It went off with a bang, and blew the back of the soldier's head out.

Chase said, 'Fuck, Santa, that was *so* Chuck Norris.'

But another Nazi found his courage, and scrambled for his gun. As Mac fired a burst of three into him, instinct flared in the others, diving for their discarded weapons. And Alpha Team engaged.

12

The GIs dropped flat to the ground, and the Nazis fired wild. Alpha Team used natural cover, gliding through it, firing precise bursts of three.

Mac took one down straight away, and while the two officers—Eisenberg and the other dick—found cover, he kept them in his peripheral vision. But then another series of bullets raked the nearest tree and he slid to his butt, twisting as he found his target. A blast that way sent the asshole running, right into Chase.

Chase shot Mac's guy in the throat, then the head, and dashed to the next point.

Thompson fell in beside Dang, who hadn't hit anything yet. Thompson's first kill of the day soon came as two tried to flank them. He took one down and nudged Dang. Although he could have done it himself, he let Dang shoot the fucker.

Four down.

Santa dragged the rebel's body with him as he went, bullets impacting dead flesh as he pulled his machine gun up and fired at the pair. He caught one with a headshot, the other in the thigh. The wounded guy tried to run, firing constantly, but then Mac found the angle and cut him down.

At the far side, as the crossfire eased, Eisenberg and his pal rolled expertly away, to the edge of the carnage. Santa gave chase, but the final two soldiers were on him. He dropped the corpse and made it to a tree stump, while Jacobs and Chase shared the final kill.

Bang.

Bang.

Two more gone.

Now, where was Eisenberg?

Dr. Lear's hands felt like rubber. Right there, barreling this way from the direction of the gunfire, was a man dressed as a Nazi captain, closely followed by a second officer. *Jesus.* This was only supposed to be a cool blast in a helicopter, some pretty scenery and possibly a surge of excitement when a depleted uranium shell was pried from the hands of a dead terrorist. Or the discovery of a natural steam vent giving a false-positive on the satellite—yes, a natural steam vent was preferable to *this.*

The captain spotted Lear, and when he clocked the three German scientists, he did not hesitate. He aimed his sidearm—at his own men— and fired three times.

Two of the three fell, and something truly odd happened: Lear assessed the past hour of his life, his legs moving without him willing it. He gave thanks that he'd had such low self-esteem as a child, a fault that spurred him to keep himself fit later in life, to be physically strong as well as mentally. The last time he experienced such instinctive clarity was holding on by his fingertips to an overhang in monument valley, trying to emulate Tom Cruise in that *Mission: Impossible* film. His line frayed, leaving him seconds to act. The three-fingered grip saved him that day.

But now he had less than seconds. Perhaps that's why he simply threw himself in front of Uhrmacher. Some instinct that burrowed into his subconscious, that maybe, possibly, at odds of billions-to-one, maybe they were right. Maybe this man was needed to send them all home.

Two shots came, and two searing hot fingers stabbed at Dr. Lear's chest, punching him backward. He landed on Uhrmacher, unable to breathe, scrabbling in the dirt to figure out which way was up, whether he was bleeding, dying, or dead.

In those seconds in which he'd leapt into action to protect a source of essential knowledge, the Swiss woman, Hawks, took cover and drew her gun. She opened fire, quick successive gunshots driving the two men back. They set off in the direction they came, but the crackle of gunfire that way cut them off. Hawks shot at them again, her barrage penning them in behind a tree.

They had no choice but to surrender.

And as Dr. Lear lay his head back, he guessed it must have been some sort of hallucination, but he could have sworn he saw something out of place, even if the impossible really had occurred to bring them here: a scarecrow, moving. Or a man, wrapped up in rags rather than a uniform, running from tree to tree. Watching them. Coming in close, checking on him.

No, that could not have been real. So instead of raising the alarm, he closed his eyes, willing the pain in his chest to go away.

13

With the Nazis all dead, Alpha Team swept through the clearing, kicking guns away from bodies. Hawks shoved Eisenberg into view, along with the other officer, who she now established was called Reitziger. Once she persuaded the British professor that he wasn't dying, that two bullets shattering Kevlar SAPI plates on his upper torso was supposed to hurt 'like bloody heck,' he was confident enough to accept the Sig and keep the sole remaining German scientist under control as they located the Americans. She found them stashing their packs at the edge of the clearing, preparing to question a bunch of survivors—more Americans.

When Captain Eisenberg saw his men—all dead—he set his jaw, and stared daggers at Alpha Team. Although little remorse filtered through for the loss of several neo-Nazi scum, Hawks did consider how it would feel to have the men for whom you carried responsibility slain without recourse. In her years loaned out to various agencies, in the multitude of what these people called 'hot zones' she had witnessed and added to body counts all over the globe. But something was different here. Civilians, ultra-right-wing terror cells, atomic power … it was not something she could have prepared for. As for the British scientist, who was still trying too hard to impress the Yanks, this must have been the most surreal and terrifying experience of his life.

Mac said, 'Huh. Took one in the vest?'

Dr. Lear's body armor hung half off his chest. 'Two, actually.'

Dang said, 'Hurts like a bitch, eh?'

'More than I would have expected, yes.'

Santa took custody of the two officers and said, 'Good work, Hawks.'

'Yeah.' Chase said. 'Not bad going.'

Hawks swallowed the pleasure of being praised and said, 'I do not need thanks. Next time, don't let them get away.' She relayed the events as they happened, but then the other Americans, those dressed in old GI uniforms, gathered themselves.

All still alive, they approached Alpha Team with caution. Likewise, Alpha Team did not holster or safety their weapons. Hawks followed suit. The two groups faced each other: 1940s GIs and 2015 Special Forces.

The sergeant extended a hand to Jacobs. 'Much obliged...' He checked Jacobs' stripes. 'Sir.' When Jacobs didn't reply he introduced himself as 'Sergeant Brown,' and then his squad: a bulky soldier was Private Martins, Private Simons the most athletic, a chubby one called Gregson, the lanky Turin, medic Peterson, and an older guy Hall—or he could just have looked older, since everyone except Hall and Brown was under twenty-one.

Eight in total.

Then the youngest one piped up, his name not mentioned. He said, 'So you're here to back us up?'

These Americans that brought her here were lost without their rules of engagement. Hawks would have spoken by now, but it was their operation. It was one time when she was happy to let them lead. Her commander back in Zurich suggested she go with whatever they said; if they succeeded, it was a joint exercise, but failure meant the Swiss were following US instructions. As for the screw-up she now found herself in the middle of, she was not about to contribute a potential black mark for her agency.

Sgt. Brown said, 'Those weapons ain't standard issue.'

'Special forces?' Martins suggested.

'That's my guess. Experimental lineup too. Not many Negroes servin' alongside reg'lars.'

Thompson said, 'Negro?'

'We don't use that word no more,' Mac said.

'What is your mission?' Jacobs asked. 'Sergeant ... *Brown*, was it?'

Brown slipped a cigar from his pocket, checked it was all in one piece, and lit it. Not something Hawks's military training unit would have tolerated. Still, if you're going to screw up, let the Americans screw it up for you.

Santa's trigger finger relaxed slightly as the one called Sergeant Brown explained his presence here. 'We got word from the local resistance the Nazis are still flyin' supplies in. Most units round here are movin' out. We aim to destroy the airfield ourselves or call in the bombers. Either way it ain't gonna exist much longer.'

Alpha Team exchanged glances. A couple of them moved to speak, but thought better of it.

Jacobs said, 'You tellin' me for sure you're fightin' real honest-to-God Nazis?'

'Umm, yeah,' Hall said. 'Who else would we be fightin'? This ain't Jap country.'

With his hands still cuffed, Dr. Uhrmacher took a couple of steps away from Dr. Lear. He said, 'Tell them what year this is.'

'Hey, Kraut,' Brown said. 'Looks to me like you're a prisoner of freedom and liberty. So shut up.'

Santa steadily took in the uniforms, the dead Nazis, Eisenberg. He shuffled in place, but held firm. 'There's resistance here?'

'Based outta that town a half-mile away.' Sgt. Brown pointed through the trees, down the hill. 'La Bastion. Don't think that's its real name, but it's what they're callin' it.'

Jacobs said, 'You in good enough shape to complete your mission?'

Martins paced towards the edge of the clearing and said, 'Ambushed us a half mile back that way, but the truck should still be there.'

'Okay, then. On your way, and forget you saw us.'

While the GIs regrouped, Jacobs brought Alpha Team in close.

Dang said, 'Sir, is that wise? We already changed history by saving them.'

'That's what we're going with?' Chase replied. 'Time travel is fuckin' dumb. They're neo-Nazi Eurotrash terrorists—'

'What about *them*?' Dang threw a thumb toward the GIs.

Mac shrugged. 'You know, guys, if it looks like a duck...'

'It's odd,' Santa said, 'but it doesn't prove—'

'*Santa!*'

Santa turned his attention to Brown, who'd just called him. It didn't strike him as odd until he did so, but he soon realized he never told Brown his name. It also took him a moment to realize that Brown was not actually talking to him.

Hawks' grasp of English was superb. But right now she was unsure if she'd dozed off and missed something of the exchange that just took place. It simply didn't seem possible.

Addressing the youngest of the GIs, Sergeant Brown said,

'Santa, you're smallest and quietest. I want you to scout on ahead. We'll follow, but you're the advanced recce.'

The skinny kid snapped to attention, eager to please. 'Yes, sir.'

But he saw Alpha Team all staring and his eyes roamed slowly over them. Hawks had listened to the conversations so far, and dismissed them as silly movie-inspired nonsense. Bickering US man-boys debating the impossible. What she, and the Rangers, now worked out ... the odds of such a co-incidence would stagger the most intelligent of mathematicians, and yet here it was. Here *he* was. She made a mental note to ask the CERN physicist later if he could calculate such probabilities, but for now she held herself in check. Better to appear unperturbed while she tried to understand how such a chance meeting could occur. If it *was* a chance meeting. If the Americans had been truthful with her government. If not, she would be ready for any outright betrayal.

Santa said, 'You're called Santa...?'

'Don't matter,' Jacobs said. 'Let them go.'

Santa strode toward the kid. 'What's your *name*? Your full name?'

The kid's eyes widened, but even as Sgt. Brown got in Santa's path, the kid answered. 'Private Anthony Santarelli, sir.'

Standing next to Hawks, Mac said, 'Anthony Santarelli. Hey, ain't that—'

'Yes,' Hawks said. 'It is the general's name.'

14

Santa stepped to the side, but Brown got in his way again. Wanting answers, needing them, Santa bumped chests with the cigar-chomping sarge, but both held firm.

'Just chill,' Thompson said. 'This might not be what it looks like.'

Santa stared, clearly freaking Anthony the fuck out. Which was fine, since Santa was pretty much freaking the fuck out himself. *No way,* he told himself. *No way could this happen by chance.*

As soon as the kid uttered the general's full name, though, he saw it. The eyes, the nose the pair shared, the kid's straight-up family resemblance to Santa's father and, indeed, a similarity to his own photos as a youngster. There was no denying it now it was out there. This smooth-faced private was Santa's grandpa. All he needed was a scar on that baby-fresh cheek.

The old bastard knew *this would happen. He had to. Co-incidences this wild do* not *exist.*

Santa's neck ached, his fist bunched. He could not take his eyes off this young man.

'I ever tell you how you got your name?'

'About a thousand times.'

Now Santa knew exactly what that meant, and why his grandpa had said it.

He knew, and never told me.

Jacobs said, 'Jonnie, pull back.' Conspicuous use of the first name. Sure. Sensible. 'Sergeant, move your men *out.* Now.'

Brown stepped back from Santa, ushering Private Anthony Santarelli aside. 'You heard the sergeant-major, people. Leave the crazy Special Forces fellas alone, and move *out*!'

The GIs departed in a practiced hustle, Santa's eyes lingering on Anthony longer than the others. When they were gone, Santa either needed to scream, panic, or keep his mouth shut. He wasn't sure which option he would choose.

Dang said, 'You see how cool that was?'

'So,' Hawks said, 'the greatest military force on the planet has sent me back in time. By accident. How wonderful.'

Again, Jacobs fingered the small item he collected from the lab inside the bunker. Under his breath, he said, 'Dammit,' and stared hard at Santa. Under other circumstances, Santa would demand to know what was in his hand, direct superior or not, but the team gathered close to Drs. Lear and Uhrmacher. They kept Eisenberg and Reitziger in view, but intel was in short supply right now.

'Okay, listen up,' Jacobs said. 'I'm gonna stake my reputation on what I say next, so if anyone disagrees, speak up. And I mean *please* speak up. I *want* to be wrong. But the way I see it, ain't any denying ... that machine inside the mountain sent us back to the year nineteen forty-five, comin' up to the end of the Second World War.'

The Rangers gave slight nods. Questioning the boss would mean offering up a viable alternative. And there wasn't one.

'The doc couldn't stop dicking with the machine,' Chase said. 'Could he? Had to see what it could do.'

Dr. Lear said, 'My IQ is higher than the American national debt. I know how to turn off a machine.'

'Doesn't matter who's to blame,' Santa said.

All turned to him. Jacobs observed from the side, no interference.

Santa couldn't believe he was about to say this, but if he didn't he would have to punch something until his knuckles bled. 'My grandpa was based in the south of France, but he never talked about it much. Every other mission, he can't stop running his mouth, but here...'

'Wait,' Dang said, 'if that was really the general, then Santa, you saved his life. You *literally* saved your own grandfather. If you weren't there—'

'No. Something else would have stopped that guy. Something must have.'

Thompson said, 'So what now?'

'We go home,' Mac replied simply. 'Sir? Don't we?'

'Right,' Dang said. 'We fulfilled our—'

'Say "destiny,"' Chase said, 'and I'll shoot you in the throat.'

As the team debated the merits of time travel, letting reality sink in around them, Santa then spotted Eisenberg's attention was not on the group. All through the quiet time after the GIs departed, the blond captain had been observing them even more intently than they watched him. His eyes moved like a bird of prey, over their weapons, their uniforms, lingering most noticeably on the iNavs on their forearms. When he found Santa watching him, he said, 'Americans, there is something you should know.'

'Quiet,' Jacobs said.

'Have it your way.'

But Eisenberg's gaze drifted elsewhere. Away from Alpha Team. His line of sight fell on their packs. Santa followed it, and landed on a figure crawling on his belly. Clad head-to-toe in ragged peasant clothing, like something he'd expect in Afghanistan or Syria, the man's hand delved into one of the packs. One at a time, on Santa's silent prompt, Alpha Team spotted him. When they shifted their weight, arming their guns, the interloper held still. He carefully withdrew his hands from the pack.

He was holding two blocks of sealed plastic clay and a box containing components.

'Ah, shit,' Dang said. 'He's taken the C-4!'

'Wait,' Santa said, but it was too late.

Dang sprinted forward, and the thief jumped to his feet and darted into the forest, quick as a greyhound.

Alpha Team rallied, checking weapons, but no one saw Eisenberg and Reitziger rise up until they were on their feet, rebalanced, and preparing to flee. They kicked Hawks to the ground, and her gun spilled. By the time anyone drew down their way, they, too, were away, crashing through the forest.

Santa didn't need an order. A lightning-quick assessment made them the main threat, and he launched after the two Nazis, hearing Jacobs' orders that followed.

'Chase, back him up. Mac, go after Dang. Thompson, with me. Rest of you, try and keep up.'

15

Eisenberg and Reitziger made it to a pitted, manmade road. A track, really, but wide enough for a tank or convoy of GIs. But the Germans were experienced soldiers, so by the time Santa and Chase hurtled into this path, the pair concealed themselves in the forest, skirting the edge, following the route they clearly mapped out before today. Instead of pursuing, though, both Santa and Chase pulled up short.

'Oh my fuck,' Chase said.

Over the trees, down the steep mountain road, the town of La Bastion unfolded less than a half-mile away. A hundred dwellings. Even from here, it was in bad shape: blown-out buildings nestled in cratered, narrow streets, and destroyed military vehicles on the route in and out. Some functional houses and properties remained standing, but not many. If there were any nagging doubts about the current year, this view knocked them flat.

Santa said, 'Quaint.'

And then he took off again, yards ahead of Chase.

The Runner took a more direct route. He pounded the foliage, leaping each fallen tree before it came into view. He glided over shrubs and rocks, skipped each tangle of roots, nimble as a deer. Dang blew after him, and although he clearly didn't know the terrain as well as his quarry, he kept the thief in sight. But only just.

The Runner wrapped the C-4 into a fold on his top and broke left. Dang felt like he was gaining on him, but then lost him for a few seconds, before catching the movement, and bolted in that direction, and—*holy shit!* That was one fucked-up town he was heading for.

Santa reached the town limits seconds ahead of Chase. Surrounded by the burned-out husks of civilian and military vehicles alike, he found cover easily. The rusted and charred metal was old, but carried the tang of a hard-fought battle. Others nearby displayed newer damage.

Chase hunkered beside him, and checked the flanks and the other direction to Santa. Through the skeletal buildings, amongst the rubble, there was no sign of Eisenberg or Reitziger.

Eisenberg, however, was watching. He and Reitziger were holed up on the second floor of a former house that, from the outside, did not look like it could support a second floor. It was the first physical contact Eisenberg had experienced in months, but he was glad for it. Glad he would get his hands on the dogs who slaughtered his men. Good men. Loyal.

Now unarmed, he had to figure out how to draw the two Americans away, bring them in close without making them suspicious.

A commotion sounded streets over. Five hundred yards, in the dry streambed, two scurrying figures whizzed by.

'It is that resistance rodent,' Eisenberg said. 'Whatever he took, the Americans want it back.'

Reitziger nodded firmly.

'That means I want it.'

'I understand,' Reitziger said, and the pair climbed down from their post.

Eisenberg steeled himself at the edge of what was left of the wall. The Americans peeked out one way, then the other. He waited ... waited until they looked his way, and—

'There!' one of them cried.

Eisenberg ran toward the town center and, as he hoped, they both pursued him, forgetting all about Reitziger.

16

Dang barely missed a stride as he rode the Runner's tail into the town itself—over a wrecked bike, through a doorway in a still-standing wall, then up an incline between what used to be shacks. The Runner rounded the corner of an intact building, and Dang lost sight him. He sprinted into the narrow street. Gone.

A clattering sounded overhead. Dang looked up. *There!* Having scaled a flower trellis and ripped it from its mooring, the Runner's feet whipped out of sight over the roof's lip, and Dang drew his Sig. He ran alongside the buildings, the walls made of sheer, grey stone, the roofs mostly red or black slates. The pursuit on the cobblestone street was probably harder than if he were up there, his ankle close to turning every five steps. Glimpses of the Runner flashed by as he dashed over the sloping surface, the wrong side for a clean shot, so at least Dang knew he was on the right track. But each time he aimed, the figure disappeared.

Then a stroke of luck: a break in the buildings. Dang sped up and aimed at the roof.

Waited.

The Runner leapt the gap. No chance to squeeze off a shot.

Dang swung a fist at nothing. 'That's not fair.'

Then a *creeee-aaaaak* sounded nearby, followed by a *crash* and a cry of surprise. Dust billowed from where the Runner landed, and slates crashed to the street mere yards from Dang. A scream pierced the air. From inside the house.

Dang didn't hesitate. He kicked the door open, and burst in, gun prepped, to find a man huddled with twin daughters, yelling in French, his ceiling caved-in.

The Runner sprinted out the back, limping slightly.

Dang said, 'Sorry,' and took after the Runner, a quick glance behind, and said, 'I mean ... je suis ... sorry.'

He barged into the next room in time to see the Runner dive through an open window.

'Wait!' he shouted. 'The C-4!'

Although military-grade explosives were generally stable, they were still explosives. You had to treat them right. Any abuse, or if you got lazy or failed one single time to fully re-spect them, that was the end for you. So Dang cringed, awaiting the inevitable.

And ... nothing.

He dashed to the window. The Runner had dropped safe-ly, rolled off the back of a truck, and launched into another sprint, albeit marginally slower than before.

Dang climbed out and clanged down on the same vehicle, and barreled up the street. The gap was bigger now, but the street was long and straight. Dang halted, breathed steadily, and adopted a firing stance. Sighted down his gun. Finger on the trigger. The Runner weaved side-to-side. Three or four bullets would compensate for that...

The Runner jagged left and was gone.

Dang lowered the Sig, almost out of breath. 'This is get-ting old,' he said, and pushed on.

17

Santa explored a jumble of alleys, Chase having taken a separate route. It was like a maze designed by a sadistic twelve-year-old. Every time he thought it was safe to venture out, the next wall had collapsed, exposing him to a potential ambush. Eisenberg held the advantage here. He *knew* this terrain.

Something in Santa's peripheral vision moved too quickly. Through a bomb-blasted building full of unfinished clay pots, a flash of uniform crept right-to-left.

It had to be Eisenberg. On the move, but slowly.

He hadn't seen Santa, who ducked through a doorway, keeping parallel. Remained low. Prepared his line of attack.

And Santa darted through the shells of two buildings, over a crumbling wall, through another door, and slammed into Eisenberg's torso. But the captain used Santa's momentum and swung him over onto his bent knee. Even through the Kevlar, Santa felt the jolt. Winded, he rolled off, was almost back on his feet when he had to block Eisenberg's swing. The follow-up jab was too fast, rocking his head back, and suddenly, he found himself on the back foot. Eisenberg pummeled blow after blow, hard and precise. The crack to his spine made Santa slow, and although he hit back once, twice, three times, the punches weren't enough against the older man. How old was he? Thirty-something? Forty? And fit. Very fit.

Eisenberg ducked Santa's kick at his head, drove knuckles into his thigh, and an elbow to Santa's jaw sent him stumbling. It was the opening the German needed. He wrenched Santa's arm up behind his back, as painful an arm lock as he'd ever experienced.

Hitler's Special Forces.

No shit.

Eisenberg yanked away the general's knife and its ceremonial scabbard. 'This is pretty,' he said. Then he gripped the iNav and jiggled it. 'It seems your flashy weapons don't train you for real combat. Perhaps the future makes soldiers soft.'

'Lemme up and I'll show you—'

Eisenberg fiddled with the straps and tore the iNav from Santa's arm, threading out his fiber-optic shoulder-cam along with it. He said, 'Care to show me how this works?'

'Fuck you.'

'In that case, I'll have to—'

Gunshots exploded nearby, bullets pinging off the wall behind.

Chase!

With his improvised human shield, Eisenberg fumbled for Santa's sidearm, but Santa used the distraction to pull out of the lock. Rather than fight on, the Nazi captain booted him sideways, and fled with the knife and iNav.

Santa dropped to one knee, and Chase skidded to a halt beside him. Checked him over quickly.

'You do know that guy is older than your grandpa.'

'Fuck,' Santa said. 'You. Too.'

With a gallows smile, Chase helped him up. 'Any idea where the other fuck went?'

'None. But I'm guessing they'll meet up. Let's catch up with Blondie, and beat the shit out of them both.'

18

The Runner flew out of a side street into what could've been a tourist attraction in 2015: working shops around a town square, an ornate but non-operational fountain, a handful of local men in once-smart clothes, milling around, smoking. And Bar du Pont—a chalet-style construction with a pointed roof, finished in dark wood, and with steps leading up from the street to its deck. It stood out amongst the other buildings on the square, largely due to its status as the only fully-intact frontage. Even in wartime, society finds a way.

The Runner bounded up Bar du Pont's stairs two at a time and crashed inside.

Dang took cover in the alleyway, assessed the square, its nonplussed occupants, ingress, egress, blind-spots, potential sniper nests.

He said, 'Runner's holed up in a bar on my coordinates.'

Hawks' voice in his ear: 'We have no satellite, numbskull. You'll have to tell us.'

In a basement room lit only by sunbeams squeezing through the gaps in the wall's slatted fascia, the man they called 'the Runner' searched around desperately for the back door. This wasn't really the plan. All he needed was intel on the Americans that passed through the town hours earlier, figure out what they were up to. He couldn't allow them to discover what the Nazis were hiding. That was up to him to figure out, him and his friends. They fought the invaders for over five years in this corner of France, and they were not about to let US troops steal the glory. At least, that's what he convinced his resistance comrades of. His real mission involved the man who bolted from the scene of death and destruction, the Nazi known as Eisenberg, and his sick colleague, Reitziger.

That bastard took way too much pleasure in the kill. Unlike Eisenberg, who treated it like a job, like his duty. He didn't gut people and leave them hanging upside-down while they died, or shoot them in the back and watch as they twitched in the dirt until the end finally extinguished the light in their eyes. No, if Eisenberg wanted you dead, he would either shoot you in the heart or head, or order someone else to do so.

Clean. Efficient. Professional.

The Runner found the rear door beside a stack of imported Russian guns and captured German weapons, mostly the common MP40s, but also a couple of 57mm *Maschinengewehr 42s* that the resistance were holding back on using—for whatever reason the hierarchy had. Sometimes it felt like they said 'no' simply to give the illusion of being in control, like real military leaders. Well, what he liberated from the new Americans would help him take things up a notch. If he was correct about what it did, and how best to use it. Similar explosives to these were not unheard of, but they were rare.

Now American voices mumbled through the front wall. It was so long since the Runner learned English that the language sounded alien, and he struggled to understand the exact phrases, but the gist was that he had little time. A minute at most. He had to risk it.

The door led to a back alley which, in turn, fed through a series of collapsed shops and a café, and from there he would pick up the former river bed. He whipped it open, casting light on the stash of weapons, and stepped out.

But Reitziger was waiting. The tip of his knife met the Runner's chin. In flawless French, Reitziger said, 'You think we do not know this bar is a resistance meeting place?' He backed the Runner into the cellar.

Eisenberg stepped in behind them, marveled at the haul. 'But we did not expect quite so much treasure. I thank you.' With Reitziger's knife drawing a pinprick of blood, Eisenberg came in close to the Runner. 'Now. Let us talk about what you stole from the Americans.'

19

Clad in black, packs stashed, and helmets in play, Alpha Team converged on the square in three groups: Santa and Chase from the east, Dang and Mac from the north, while Jacobs, Hawks, Dr. Lear and Uhrmacher arrived from the south. There was no westward ingress. The second floor of an intact but abandoned building furnished Thompson with a nest for him and Delilah, his loyal weapon's regular sight aimed at Bar du Pont. The experimental scope was back in its figurative box, the professional marksman unwilling to risk it now their mission had deteriorated into a surreal life-or-death scenario.

Jacobs asked for a status update.

Santa said, 'Blond bastard got the drop on me. Took my iNav, and we lost him.'

'We?' Chase said.

'Dang followed the thief to this location, and we think he's penned in. Can't see a back way out.'

'Your iNav,' Jacobs said. 'Was it disabled?'

'Negative, sir. It was still active from the bunker approach. And the battery has a good twelve hours left.'

'Okay, I want everyone to secure your touch screens. Fingerprint access.'

As Mac followed the order he said, 'Wouldn't worry. If this is the forties, it'll be like a caveman tryin' to figure out a TV.'

Santa lowered his voice, hoping the shame didn't transmit

too obviously. 'I'm not so sure about that. This guy, he's ... he's not stupid.'

'By the numbers,' Jacobs said. 'No mistakes from here on out.'

In the same way they approached the Nazis in the forest—run, cover, touch, repeat—the team advanced on the target. The dozen or so local men, five of them armed, remained in place, observing with curiosity, but not fear.

Thompson said, 'Guessin' this ain't their first rodeo.'

'More reason for caution,' Santa said, now at the bottom of the stairs with Chase, Dang, and Mac. 'Dang, there.' He chopped his hand toward a narrow passageway between the bar and the next building. The rubble in front concealed it from the square, but it clearly led around back. 'Take that route.'

Dang and Mac scrambled over the debris and, once they confirmed there was a back way in, albeit a climb up a drainpipe and through a window, Santa prepared to breach.

Up to the deck, he and Chase took one side of the door each. Submachine guns armed, laser sights active, Santa tried the handle. It was unlocked. He pushed it open, but both men held back, aiming inside.

Their dots swept around the interior. The tavern was large enough to seat fifty people in an establishment with virtually no decoration, but structurally intact. A woman with long dark hair wore a black dress behind the bar. She was in her early twenties, but this was very much *her* bar. Her eyes flared at Santa's intrusion.

He advanced inside, meeting her gaze, finger to his lips. Her fists bunched on her hips. Joined by Chase, Santa moved deliberately over the floorboards, planting each foot silently.

Tables and chairs sat empty. A cast iron fireplace with large marble hearth filled the place with the scent of wood smoke, mingling with the booze and cigarettes from the previous night. The bar itself was stocked sparsely with wine and beer and spirits.

Mac stalked in from the rear. He, too, got the stink eye from the proprietor.

Santa covered each corner, while Chase guarded the doorway behind him. Mac took his section slowly as well, all under the watchful eye of the dark-haired barmaid. She loudly clunked a glass on the bar.

She asked, 'Un boison, monsieurs?'

Boison, Santa thought. *Drink?* He said, 'Ma'am, do you speak English?'

'Non.'

Mac said, 'I think that means no.'

Dang emerged from in back. 'Storeroom's clear.'

The woman lingered on Dang as he joined Santa, Mac, and Chase. Dang smiled and gave a little wave. 'Hi.'

'Don't get too excited, kid,' Santa said. 'Doubt she's ever seen Cuban skin before.' Dang dropped the smile and Santa asked, 'Doc, you speak French?'

Dr. Lear came through sub-vocal. 'I'm fluent in German, Dutch, and Mandarin. Only schoolboy French. Sorry. She did offer you drinks when you first arrived, though.'

Dang said, 'Lemme try.'

'She ain't no Klingon,' Mac said.

Dang closed his eyes for a second, then said, 'Ou es ... le...' He waggled two down-turned fingers. 'Running man. Un garcon. *Running.*'

The woman wiped down her bar, muttering in French.

Dr. Lear said, 'She called you a ... and I'm quoting directly ... a fucking idiot.'

'Great,' Dang said, and looked to Santa. 'What next?'

With muffled voices warbling through the beams above, the Runner kneeled under Reitziger's gun. Eisenberg wielded one of the German MP40s, stalking around the cellar. Each time a footfall dislodged a mote of dust or creaked above them, he pointed at it with the gun barrel.

This man was not sick, but he was always prepared, and always willing to do whatever he deemed necessary. And that was exactly what he did next.

20

Jacobs entered the bar from the front, checking behind him one last time. In the square, the two docs and Hawks held back, while in his nest, Thompson aimed Delilah.

Thompson said, 'Still looks clear.'

Jacobs approached Desiree. A hundred 'hearts-and-minds' training simulations ran through his head, but right now he couldn't think of a single appropriate way to ask a French woman in 1945 why the fuck she was hiding the scumbag who just swiped enough C-4 to gut two buildings.

He said, 'I'm Sergeant Major Vince Jacobs, and I want to help. Who are you?'

Her head lilted to one side, lips pursed. 'Je ne parle pas Anglais.'

She already said that, but Jacobs figured the 'nice' approach might loosen the *Anglais* if she was faking. Santa had managed to ascertain her name was Desiree du Pont, but nothing more.

Dang said, 'I tried everything I know.'

'Near as we can tell,' Santa said, 'the Runner must've headed straight out the back, the way Dang came in.'

Jacobs raised his chin Desiree's way. 'That right?'

'Je ne parle *toujour* pas Anglais.'

Dr. Lear said, 'She said she *still* doesn't speak English.'

'Copy that,' Jacobs replied. 'Anyone got good news?'

Mac jabbed his thumb behind him. 'Sir, all's back there is an empty storeroom and one a' them foreign johns means you gotta squat to take a dump.'

Santa paced toward the end of the bar, gun up. '*Empty* storeroom? You sure it's empty?'

'Except for some cleaning shit, yeah.'

Jacobs spotted it a couple of seconds after Santa.

Santa said, 'Where's all the alcohol come from?'

The bottles behind the bar, wine, spirits, beer. Frequent booze runs weren't exactly practical, although in all war zones throughout history, a central focal point for socializing was something regular people risked their lives over.

Chase hopped the bar to a 'Hey!' from Desiree.

In the cellar, the *thump* from Chase landing sounded above. His voice, muffled, came through: 'Little lady here's standing on a hatch. There's a fuckin' basement.'

Eisenberg and Reitziger separated, both with one eye on the Runner, exploring the ceiling, trying to work out the Americans' positions.

'*Course there's a basement,* Thompson thought. *It's a bar.* That none of them nailed it sooner made him act faster than he liked. Moving this rapidly, with precision equipment, rarely ends well. But even though they didn't say it, the boys in there needed him to check something. And quickly.

He swapped out the regular day scope for the Hobbit, taking a long ten seconds to complete the trade, then adjusted his sight to focus. He switched between the view optimized for imagery, to one optimized for picking up vibrations and movement. The guys inside the bar morphed into ghostly black-and-white avatars, but nothing in the basement. It was blocked with boxes and too many wooden beams and the daylight was too bright firing for standard infrared. But, flicking the switch to that designed for desert conditions, this overrode the infrared warnings, and faded the black-and-white image into red and green. The structure turned translucent.

And revealed three people in the cellar.

'Contact. Three bogies, *right under you.*'

Right under them, the two Germans heard the sudden scrabbling overhead.

Eisenberg said, 'They know we are here.'

He opened fire upwards, the booming machine gun spitting round after round. Reitziger shot from a different angle, filling the space with smoke.

Bullets exploded through the floor. Santa and Mac hit the marble fire hearth, and Dang sprinted for the back. Chase was safe, although he had to cope with Desiree's screaming.

Jacobs remained close to the bar.

Underneath them, the Runner lunged into Reitziger, a thudding shoulder-barge that sent the officer's blasts wild.

The new angle of the bullets covered Dang, just before he made it through to safety. A 9mm slug tore through his thigh and he stumbled, then face-planted short of the corridor. He writhed there, trying to push himself along, leaving a trail of red as he went.

Jacobs hugged the bar, saw Dang go down. Moved towards him.

'Sir,' Santa cried from the hearth. 'Get over here!'

But even as he said it, he knew Jacobs wouldn't leave Dang to bleed alone. He'd lost plenty already.

With the Nazis off-balance, the Runner snatched his bag and fled out the back. Reitziger righted himself, about to pursue, but a shadow moved across the bullet holes above.

'There!' Eisenberg said.

Santa and Mac fired blindly into the floor, hoping to take out whoever it was. The Runner? Was he that desperate to escape?

Under their covering fire, Jacobs ran toward Dang. His smaller pack slipped from his shoulder to pull out the gauze and bandages the kid would need. He'd taken three steps when the wood beneath him splintered.

The blasts from below ripped through his legs, bloody chunks of flesh spurting. He folded, crashed to the floor, and bullets peppered his vest, his arms, his legs again. He spat blood and tried to roll, but it was no use. They would not give in now they had him.

21

'*Sir!*' Santa skirted the edge of the room, Mac firing into the floor.

Santa leapt over the bar. Chase wrenched open the basement hatch. From across the floor, Mac tossed Santa a flashbang grenade. Santa popped the pin, dropped it in. Chase slammed the hatch shut. It blew as expected, like lightning through the bullet holes. The firing from below stopped, and Mac did likewise.

Chase reopened the trapdoor. Santa stepped in, slid down the wooden ladder, landed in a crouch, and swept all around with his SCAR-M. Smoke swirled, the acrid tang of gunpowder stinging his nose. A ton of guns were stacked neatly nearby, including a *Maschinengewehr 42*. His grandpa owned a decommissioned one in his study, mounted on the wall. Weighing in at around twenty-five pounds, armed with 57mm rounds, the MG42 was a monster of a weapon. He doubted it belonged to the barmaid up top.

He found Hawks in the open doorway, her Sig pointed at Reitziger curled by her feet, his ears bleeding.

She said, 'I thought there may be another back door. The blond one ran out that way, but this one was still here.'

Chase dropped into the basement, took in the scene. 'Fuck.'

'The C-4's gone,' Santa said. 'Good work, Hawks. Get him out front.'

She gripped the scruff of Reitziger's neck, yanked him toward the exit. But he jumped up way faster than anyone expected. Santa aimed. Chase aimed. Reitziger seized Hawks by the throat, a knife on her skin.

'Let her go!' Chase's sight painted a dot on Reitziger, but the German kept moving his head.

Hawks said, 'I have got this.'

Reitziger edged sideways for the door, dragging Hawks along as his shield.

'Freeze!' Santa shouted, but then he saw what Hawks meant.

She eased the hilt of her knife out of her belt.

Eyes narrowed in pain, Reitziger said, 'I go now.'

'Yes,' Hawks said. 'You do.'

Snickt—the blade popped out. Hawks wedged her free arm into the crook of Reitziger's elbow and jammed the blade in his leg. Reitziger howled, and Hawks pushed free, and the pair faced-off with their knives.

Spittle sprayed from Reitziger's lips as he attacked. She parried and slashed at his ribs, drawing blood. He dropped his shoulder and punched her in the side of the head, but she almost ducked it; a glancing blow. Their blades clashed like swords, hard and fast, Reitziger a rabid animal, Hawks weaving like a dancer.

Chase bobbed his head toward them and asked Santa, 'Should we—'

'I think it'd piss her off,' Santa said.

Reitziger slashed. Hawks bent back at the hips, his knife close to her face. She was off-balance, ripe for a killing blow. But she used the angle, twisted, and booted him in his wounded leg. He pitched sideways. She kicked him in the sternum. He landed on his back, cracking a stack of wine crates. Hawks lunged forward and, with two hands, she thrust the blade into his chest, pushing it down right up to the hilt.

Reitziger's eyes bulged, his mouth open in surprise. And then his whole body went slack. It was over.

Chase whistled, impressed. 'Fuck me, Hawksy, that was—'

'I told you,' she said. 'We like our knives.'

'Is it wrong that I'm kinda turned on by that?'

Blood dripped from above. Santa followed the droplets to the boxes, the guns, the dead officer.

Hawks pulled the knife from Reitziger's chest. 'Who...?'

'Jacobs,' Santa said. 'They got the boss.'

22

When Santa returned with Chase and Hawks, Jacobs was barely hanging on. Mac tended to him with a field med-kit, while Desiree hurried to the scene with an armful of bar towels. Mac accepted them and layered as many has he could over Jacobs' wounds, cinching them tight, telling him to hang on, it'll be fine.

Thompson rushed in, pulled up short. 'Square's clear. Jesus ... I'm sorry. I should have spotted them.'

Jacobs worked his jaw, barely able to focus. 'Forget it...' He moved his wrist. 'Someone...' He pointed. 'Help ... Dang...'

Desiree ran a couple of towels over to where Dang lay, and helped him stem the flow. Chase and Hawks assisted by strapping the padding tight.

'Santa...' The sergeant-major shifted his hand to his pocket, an effort that made him wince.

Santa knelt beside him, blood soaking into his trousers. 'Stay still, sir.'

'I don't take orders from you.'

'Sir...'

Jacobs slid his hand into view, and drunkenly pulled Santa close. Palmed him the item he'd been messing with since the bunker. He coughed out the word, 'Everyone!'

Chase and Hawks helped Dang limp over, a proper gauze and a towel taped to his wound. All gathered round.

Jacobs said, 'Santa's ... in charge now...'

Mac and Chase both glanced at Thompson, but the team's official second-in-command held still.

Santa said, 'I told you—'

'It's time,' Jacobs said. 'And it's ... y'know ... an order.'

Santa bowed his head.

'About your grandfather... Moscow.'

'What about him?' Santa said.

'The nukes. The story ... it's *true*. It really happened.'

'How can you know that, sir?'

'You ... saved his life today. And he stops the launch. He ... *will* stop the launch...'

Santa pressed on one of Jacobs' larger wounds, but the blood pumped around the compress. The color showed it was arterial. That he'd held on this long was a miracle in itself.

'How do you know that about my grandpa?'

Jacobs said, 'Because I was there.'

Stories about General Santarelli were popular all over the world these days, and a sort-of cult sprang up around them. Some called him a true hero, while others thought of him as an American Baron Munchausen. Once an incident was no longer classified, he would write an account of it, with a flair that occasionally ranked him, critically, alongside Tom Clancy, but his insistence on publishing the stories as non-fiction meant he never reached those literary heights. While the government issued no comment on his version of events, people dug for facts, coming up empty as often as corroborating him, and some pointed to the government's silence as proof of a network of super-agents operating around the globe, influencing world leaders, and shaping the population's lives to their own ends.

To Santa, he'd always been Grandpa. An eccentric fool

who invested his earnings well, could train a boy to gain the fitness of a pro soldier, and make a little girl laugh until her ribs ached, but who had never seen a real person speak out for him before.

'Sir,' Santa said. 'Just because my grandpa thinks I should be pushing myself, it doesn't mean—'

'When a general speaks...' Jacobs started, but took three shallow breaths to complete the sentence. 'You listen.'

'What? Sir, that's what he told...' Santa's tight face relaxed, a chill sweeping through him.

Chase said, 'You were the fuckin' driver?'

Jacobs grinned. 'Swore me to secrecy ... he ... liked the ... ambiguity.' He coughed again, and a fine red mist bloomed, then faded. 'Santa ... the general is right ... about you. I need you to take lead. You are ... the only one capable.'

Thompson turned away, then back again. Swallowed.

'I'm sorry, Thompson.' Jacobs gripped Santa's hand. 'Get them ... home.'

Jacobs retched up a slew of blood. His grip slackened. The light faded from his eyes, and he died, there on the floor of Bar Du Pont.

Santa's fingers were curled so tightly around the object Jacobs gave him that it actually helped hold back his anger and grief.

Chase said, 'What'd he give you?'

'He picked it up in the bunker. Before we got stuck in the chamber.' Santa slowly opened his fist.

A set of US dog tags.

Santa frowned. Fished into his own uniform.

Chase said, 'So come on, whose tags are they?'

Santa looked at his own, and back to the ones in his hand. Stared at nothing in particular as he understood why Jacobs acted the way he did. He held up the tags so everyone else could see.

He said, 'They're mine.'

23

As darkness descended over the town, Santa sat alone on the top step of Bar du Pont, fiddling with the dog tags. Soft *whumphs* rode in from the west, allied bombs driving back the final vestiges of German invaders. Although it sounded like they were only a couple of hills away, the muffled explosions meant they were much further, and only carried this far because of the thin air, and the elevation.

Desiree had hung a sign on the bottom rail declaring the bar closed, and occasionally a local would happen by, often with a gun on his shoulder, read the notice, give Santa an irritated shrug, then go on his way. Mostly men. Only two women came by in the hour he loitered out here. The rest of the team wanted to toast Jacobs, but Santa's first order of his unwanted command was to ban alcohol until they returned home. 'We'll drink to his memory back in twenty-fifteen, and not before,' he said.

The order was met with silence, until Thompson said, 'Yeah. Santa's right. Let's keep a clear head.'

And the French girl, Desiree, said she'd brew some coffee.

Inside, Desiree opened up the rear of the bar to reveal a stove with two wood-fired rings and a couple of huge pots. She directed Dang to chop and peel with gestures that left no room for interpretation. A morphine shot allowed him to stand without pain, and the dressing halted the bleeding, but he still kept his foot raised, sat on one stool with his ankle on another. It was awkward, but the activity helped him concentrate on preparing this meal, and allowed the team to put away their ration packs. Who knew if they'd need the packs later? With home-cooking on offer, preserving supplies became less of a chore. If it weren't for Jacobs' body under a bloody sheet, it would have been a happy anecdote to tell the boys back home.

Dang was more concerned, though, that the team had split into three distinct groups: Mac and Thompson talked in low voices at one end of the bar, while Chase and Hawks discussed knife-fighting techniques at the other, and Dang took part in that before Desiree dragged him away to help with dinner; finally, Drs. Lear and Uhrmacher hunched over one of the tables, comparing notes in the old diary Lear brought, against the shiny new equivalent Dr. Uhrmacher carried in his pocket.

Perhaps a meal might bring them back together.

Desiree babbled something in French and when Dang held the short knife up, she guided his wrist and taught him how to slice the garlic bulb as thin as she required. Once he'd performed what he took to be an adequate job and she scraped the slivers into the stew, he suddenly felt a tingle of excitement. He checked in his pockets and found his iPhone was still intact. It was always switched off during operations, and if Jacobs learned of its presence, the sergeant-major would've chewed him all the way out. Even if Dang wasn't actually captured, jihadis were able to pull the signals out of the air, and enjoyed little more than taunting relatives of US soldiers—it had happened before. But now he had a real-world use for it, providing it didn't require a 4G connection to work the app he was thinking of.

Desiree held herself stiff as Dang showed her the phone. As

the colorful tiles bloomed to life, he thought this was how Picard or Kirk must have felt encountering a primitive alien species for the first time. At least the US Army enacted no 'prime directive' for dealing with people from the 1940s, so he wasn't breaking any rules.

He tapped on a translation app and typed, 'We will not hurt you. You are not a prisoner. We need to find the man who stole from us.'

The phone relayed the message in mechanical French, and Desiree stared at it, then at Dang. She continued stirring, but spoke French at the phone. Dang held up a finger—*wait*. He engaged the microphone, and made a 'patting' gesture. She understood, and slowed her speech.

The phone interpreted her words as, 'He is resistance. He raids German supply runs with the other brave men here. I do not know him.'

'Now we're getting somewhere,' Dang said, and the handset translated for him.

Between the cooking and a lot more iPhone-assisted chatting, Dang drew concerned looks from the two scientists, obviously worried about engaging a primitive culture with technology that must appear magical to them, but in Dang's limited experience you could take a child who'd never seen electricity in 2015—there were millions of them around the world—and show him a Pixar movie projected onto a sheet, and once the initial sense of wonder wore off, the kid simply accepted it. The impossible, made possible before your eyes, always became the norm eventually.

The door opened. Everyone fell silent. Santa's face was blank, those weird-as-hell dog tags still hanging from one fist. He took in the disparate groups and stood equidistant between them. 'So what have we got?'

'Dinner,' Thompson said. 'Least, I think it's nearly ready.'

'Hope so,' Mac said. 'Dang, you ready?'

Dang showed Santa the iPhone, and demonstrated his back-and-forth with Desiree. The phone said, 'Ten minutes.'

Dang said, 'But it's not just cooking we've been talking about. You want to know who took our C-4?'

Santa lowered himself into a chair by a long table. 'Why not. Let's hear it.'

'Cool. So. Resistance fighters have driven a lot of the Nazis out. The allies won't make it out to these remote outposts, so it's up to them.'

Santa said, 'More likely the Nazis got recalled to help fight in more important areas.'

'Whatever. Most flew out. Left the locals to rebuild the town, and mostly left 'em alone. But like the GIs said, supplies are still coming in.'

Uhrmacher said, 'The new equipment and food is for Eisenberg and his men.'

'No shit?' Chase said.

'The Allies,' Dang went on, 'are about a hundred miles west of here, but Desiree heard about some advance party, which I guess means your grandpa. But two weeks ago, with the allies close by, Eisenberg shipped in troops to fight the resistance on their terms. Hand to hand, tree to tree.'

Thompson said, 'So we got bad guys at the airfield and unknown numbers in the forest fighting a guerrilla war with insurgents.'

'How's that help us?' Mac asked.

'Well, we have a person willing to help,' Dang said. 'She's picked this up so quick, she's obviously real smart.'

'Uh-oh,' Chase said. 'I think someone's in luurrve!'

'Shut-up, Chase. Let's concentrate on avenging Jacobs.'

'Avenging him? Who the fuck are you? Iron Man?'

Before Dang could reply, Mac said, 'We took 'em all out at the bunker, and Hawks turned his officer buddy into kebab-meat. He's probably running all the way back home over those mountains.'

'Unlikely,' Uhrmacher said.

Santa pulled his seat closer to the scientist. 'Really? Why not?'

Uhrmacher removed his glasses and rubbed the bridge of his nose. 'It is more likely that Project Return Fire is now active.'

'Oh.' Thompson stepped down from his stool. 'You figured you'd bring that up now? Why'nchu tell us all about "Project Return Fire"?'

Although Santa offered to help several times, Desiree insisted on serving them as guests. Sitting himself at the longer table meant the team all grouped together, with Thompson on his right and Chase on his left. While Desiree brought out metal plates topped with a potato and vegetable stew, Uhrmacher presented 'Project Return Fire.'

'Simply put, if news reaches us that Germany loses the war, or if it is impossible to win, Captain Eisenberg will take his men to the spike we created in 1939, and see to it that no one but Germany can emerge victorious.'

'What's a "spike"?' Dang asked.

Hawks said, 'More importantly, what will he do in the past?'

Uhrmacher spread his palms and shrugged. 'I am nothing more than a scientist. They do not share such plans with me.'

'Okay, wait,' Chase said. 'If the Nazis have this fuckin' obscenity, how come they don't win?'

'Because we stopped them,' Dang said.

Santa swallowed the most delicious potato he'd ever encountered. 'More likely my grandpa's unit did. They're here, the war is pretty much over. Someone stopped Eisenberg first time around without our help.'

Dr. Lear nodded agreement. 'It's likely he was killed by the bombers at the airfield. He requires specially-manufactured rods to work the machine. They are stored there, away from the bunker.'

'For safety,' Uhrmacher added.

Forks clinked on the plates, and chewing and swallowing followed. The veg was moist but not sloppy, rich with gravy and oils, and garlic topped it off a treat.

When his mouth was empty, Santa said, 'Still doesn't explain why they didn't go back when things went bad for them on D-Day.'

Thompson said, 'And why's it way out here, not back in the Fatherland?'

Uhrmacher put down his fork and wiped his chin with his handkerchief. He said, 'The answer to both questions is that we are dealing with a crystal of enormous power. Of unknown origin. Some say an expedition to Egypt uncovered it, but we cannot be sure.'

Mac said, 'I think I saw that movie.'

'That is unlikely,' Uhrmacher said. 'But wherever it came from, would you want to keep such an unknowable object in your homeland, or rely on it to conquer a world?'

The rest of the meal took place in silence. At first, they all looked to Santa, but he encouraged them only to eat. After, as Chase and Mac cleared the plates, Thompson insisted Santa make a damned decision.

'I need more information,' Santa said. 'We don't even get how this thing works.'

Dr. Lear stepped up, shaking the notebook. 'Sounds like my song. The physics are so complex I doubt any of you will grasp it, but if you would allow it, perhaps I can put it in layman's terms?'

They all twisted their bodies to face him. Pissed.

'No need to be like that,' Dr. Lear said. 'I need your attention.' A piece of chalk in his hand, he asked Desiree, 'May I?'

Through the phone she said, 'Go ahead, you cannot hurt my business any more than you already have.' She spread her arm to indicate the hole-riddled floor.

Lear drew a simple stick figure diagram as he talked. 'They have generated many fixed points, or "spikes." Anchor points in time. Each spike can only be used once. The first one exists in 1939, but now this Captain Eisenberg fellow needs to refuel the machine.'

Dr. Lear's diagram showed stick figures of Alpha Team in a tunnel branching from one crystal to another.

'The crystal,' Uhrmacher said. 'We experimented on it, but could not even chip off a fragment to examine. We ran high levels of energy through it, enough to power a city for a week, and we watched as it faded away, then back into a solid state. We connected objects to the crystal—a pen, a soft toy, a live gerbil—and whatever was attached faded too, and returned with the crystal. It was only when we tried this with a wristwatch that we noted the time difference.'

'These anchor points,' Dr. Lear said, drawing connecting lines between past and present, 'create an exit point. In the future, we created an entrance. When the two linked up—'

'A wormhole,' Dang said.

'Yes, yes.' Uhrmacher was growing excited. 'We call it a tunnel. Like a mole. But worms too, yes, this works.'

'The copper chamber,' Dr. Lear said, 'keeps the crystal's energy contained but also spreads it around.'

Santa realized he had shuffled forward, sitting literally on the edge of his seat. 'Because it's both conductive and reflective?'

'Ah, someone paid attention in high school physics. Exactly.'

'Right,' Chase said. 'That's a long fuckin' way round of sayin' we go back up the way we came.'

Mac fist-bumped Chase. 'Yeah, let's close ourselves in and—'

'Not possible,' Uhrmacher said.

Chase flipped him his middle finger. 'Shut the fuck up. Get to working out how to—'

'Not helping,' Santa said.

Thompson said, 'Boys just wanna go home.'

'You think I don't? I have Lily to consider.'

'I don't have kids,' Mac said. 'But I still wanna get back.'

'I got a wife,' Thompson said. 'Think she ain't worried?'

'My mom's sick,' Dang added. 'Mac's started seeing this girl a couple months ago too.'

'Actually, we split up,' Mac said. 'Thought I might find a nice British chick—'

'*You cannot go home!*' Uhrmacher said suddenly. 'Not ever.'

Hawks said, 'I do not want to be here with you in 2015, now I have to live with you in olden days? Wonderful.'

Dr. Lear tapped his lip, flipping through the notebook. 'Sadly, gentlemen, I think he may be correct.'

24

'I am sorry,' Uhrmacher said, 'but the machine is not fully operational.' He raised his hand to his brow and rubbed as if he was enduring a migraine. 'All effort was put towards making it go *backwards*. There were no plans to ever go forward. There was no need, not for Project Return Fire to proceed. In time, maybe they would let us experiment, but for now, we do not even know if it *can* go forward.'

Chase stood up and kicked over a chair. 'Well, isn't that a fuckin' boot in the balls.'

Desiree stepped in and Chase held up 'surrender' palms.

Thompson said, 'Dr. Lear, what do you think?'

Dr. Lear was still thumbing through the notebook. 'As I say, he *may* be correct. It looks like there are *designs* for forward journeys, but—'

'Theoretical,' Uhrmacher said. 'We never stop thinking about the possibilities, but—'

'It would require more than twice the power of backwards-travel.'

'Yes, and we do not have that capacity.'

Hawks said, 'What about the fuel Eisenberg needs in the airfield?'

Uhrmacher removed his glasses once again, this time aging him ten years. 'Even if we acquired these extra fuel rods, it still would require us to overload the system in order to generate the required power. This would result in a meltdown.'

'What does that mean?' Mac asked.

Chase picked up the chair he kicked. 'Radi-fucking-ation everywhere.'

Outside in the town square, the team lay Jacobs' shrouded body in the dry fountain. A half-dozen locals watched from the sidelines. It was fully dark now, and little had been said since the kick in the balls back in Bar du Pont.

Desiree furnished Dang with a walking stick, and he was able to stand beside Santa as their new leader poured a couple of slugs of fume-heavy moonshine on their former CO—the only liquor Desiree would give up. Dang asked, 'What's next, sir? After this?'

'Doesn't matter,' Santa said.

'Of course it matters.' Dang accepted the bell jar of clear alcohol. 'We changed things, you know. We have no idea what's going on tonight. What if Eisenberg was supposed to die at the bunker this afternoon? Maybe one of the GIs got free. Or that resistance Runner guy coulda' saved the GIs and then they destroyed the airfield, and everything was fine. But now it's all changed…'

'We don't *know* anything.'

Chase took his turn with the liquor, slopping a portion into the fountain. 'If we changed something, how come we're still here?'

Santa said, 'We interfere more, we might make it worse.'

'True,' Dr. Lear said, stood to the side with Dr. Uhr-macher. 'There are many theories about this, but it is impossible to prove any. Maybe it already *did* change, and our brains assimilated the new reality without us seeing it. Or perhaps we exist outside the future time stream now we're here. A reset, so to speak.'

'Also,' Uhrmacher said, 'we worry that nothing we do will change anything. Everything that will happen has already happened. It is possible that, if Eisenberg goes back, he has *already* gone back, and history will play out regardless. He could step out of the bunker, and instead of making his way through Switzerland, he might die in an avalanche, or be caught before he can deliver victory to Germany. Many possibilities.'

'So do nothing,' Thompson said, dribbling his share onto Jacobs. 'That's a plan?'

Dang looked to Santa. 'Sir—'

'Don't call me that.' Santa took a flare from one of the packs.

'But you're leading now.' Dang appealed to the other guys, ending at Thompson, who shrugged.

Thompson said, 'Jacobs' orders were clear—'

'I don't care,' Santa said. 'My grandpa's unit is here to blow up the airfield, which is where the fuel rods are, and we're certain Eisenberg never changed history. He *can't*. He's gonna die. We don't have to do a thing.'

Mac poured on the remaining liquor. 'So that's your plan? We *wait*? And hope? We're *Army Rangers*. We got a job to do.'

Santa said, 'Our job is seventy years away. Not here.'

'What about the rods?' Chase said.

'What about 'em? We can't use them. Better they're buried in a mountain pass than out there for everyone to see.'

Thompson said, 'Eggheads said "probably" a lot. And "maybe." While there's a chance, Santa, we should be trying.'

Santa struck the flare. It bloomed an angry purple. All focused on the searing flame in his hand.

115

'Dr. Lear,' he said. 'What's the best case scenario? If we tried?'

Dr. Lear stepped away from the smoke. He said, 'The spike exists in the future, but we would need to create another spike now, cut a separate tunnel, or wormhole, and bypass our incoming selves... it's possible. But I'm certain it would require more energy than the machine can handle.'

'Odds?'

'I'm seventy-five percent certain of a mushroom cloud situation.'

Santa tossed the flare into the fountain. Flames flickered to life, dancing up into the dark. Then the liquor took hold and the fountain filled with fire.

Thompson came in closer to Santa, patience wearing thin. 'You wanna keep this up, fine, I'll follow orders. Just understand this ain't some trainin' mission or cakewalk. You're responsible for us all. But if you write Jacobs' order off as a dyin' delusion, no one back home'll blame you.'

Mac said, 'Thompson's right, guys. He's senior, he's more experienced. No matter what Jacobs said. He'll make a decision.'

Santa stared into the flames. Relinquishing a command he never asked for meant disobeying orders. But if the orders were questionable, issued while the person was of unsound judgment, like illegal orders, he would be in no trouble should he disobey. Theoretically. Thing was, Jacobs had given him command a number of times, and Colonel Johnson approved it just before they hit the LZ.

Uhrmacher watched the soldiers. It would be easier if Santa could really unpick that guy's mind. He seemed to be cooperating, but he was still a Nazi. If he was being genuine, he was a risk-averse type, so he might have been over-egging the danger.

With the flames consuming Vince Jacobs, the German squeezed his lips tightly, almost as emotional as they were. Could he fake such compassion?

'Well?' Thompson said.

'I...' Santa closed his eyes. Couldn't speak.

Then the whole world flashed white.

A single strobe burst.

They all staggered, an invisible icepick through their brains. As soon as they could see straight again, Alpha Team pulled their weapons, and faced outward. But there was no enemy. Just a bunch of scared Frenchmen with guns, afraid to touch them.

Chase said, 'What the fuck was that?'

Mac rubbed his brow with his free hand. 'My head! Felt like it was gonna explode.'

'What *was* that?' Hawks said. 'What have you people started now?'

'The time stream,' Dang said. 'Has to be.'

'What happened?' Uhrmacher asked, apparently unscathed.

'In the light,' Dr. Lear said. 'I saw myself. On fire.'

Still shaky from the experience, Santa realized he saw something too, burned on the inside of his eyelids, like the aftermath of a camera flash. Only, this time it was an image of Lily, standing before the destruction of a city, and deep in his gut he could not shake the sense that everything was lost.

Thompson unpacked Delilah and disengaged the Hobbit scope, using it to sweep the square. 'Doesn't matter what it was. We need to take *action*.'

Mac said, 'We gotta go for those rods.'

Chase said, 'Your call, Santa.'

'Gentlemen,' Dr. Lear said. 'I don't know what that flash was, but it must have to do with our trip here. Either time is being altered and we need to make a decision, or we need to desist in our current actions. It occurred when Santa was dithering so perhaps doing nothing isn't an option, or...'

'Or what?' Santa said.

'Or we all have massive brain tumors from the radiation.'

'Damn it, Doc, this is serious. What the hell was that?'

'Okay, fine.' Dr. Lear paced, pointing as punctuation. 'They have this *awesome* machine that can swing history in their favor. They can warn the high command about D-Day, assassinate Winston Churchill, bribe some senators to vote against America joining the war ... whatever Eisenberg is doing, he can only do it if you chaps don't stop him.'

Hawks coughed.

Dr. Lear said, 'I mean "chaps" in the ... "people" sense. My point is, if those flashes are down to our actions, or more to the point, our *inaction*, maybe we need to try.' He gave Uhrmacher a pleading look. 'Even at twenty-five percent.'

Santa replayed events in his head: *Lily giving him that beaming smile; the flash in the time chamber that knocked them out, so similar to the strobe that hit them; grabbing the arm of the Nazi soldier about to kill the young Anthony; firing the gun; the general, asking him yet again, 'Did I ever tell you how you got your name?'*

Each moment caused Santa's grip on the tags to tighten.

Sergeant Brown, in the aftermath of the fight beside the bunker, telling them their plan. 'We aim to destroy the airfield ourselves or call in the bombers. Either way it ain't gonna exist much longer.'

'My grandpa,' Santa said now. 'He's going to blow up that airfield.'

The bullets firing from the floor in Bar du Pont; Jacobs, bleeding; 'It's true ... it's all true...'

'Eisenberg was there,' Santa said. 'When the sarge told us

about blowing up the airfield. Eisenberg was present. If he heard...'

'Shit,' Thompson said. 'They know the GIs are coming. They'll be waitin' for 'em.'

Chase said, 'Meaning...?'

'Meaning,' Dang said, 'we can't *not* interfere now. The general is in danger. If he dies...'

'Dr. Uhrmacher,' Santa said, 'do you know exactly how much we need to power our way home?'

'At least two point five times what it took to bring you,' Uhrmacher said. 'You would need all the rods stored at the airfield. Not just those Eisenberg will collect.'

'Hang on,' Mac said. 'You're sayin'—'

'Yes,' Uhrmacher said. 'Why not. If Eisenberg returns to 1945, we are all lost.' He gave a short, chuckle. 'It may kill us all, but maybe ... maybe, once you make certain Eisenberg is dead, I can send you all ... *back* to the future.'

At funerals, it is not unheard of for some minor blip of an incident to occur, to set of someone giggling; a trip, a child's comment, a louder-than-intended fart. It is a result of so many stored up emotions, that when a release valve is turned, it is difficult to switch off. Here, with the flames consuming Sergeant Major Vince Jacobs' body, with Uhrmacher's accidental quote from the 80's movie, Mac was the first to snort, then hold in a giggle. The others kinda smirked too. Then it rippled throughout the gathered team, no one making eye-contact lest they burst out laughing completely. The breaking of the tension, the relief of a decision finally being made.

Attempting to smother full-on laughter, Santa stared into the flames one last time. When he faced the others, he was stone-cold serious. From a pack at his feet, he pulled a paper map and brought Uhrmacher and Hawks together.

'Okay,' he said. 'This is a map from 2015, but the topography should be accurate. Doctor. Show Hawks where that airfield is. We need to make sure my grandpa makes it through this. Or God help us all.'

25

'Okay,' Santa told them as they prepped their weapons and packs inside Bar du Pont. 'A story. If you're all sitting comfortably ... once upon a time, toward the end of the Second World War, a US Army private called Anthony Santarelli was stationed in Southern France for six months. Whilst there, he received a letter containing the tragic news that his fiancée, Sarah, died in childbirth. A son, conceived on the night before he shipped out. And Sarah's devoutly religious parents wanted to give the bastard baby away.

'Yet, after the war, Anthony raised the baby himself. His own parents died a couple of years before he enlisted, but he had good friends, and a family known as the US military. He never married. He stayed in the service of his country, rose through the ranks, and took part in some of America's key battles through the years.

'He planned the Ying Mao offensive in Korea, managed some key victories in Vietnam, without ever deploying napalm. Heck, he even advised the president against the Bay of Pigs. Guess the president should have listened to him.

'Later, he worked in intelligence. I heard his stories a million times and each version got wilder and wilder. Figured it was mostly bullshit, but Jacobs ... he said the Glasnost story is real. So now I'm guessing others might be too.

'In the meantime, his son Mike, raised pretty much entirely by the Army, rebelled and became an investment banker. He got rich over the years, and although he left it late to start

121

a family, he went on to marry a much younger woman named Marie, and together they had a *very* handsome son, called Jonathan.

'Jonathan ... Named after the soldier who saved his Anthony Sr.'s life in France, nineteen forty-five.'

I ever tell you how you got your name?

Chase said, 'Think the old coot knew?'

Santa thought about it. 'Yeah, he knew. When I was thirteen or fourteen he started pushing me physically. That's when his stories first got more spectacular and glamorous sounding. I must have begun looking like that memory of his when I hit puberty. He didn't persuade me directly, but I was young when I joined the Army. Wanted to get away from my dad's Wall Street life. But Grandpa ... he definitely influenced me. All along, he knew. He knew I would grow up to save his life.'

Having trekked above the snow line, and changed back into their whites, Alpha Team double-timed it through the woods. The shrieks and cries of nocturnal wildlife accompanied them, while a crescent moon watched on overhead. Their footfalls were practiced, virtually silent, and even the two docs managed to keep it light, Lear the adventure sport enthusiast making light work of it, though Uhrmacher stopped for breath more often. The only person not present was Dang.

Back inside Bar du Pont, as the team slung on their packs and stowed their weapons, Thompson caught Santa's eye and twitched his head at Dang. While Santa wasn't happy about it, Thompson was correct. He brought Dang aside, and told him, 'Sorry, buddy, but you're sitting this one out.'

'What? No. I can walk.'

'On foot, that airfield is two hours at regular speed. We're gonna have to put in some serious cardio. Uphill.'

'Then you go ahead, I'll catch up. I can still be useful. You know I can. That Uhrmacher guy can't keep up. I'll watch him.'

'He assures us he will. He doesn't drink, and he hasn't had a bullet rip through his thigh muscle.'

'It's a flesh wound.'

'It is. And they're nasty. They stop you from running.'

'Santa's right, Dang.' Thompson joined them, the rest of the team now aware something was wrong. 'Why'n'chu guard the civilian.'

Desiree paused washing a glass as she felt their eyes upon her. 'Oui?' They went back to their business, and she returned to hers.

After more back and forth, with Dang and Desiree watching on from the bar's stoop, Alpha Team jogged away, fully armed, ready for combat. As they left the square, Santa caught sight of at least four locals heading for the bar. Desiree would do some business tonight after all.

Now, as Hawks led the way, she checked the map again. Held up a fist. The team hunkered down behind a large rock. Listened. They were high up now, but in a valley, the mountain pass in which La Bastion was built, and which the Nazis chose as the site for their landing field. A good choice, as the US Army would attest in seven decades' time; it was where the Black Hawk would be waiting for them, if they ever made it back up the tunnel. The pass dropped in increments. Beyond the town, it plunged even further. In the late summer months, a river flowed, and would probably flood the streets on occasion, but for the time being it was dry, and

Alpha Team used it as a guiding path to—hopefully—get ahead of the GIs.

Santa said, 'Do you smell cigar smoke?'

'The other Americans?' Hawks said.

'Maybe.' Santa pointed at Thompson. 'You see a nest?'

Thompson spent a few seconds checking the area, gave Santa the 'Okay' sign with his thumb and forefinger, and slipped away toward an outcrop of intertwined trees growing out the side of a rise.

Santa crawled up the rock and over the top of the trough formed by the hibernating river. Using the zoom on his night vision goggles, Santa watched the eight-strong team, including the young incarnation of the man who would prevent World War Three, advancing through the woods. They were less than a thousand yards from the edge of what Dr. Uhrmacher assured them was an airfield housing a battalion of German soldiers, and enough uranium to blow up the mountain ten times over.

'Thompson,' Santa said. 'I'm gonna need the best report you ever laid on us.'

26

The image down Delilah's Hobbit scope turned red-brown. The GIs' bodies glowed white with a misty red aura, the sergeant using a bulky radio to make a call. No doubt to the bombers they promised would wipe the airfield off the map.

Thompson still wasn't sure about the tech. His old scopes had none of this: one regular for daytime use, and one infrared, much like the goggles. The new viewing modes gave him the bog-standard settings, plus ultra-high-def low-light penetration, and this oddity: intense infrared, which essentially took the input normally associated with the green computer-game-style view where minute amounts of light returned clear images in their new hue, but this worked in even darker circumstances, shooting out body heat and movement and converting it to imagery. Somehow, it differentiated between small animals and humans, filtering them out. It was for shit in terms of actually aiming at something to shoot, but as a method of identifying a target, he conceded it was pretty good.

Only thing was, he wasn't sure they should be targeting anything.

Okay, today had been one hell of a head fuck all round. Not only the time travel, but Jacobs passing him over for a battlefield promotion in favor of a kid whose only real qualification was his kick-ass grandpa. A grandpa who Thompson now watched in the form of a weird reddish ghost.

His problem was not that a younger guy was in charge, or that he was passed over; Thompson was pretty happy at his current rank. He just questioned what made Santa a better leader to get them out of this. And now the kid was making a potentially deadly mistake.

Sure, Thompson pressed Santa for a decision, but he didn't expect him to go all bat shit crazy. One minute it's 'let's do nothing' and the next he's jumping in with both feet, wanting to blow ten tons of shit out of the time stream.

The time stream. In his ten years with the US Army, he'd never known such a dickish thought. It was like they'd all woken up in one of Dang's wet dreams. Time travel, a firefight, now the kid was all alone with an exotic chick, communicating via a device that was probably like an alien's toy to her. Meanwhile, here they were, about to crack open the space-time continuum.

Yeah, *space-time continuum*. If you're gonna talk shit, may as well commit to that shit.

All he wanted was for the kid to set up an ambush, take the rods off the Nazis when they showed, and go the fuck home. Arrowing headlong into a battle that resolved itself seventy years earlier was dumb-dumb-*dumb*. If the general died here, because of them, they'd have felt more than some split-second migraine. The world would have crumbled around them.

No, all those damned flashes meant was that they needed to *go home*. Not fight the goddamned Nazis all over again.

He zoomed out and panned right to where the airfield loomed a thousand yards away. The visuals were dull so he flicked to the green infrared and the moonlight revealed three actual planes lined up on one end. Two big-bellied whales and a sleek bomber. Two towers equipped with floodlights, sandbags, and mounted machine guns, both in darkness. Nothing moved. No wildlife, no people.

'Looks deserted,' he told the team. 'Gimme a minute.'

He swept the field, summarizing all he saw: the runway stretched backwards somewhere between five and seven thousand feet, dotted with buildings. Barracks large enough for twenty or more men lay off to one side, while a guard tower lorded over the place from where the terrain made a sharp turn upward, a hill starting to transform into a mountain.

'Can't be abandoned,' he said.

'No,' Santa replied. 'I seriously doubt it.'

'Unless he's been and gone already. Taken his guys back to the bunker. Where we should be.'

'We worked that out,' Dr. Lear said. 'It would take too long.'

'Still...'

Santa said, 'Thompson, I know you don't like this, but if we're doing it, we're doing it. I can't go home until we're sure everyone in that future is safe. Including my grandpa.'

'Roger that. Stand by.'

Thompson made a scan of the perimeter. Stopped on a fuzzy blur. He flicked back to the intense infrared mode and found a shimmering white blob spilling from the belly of the German bomber.

'Hmm. Got somethin'...'

At the thumbing of a dial, the image turned black and white, the effect of ultra-high-def low-light penetration. The lines forming each object took on a thicker quality, like someone traced around the scene with a Sharpie. It picked out hard edges and regular lines with a clarity that left no doubt: the blob had been surrounding the 20mm cannon the bomber would have used against fighter planes trying to shoot it down.

He zoomed in on the toughened glass bubble through which the gun was poking. Focused the scope. A man's hand grew clearer around the weapon, inches inside. In another hand, raised to the Gunner's mouth, was a radio.

'Ah, shit,' Thompson said. 'Goose steppers definitely know they're coming. It's a trap.'

He swung his scope to the GIs. They all advanced up the hill, closing in on the nearest tower. Two of them, Martins and Simons he seemed to remember, ran ahead and took cover at an overhang.

Thompson switched back to intense infrared and swept left.

The red mode picked out another body, lying down on a camouflaged building. Another to that body's right, and more. Then night-vis revealed a rifle. Every location was armed, troops awaiting an order.

Santa said, 'Okay, all move into position.'

'You sure?' Thompson said.

'We need to back them up here.'

'Doc, are *you* sure we should be doing this?'

Dr. Lear said, 'I'm not sure about anything. This is unprecedented. When I get round to writing my paper, there won't even be an opportunity for peer review because to peer review it, someone would have to come back and try to change history. If that happens, I might not come back, and never write the paper—'

'Just answer the question,' Thompson said.

'The answer is that I do not know. If we interfere, we might destroy the future. If we don't interfere, we might destroy the future. We're in guesswork territory. Not really my field of expertise.'

'Thompson,' Santa said. 'I need you on this.'

Mac said, 'Maybe he's right. I mean—'

'No,' Chase said. 'We kick more Nazi ass, then go home. That's the plan.'

'I'm sorry, Santa,' Thompson said. 'I have to listen to the doc on this one. Let it play out.'

Santa said, 'Back in town you wanted to take action, now you're going to disobey an order because of a fifty-fifty guess?'

Thompson trained his sights on Santa, infrared pulling his frustrated expression into clear focus. Thompson said, 'Let *this* play out, and *then* go get the fuel rods. *That's* the action we take.'

Santa peeked up over the bluff, now watching the GIs from behind as they crept closer to the airfield. He said, 'In position. Prepare to engage.'

'Hold that order,' Thompson said. 'I am taking command. Do not engage. I repeat do *not* engage.'

'They're going to die!'

'Some of 'em, sure. But this already happened.'

'You saw the deal with my name, Thompson. I saved the general. How do you know we're not here to save them too?'

'I don't. But we'll find out in a—'

One of the huge floodlights crashed on, illuminating half the forest, and the anti-aircraft gun in the belly of the bomber rattled to life.

27

The 20mm steel-jackets ripped through the GIs' medic who was darting to a second cover point. The older guy, Private Hall, jerked hard as his chest popped with three fist-sized holes. The chubby fella, Gregson ran forward alongside his lanky pal—Turin. Where these names were coming from, Thompson couldn't say. They were all dying right before him, but he told himself they died seventy years ago. Sad, yet the whole country honored their deaths every Veteran's Day. He wasn't *letting them die*; he was *observing history play out*.

Gregson and Turin made it to the other side, a trail of anti-aircraft bullets blasting behind them, before finally tearing up the tree trunk that hid them.

On comms, Hawks said, 'They cannot survive this.'

'Thompson!' Santa said. 'I need you to lay down some covering—'

'I can't,' Thompson said. 'Court martial me if we live.'

He switched to hi-def black and white and shifted his view to the airfield. German troops streamed from their buildings, ran back and forth, arming themselves, taking cover.

A Gatling gun blasted to life. The nest guarded the airfield's outer-perimeter, to the left of the GIs' attack, ideally-positioned for such an incursion. A white-clad Nazi soldier hid behind a sheet of metal through which his gun pointed, bullets feeing in, shells spitting out.

Down at the edge of their assault point, Sergeant Brown ducked against the massive rounds that gouged dirt and wood out of his immediate area. He fired his machine gun. The others joined in. All fired blind, some shots coming close to the nest, but the GIs' bullets just pinged on the metal.

Over the gunfire, Brown yelled, '*Flank him! Now!*'

Brown and Anthony laid down covering fire, drawing the Gatling gun and the bomber's weapon to their hole, while Gregson and Turin ran to the edge of the field. This drew the attention of both gunners, allowing Sgt. Brown and Private Santarelli to make it up over the ridge to the first parked airplane.

'Not bad,' Thompson said. 'Hey, Santa, turns out your grandpa was a badass even as a skinny runt.'

Anthony Santarelli wanted to curl up into a ball and wait for it all to end. Preferably with someone else doing the work. He'd just seen two of his best friends die, their bodies literally steaming in the snow. Now Gregson and Turin had drawn the Nazis' fire and gotten themselves pinned to the ground, in between the roots of an enormous pine, mercifully hidden from the big gun. He couldn't let them down. He *wouldn't* let them down.

He said, 'Sarge, I can get a grenade in that nest.'

Brown pointed at the corners of the airfield. 'Negative. Concentrate on planting the flares. Two or three is better than none.'

'Yes, sir.'

Before Anthony could make the dash, Gregson cried out in pain. His shin pumped blood from a bullet wound. Turin moved left. A second shot exploded his shin, spraying red.

Anthony suppressed a scream, and pulled the football-sized knapsack tighter to his shoulder. He said a prayer, asking God to watch over him as he guided the bombers to this place, but if He was busy elsewhere, and Anthony bought it here and now, it'd be great if He could look after Sarah and the baby once the war was over. *Please*, he thought, *I'm going to die. They need someone.*

Sergeant Brown aimed his gun in the general direction of the sniper bullets that disabled Gregson and Turin. 'When I get into the shootin', you run like the devil himself wants to bite your ass. Got that?'

'Got it,' Anthony said.

He bent his knees, dug in his toes for a faster start. Focused on the most important sections of the runway, where the B24s would need to aim their payload.

'Ready, sir.'

'Okay, and—'

But a bullet pinged through the fuselage inches from Brown's head. He ducked back down. A second shot slammed home nearby.

'Damn it,' Brown said. 'They made us. We're pinned.'

So this was it, Anthony figured. The end. Except, as usual, the Sarge surprised him.

'Listen up,' he said. 'I got a plan.'

As soon as Santa saw the two GIs take serious caliber rounds to the legs, Santa said, 'Thompson, they have a sniper. You need to make him an ex-sniper.'

Thompson did not respond.

For fuck's sake, the guy was pissed at Jacobs' order, but it *was* an order. Santa understood, but that didn't excuse it. If the backup solid state drive in Hawks's pack was able to function without contact from mission control, then everything they said on sub-vocal was recorded, and Santa would have no choice but to bring his friend up on a charge. The colonel might go for the full court martial after all. This wasn't like Thompson, but then it wasn't like any situation they'd trained for. Even the cleverest people in the room, the egghead docs, could only guess at what course of action to take. Those flashes were too random to be classified as proof, too vague to guide them. But it meant *something* was wrong. That doing *nothing* was as bad as doing the *wrong* thing. Right now, he was sure they were on the wrong course. And as the young Anthony readied himself to break from cover, Santa's head pounded.

He raised his voice. 'Thompson!'

The guy with the burst shin screamed in pain, another wound, this time his shoulder.

Mac said, 'Come on, Thompson, you know I'm with you, but ... they're torturin' them boys.'

Santa checked again through his night-vis goggles, able only to watch as Sergeant Brown stepped out from cover, hands raised. The pair who'd tried to flank the field the other way also came out, weapons to the side. Brown walked slowly over to them, so the three stood together, clearly no threat. All munitions were silenced.

In the dark, under the German plane, Anthony remained hidden, hoarding flares, ready to run, as soon as the distraction took hold.

The other floodlights whumped to life, casting this small group in a bright spotlight. The Nazi soldiers, who were taking up positions nearby, ventured closer to watch.

From one of the huts, Captain Eisenberg strode out. Three lookouts stood a few meters apart, and signaled to Eisenberg, some gesture that meant 'all clear.' He was holding something, talking about it to Sergeant Brown.

Thompson said, 'Son of a *bitch*.'

'What?' Santa said. 'What is it?'

'I'm sorry. I couldn't have known. I'm so sorry.'

Sergeant Montgomery Brown did not know what the hell that contraption was, but he sure as hell wished the Eisenberg asshole would shut up about it. He already expressed his annoyance at the easy surrender, but now he insisted on blathering on about some portable radar unit.

'This technology is truly remarkable,' he said.

Asshole.

In his hand, Eisenberg held one of those units the Special Forces guys were wearing. What the hell were they doing here? He'd figured on an extraction mission, getting some valued resistance asset out before the real fighting started. The unit showed images, though, a camera that penetrated the dark. When Eisenberg pointed a tiny lens on a cable at him, his own bored features appeared. He'd seen TVs back home at the state fair, and a few of his fancy-pants neighbors wheeled them into their homes now and again before waxing about how wonderful they were at the next barbecue, but he didn't see what the big deal was. Huge TV box in the living room, a little one on your arm. A TV's a TV. Shut up about it already.

Eisenberg paced a tight circle around Brown. 'I believe they call this an 'iNav', or some-such. I cannot think why they would name it that, it doesn't matter. What matters is, with this in my hand, I can see in the dark, and there is nowhere for anyone to hide.' He stopped, his face so close to Brown's that their misty breath mingled. 'Where is the other unit? I would like to thank them personally.'

'Yeah,' Brown said. 'You an' me both.'

'That's my iNav,' Santa said. 'That means—'

Another wave of searing white engulfed the team. It was as if his headache was a precursor, an initial shockwave before the tsunami hit, and the entire world exploded in light.

He emerged from the flashes, the images strobing; a mental disco acid-trip. His grandpa's scarred face flickered within the strobe ... in full uniform, looking down on him. Disappointed.

Mac watched helplessly, as the glare morphed into a farmstead. A beautiful woman in a breezy dress stared right at him. She mouthed, "I love you."

Hawks leapt out of her vision on skis, an expert, zigzagging down pristine powder, a frozen lake in the distance.

Chase shielded his face from the lights. Lots of lights, all illuminating him. Beyond the bulbs, an audience cheered in a small club ... laughing ... at *him*! He was holding a mic...

Dang was sitting the bar when the flashes hit him. A smattering of locals jumped back as he yelped, dropped his drink, and bent over to make the pain stop. He found himself on a white-sand beach, women surrounding him. No, not surrounding *him*, just ... all up and down the beach, and the feeling he could get up and talk to any one of them without fear. Some men, too, of course, but he barely saw them. He lifted a beer to his lips, one thought prevalent: *Ahh, this is the life..*

.

As Santa cinched his eyes tight, Lear also succumbed. He stopped fighting seconds after everyone else, and all he saw were flames. Nothing but flames ... everywhere!

Santa stifled a cry of pain. Hands to his eyes. He was emerging from the glare, when some force sucked him back in. *Blackness.* A cold surface. Then his view emerged from behind a rock ... standing over Yosemite National Park, the trip he'd been promising to take Lily on all year. And here he was, holding Lily's hand, but something was wrong. The ground shook. A blast of dust hit them head on. And, in the far distance, a mushroom cloud boiled into the sky—

In the forest, Santa sat up with a start. He was on his back, Uhrmacher leaning over him. He was the last to recover, the rest of the team having resumed their positions.

Mac said, 'I never been on a farm.'

Hawks armed her SCAR-M. 'Skiing makes me want to punch people.'

'I can't do comedy for shit,' Chase said.

'We know,' said Thompson. 'We've all seen the YouTube clips.'

'Fuck you.'

Santa said, 'Those were our memories.'

'I'm sorry?' Dr. Lear said.

'Our future memories. Things we *will* remember if we fuck up. We were *meant* to be here. We are part of history. By doing nothing, we are *changing* it. We need to help them before something catastrophic happens.'

'He's right,' Thompson said. 'I'm sorry, I ... I'm with you now.'

Santa snapped into gear, his head focused like a laser, and

every part of his body flooded with adrenaline. 'Okay,' he said. 'Thompson, take out that sniper. Mac, you and me on the big gun. Hawks, Chase, when the high ground's ours, it's open season. Clear?

Chase held his SCAR-M in one hand, Sig Sauer in the other. 'As fuckin' crystal.'

28

Santa and Mac crawled through the underbrush, skittering like insects, night-vis goggles showing the way. They also showed Anthony Santarelli cringing behind a plane, helpless. Then, to the right of him, Eisenberg shot the crippled Gregson through the head.

Santa knew their names now, close enough to hear them spoken. Turin was the other guy down. Plus Simons, Martins, Sgt. Brown. Higher than the camp netting, not quite at the gun-nest, he could only watch as the German captain shot Turin dead as well.

'Okay,' he said. 'I'm in position. Thompson? Take those bastards out.'

Eisenberg gave an order and one of his soldiers aimed at Martins. A smile from both men made Santa's gut curdle. Even seventy years later, people like this continued to exist. Sadists, who took pleasure in others' pain. In the twenty-first century it was bastardized by religious indoctrination and race-hate and misogyny; here, it was in the name of empire-building, of making one's country great. But, beneath the surface, it was all the same: an excuse to do evil.

Bloody chunks thumped out of the Nazi's chest in a tight double-tap. No need to compliment Thompson on it; he knew what he did.

While the surrounding troops split back and forth in a panic, Eisenberg reacted by calmly ducking into the camp, shouting in German, '*Kill them all!*'

He reached the camouflaged hut from which he came, and made it to safety as Thompson's shells raked the structure. Once Eisenberg was gone, the shots landed higher, blowing out the floodlights, and before the bomber's machine gun had a chance to light up again, a tight grouping shattered the glass, splattering red inside. No bullets came.

In the confusion, the GIs saw a window, retrieved their guns, and sprinted for the tree line. Sniper fire kicked up dirt as they ran, followed by the Gatling gun battering their path. Soil, wood, and snow shredded under the barrage, cornering the GIs waiting for backup on the ground.

'Thompson,' Santa said. 'Get that sniper. We'll take the big gun.'

Thompson focused through his sight. 'Okay, bitch. Where are you...?'

Nothing on ultra-infrared, so he switched to standard, which showed no movement. The eyepiece fizzed with static for a second, the image splintered.

'Oh, not now.'

He flicked to low-light black and white, which showed nothing manmade or any hint of a body. He switched back to the ultra-infrared and made another pass, but every time he panned even an inch, the Hobbit's visuals cracked and shook.

Standard infrared showed nothing. Before he could establish anything useful, this died too.

Thompson found the regular vision, and observed the battery icon flashing red. The thing was dying ten hours early.

Field test failed, he thought as he swapped out the Hobbit for his regular night vision scope. He found his previous point, and searched more slowly for the sniper. There was image blur. Like when those dumb-ass 3D movies try to get you *inside* the action, but the scenes just end up as a series of whizzing colors smashed together. So he had to move slower than with the hi-tech toy. And it was a lot harder.

Whoever this guy was, he was good. He must have positioned himself high up, and the most advanced scopes of the olden days were little more than telescopes with a cross on the lens. No night-vis, so Thompson theoretically still had the edge.

A little to the right ... something ... a flash.

The guy's camouflage, cream, and whatever mud and crap he built his nest from, more than likely masked his body heat, and the netting probably obscured the straight lines from the Hobbit's low-light sensors, but launching a bullet would always generate heat, and movement. And that's all he needed with his trusty old girl.

'Thompson,' Santa said, 'they're in a hole here.'

Thompson breathed. Finger on the trigger.

Another tiny muzzle-flash flared, but the grainy night-vis was too imprecise. He marked the spot in his memory, then swapped out the night-vis to the scope he would use in daylight, something similar to what the German himself was likely watching through, and repositioned himself. Found the mental marker to pick up where he left off, and recognized the spot he would have chosen himself.

The nest was seriously professional. You would never identify it if you didn't already know what lurked there. Sufficient moonlight to spot the sniper's hand inch into frame, loading more bullets. From here, Thompson determined his position, his angle, and where his head probably lay. And squeezed the trigger. Through the suppressor, Delilah made that familiar noise, like someone flicking the top of their ear.

Something in the nest sprayed red, and the rifle pitched sideways.

Nothing else moved.

Thompson nodded to himself. *Score another for the twenty-first-century boys.*

A couple of feet beneath the machine gun outpost, Mac heard the gunner giggle between bursts. An actual *giggle*. The GIs were pinned down, and Santa's covering fire meant Mac was able to sneak in unseen. Not that Mac did much sneaking, of course, but in this case, it wasn't that hard. He was nimble for a big guy, and large-caliber munitions going off every which way gave him an edge. Heck, he always had an edge. Alpha Team were too good to go down to these guys.

Mac casually unpinned a grenade's pull-ring but held the spoon in place. He spent a couple of seconds savoring the notion of a 1940s soldier encountering an M67 fragmentation grenade, and had to remind himself that people were dying. He released the spoon, counted to three, and tossed it back. The shooting stopped and Mac jammed his fingers in his ears.

The nest above him exploded, raining body parts on the surrounding forest.

As he was considering the Hollywood depiction of a grenade going off—namely a soldier somersaulting through the air—he thought he had a great idea.

Chase and Hawks dashed into the camp, firing quick, lethal bursts. They stayed low, used natural cover, and could not believe their luck as the Nazis scrambled to get away. With Thompson laying down a storm of accurate shots, and the

GIs now free to advance around the side, the Germans dropped one by one.

'Guessin' he ran out of those Special Forces fuckers,' Chase said.

Three Nazis rushed into view. Neither Hawks nor Chase raised their gun in time. Chase was a split-second away from finding religion, when Santa leaped into the snow from up high, and shot down all three.

'Thanks, boss,' Chase said.

'Keep taking these bastards out,' Santa said. 'I'm going to make sure they don't call those bombers in until we have our fuel.'

Santa ran flat out across the field, trusting in Thompson, Chase, and Hawks to keep the lead out of his back. Mac already took out the gunner's position, but he was nowhere to be seen, and there wasn't time to waste on the sub-vocal. That was now reserved for immediate threats.

He made it to the tree line, yards from where he last saw Anthony under the plane, waiting for his chance. But he was gone. Instead, Sergeant Brown guarded this section.

He said, 'Help you?'

Anthony's bag lay on the ground. Empty.

Santa said, 'Where's ... your guy? Private Santarelli?'

'Doin' his job.'

Anthony ran headlong into the darkened camp, hugging the flares. Martins and Simons backed him up with wide volleys. Nazis fell, partly through their efforts, partly through the Special Forces team. All it would take would be for one of the enemy to organize something, to get a group of them to stay still long enough to pinpoint the threat, and that would be the end. But their leaders were gone, taken out quickly, and then scattered. Did they get the one who killed Turin and Gregson in cold blood? Anthony sure as heck hoped so.

Dirt erupted around the three GIs, great baseball-sized clumps. From behind the small hanger, a tank—an actual *tank*—trundled its way forward, firing its machine gun. They all ran, heads down, legs pumping. Hugging the darker line, they made it into a rocky crevasse between two huts. It was safe, but they were stuck.

And, as Anthony feared, the panic was easing, and a group of five Nazis spun from the evacuation stream, and headed their way. Martins and Simons fired, dropping two straight away, but both needed to reload at the same time. The remaining three troopers sped up, almost upon them, when two of the special forces—the potty-mouthed man and the woman they assumed to be a nurse—stepped in, cutting them down with those sleek black weapons.

'You're fuckin' welcome,' called the man, as they sprinted to the side.

The tank swung its big gun toward their saviors.

'Crap,' the man said.

Martins said, 'Go.'

Anthony ran again, jammed one flare into the floor, Martins and Simons providing covering fire. Before he could strike the first flare, the guy with a similar name to him arrived, and dived to the ground beside him. *Santa*. Another person with that odd nickname.

'Listen,' he said. 'We're trying to stop something very bad. Don't set off those flares. Let *us* clear the base.'

'But ... you can't,' Anthony said. 'The sarge ... I have orders.'

Then a tank shell exploded nearby, showering them with dirt.

'Dammit,' Santa said in Chase's ear. 'Chase, Hawks, where are you?'

Chase replied, 'Kinda tied up right now. Hold, please.'

Motherfucker, can't he see?

As Chase barreled between the barracks, using the largest buildings as cover, the tank maneuvered like a lame fuckin' cow, trying to pin him down. As they planned, once it was concentrating on him, Hawks ghosted into the tank's blind spot, and threw a pack of C-4 into the barrel. Then she ran like hell, holding the detonator. The machine gun fired at Chase once more, and she flicked the switch.

The top part of the tank blew apart, the main gun wrenched from the body, great cracks spewing smoke.

Is it wrong that I'm totally aroused right now?

Chase ran over to high-five her when a posse of six troopers streamed from a stone doorway in the mountainside and opened fire. Regrouped chickenshits, or reinforcements? It didn't matter. Chase and Hawks ducked by the hot tank wreck for cover.

'Mac,' Chase said, 'where in the world of fuck are you?'

'Coming,' Mac replied. He sounded like he was running. 'Honest.'

The newcomers spread out, evading the suppressing fire from the GIs. The heat radiating from the twisted metal forced Chase and Hawks backwards—no way to reposition themselves.

The first of the Nazis rounded the tank, him and a buddy getting the drop on them. They had nowhere else to go.

But then in a torrent of cracking twigs and flying leaves,

from uphill and behind the wreckage, Mac bounded out of the trees. The Germans spun around to see what the hell that was. Mac said, 'Hey there, little buddies,' and grinned, hefting the Gatling gun salvaged from the nest.

Chase laughed. 'You big cheesy bastard.'

Mac couldn't speak a word of German. Well, maybe 'nein' and 'heil Hitler' and he had a vague notion that when a panicking officer yells, '*Schnell! Schnell!*' at subordinates, he's pissed as all hell. But one of the Nazi soldiers ten feet below him said something in German that sounded a lot in tone like, 'Oh, fuck me.' Which was appropriate.

And Mac unleashed a hail of lead that staggered him at first. The massive slugs ripped through the soldiers so powerfully that they didn't even have a chance to try and remain upright, or to flee; the barrage just dropped them where they were, full of holes.

In Mac's youth, and even in his adulthood, Nazis were just inhuman creatures from the past. We never think twice about killing such cannon fodder in movies or video games. But these were human beings with chunks of meat and even bone punched out by hot metal. It took Mac a few moments to realize this. They weren't on a movie screen or a video game. Like every other piece of shit he'd disposed of in his career, they were right in from of him. In the flesh.

But this was still life or death. And as the gun spewed its huge payload, he pushed back those notions of mortality. As he always had to at times like this, he hoped they were all assholes to their families, that they had no friends outside their army, and that he could keep his head in the game, for the sake of his friends.

He swung the weapon's firepower to the stragglers, the

Nazis trying to find cover, those shooting at Santa and the young general-to-be, and the other GIs. The Germans popped apart like water balloons, their shacks splintering, metal turned to honeycomb. He didn't stop until every last moving human was lying dead on the ground.

When he first appeared with the gun, Chase seemed impressed. Excited, even. And although killing all these people was the right thing to do, Mac didn't really feel like celebrating, or even particularly excited. Maybe he'd call the shrink the girl he just dumped suggested after all.

But he was *Mac*. The team's nominated *tough-guy*. Their hard-assed *warrior*. So he snapped back into character, held up the gun on one shoulder, and said, 'Was that worth waitin' for, or what?'

When he reached Anthony, and the shooting recommenced, Santa lay on top of him, and refused to move. He growled strange things, repeating that he could not allow Anthony to die, and that he would not let the fuel be destroyed. Somewhere, in one of these hangers, or one of these huts, he told Anthony, was the means to send his team home, and for him to attend the party he promised his little girl. Whatever the heck that meant.

Now safe, he rolled off Anthony, and sat him up. 'You okay?'

'I'm fine,' Anthony said.

The whine of a plane sounded overhead.

'Okay,' Santa said. 'Get your sarge to call off those bombers.'

Anthony backed away from Santa. He still held the flares.

'Wait…'

'I have orders,' Anthony said.

'No. You don't have to follow them.'

'Of course I do. They're orders.' And, in quick succession, he ignited the flares.

The plane rumbled closer, louder

Santa said, 'No. Put them out. Do not let those bombs land!'

But Anthony was done with fear. All he knew was what he'd been taught since day one: to trust the chain of command. To follow orders. And with no one to countermand those orders except some weirdo Special Forces guy, Anthony tossed the flares as widely as possible, lighting up the ground for the B24 to unleash its payload.

And judging by the noise, they had about thirty seconds.

29

Santa ran alongside Anthony, calling to the team, heading deeper into the airfield's camp. Chase, Mac, and Hawks joined him, and Thompson jogged in from the trees. As the overhead whine increased in volume, Brown charged in from the side.

'If it ain't escaped your notice,' he said, 'we got birds comin' in hot. I reckon we should be movin' *that* way.'

Santa said, 'We need something from here.'

'Who exactly *are* you people?'

'That's not important. How much time do we have?'

The bombers sounded so close, the engines echoing through the mountain pass.

Brown said, 'You don't wanna go up with the Krauts who just killed four good men, I suggest we all run. Now.'

Dr. Lear said, 'Uh, hello?' It was in Santa's ear. 'You may want to listen to him. I thought when Dr. Uhrmacher said they kept the rods in a safe place, he meant, well, a safe. But if they are stored in one of these buildings—'

'Mushroom cloud situation?' Chase said.

'You need a more serious reaction for that, no. But there will be fallout.'

Mac said, 'What? What do you mean "fallout"?'

'If the bombs hit that depot, at the right point, it could rupture the uranium, causing it to disperse. Essentially creating a—'

'Dirty bomb,' Santa said. 'We gotta get those rods out of there—'

But the planes were now overhead.

Thompson said, 'Shit, too late.'

Whistling sounded.

With the GIs around them, Alpha Team ran in a group, arrowing for the drop-off into the trees. The first of the bombs hit some way off-target, the next closer, exploding so hard the ground shook, and everyone staggered to remain upright. All zigzagged, heads down, sprinting for the forest, as a second sortie nailed the flares with four or five bad boys.

The succession of explosions sent shockwaves over the fleeing people, lifting them off their feet and knocking them over as they reached the edge of the woods. Those who fell leapt up, and dived over the steep drop. Flame, shrapnel, and debris sailed through the air, to the whoops and cheers of the GIs. It pattered down for hundreds, maybe thousands, of feet in all directions.

As the aftermath of drizzle petered out, Santa crawled back up the ridge, watching as a third bombing run strafed what was left. The first two lit up the ground, and gave them a better sight of what to destroy. And destroy it they did. Alpha Team could do nothing but stare as the Nazi airfield and camp erupted in a series of blasts, destroying the small buildings, vehicles, weapons, tearing up the surface, until they'd have had more luck landing a Focke-Wulf Condor on the moon.

And as the bombers' engines faded, and the ringing in their ears echoed more quietly, everyone observed the craters and flaming shells of twisted metal. The GIs nodded firmly, puffed out their chests. Brown tossed a cigar in his mouth and lit it.

Alpha Team turned from the devastation, no words to be

said. Santa took out his rad-pen, and the others followed suit. Santa said, 'Okay, let's see how bad this is.'

30

A droopy mustachioed Frenchman stomped through the door of Bar du Pont, an old bolt-action rifle on his back. He walked over the floor peppered with bullet holes, placing his feet carefully, as if the wood might splinter and crack around him. Other raggedy locals drank in small groups, raising their heads to acknowledge a fellow regular. They mostly carried automatic weapons, and smelled like rotten vegetation. Some tan-skinned, others pasty-white, they filtered in slowly, the first of them only moments after Alpha Team vacated the vicinity. Well, most of Alpha Team.

Desiree explained to Dang that these men were not all resistance, though some of them probably would be. Dang asked about The Runner, and Desiree reiterated she did not know who he was; she kept her head down, and did not involve herself in such matters. She allowed anyone to drink here; those residents who had not fled, resistance fighters, even the odd Nazi who ventured this far, though they were rare. It was how she became the wealthiest person in La Bastion. It also helped that she ruled this place with an iron fist that would make Colonel Johnson himself think twice about questioning her authority, having already ejected two gruff drinkers who had given themselves a head start on the booze before arriving. She drew cheers from the less inebriated locals, and made Dang dubious about her claims of not being involved with the resistance. A woman in this phase of history commanding this much respect was unlikely, though not impossible. Maybe she was just as she appeared to be: in charge, immovable, and with the backing of the majority of customers, untouchable.

All conversation faded as the muffled *whumpf* of bombs going off up the mountain drew their attention. They listened, not drinking, and Dang figured they were probably waiting to see if the danger was heading this way. He guessed they won, since that weird flash and vision of what could only have been a possible future or fractured timeline had not repeated itself. Or maybe they were his original memories, and his current ones were the new normal, their actions having altered something he could no longer recall.

He sat at the bar in civilian clothing provided by Desiree, a size too big; her late father's. With his leg elevated, he sipped coffee, ashamed that he'd sampled the local aniseed-like liquor and coughed half of the sharp fluid back up. He wasn't ashamed at the reaction, but at spiting Santa's order that no alcohol be consumed. He told the new boss man he wanted to help, and meant it. Booze would make a lie of that. So he chose to remain sober, and awake, to the extent that he injected the smallest doses of morphine he could manage, although he had little experience with this sort of thing.

The closest he'd been to getting shot before was when a slug embedded itself in the brick wall of a goat herder's property on the Pakistan border, showering him with shrapnel that drew blood but left no scar. His current injury most certainly *would* leave a scar—at least he hoped so. Nothing cooler than a scar with a heroic story to go along with it, providing he treated the rupture correctly, and did not inflict permanent damage. Rather than numbing him entirely, the smaller volume served to dull the sensation to that of a small rodent chewing at his thigh, reminding him what happened with each incremental movement. He reasoned that, while the field dressing was tight, if he forgot about the injury he might try something dumb, and further pull his tissue apart.

The bombing ceased as suddenly as it commenced, and Dang raised his cup in a toast to anyone who had potentially fallen, hoping so badly the casualty count was zero.

Desiree served Monsieur Droopy Mustache, who glanced once at Dang, but no more. Not interested. When Droopy Mustache retired to a corner alone with a book he dug out of a battered knapsack, Dang sighed, and Desiree came to him.

'I'm not a kid,' he said. 'Santa should be able to see that. I mean, I'm not *that* much younger than him.'

Desiree smiled and shrugged—no idea what he said.

Dang tapped a message on his iPhone. 'I should get some sleep. Santa may need me.'

Desiree tapped on the phone in reply, fast as a teenager already. 'Upstairs on left.'

Dang checked the battery. Down to a quarter. These conversations wouldn't last much longer. Not unless they got power sockets for an Apple device.

He heaved his leg down from his chair, but as he did, Desiree typed another message.

'You are so young. One day you will understand these things.'

Dang shrugged, took the phone. *Sure, whatever.* Same story: getting patronized as usual, even by an ancient French girl. He pressed the power button to switch it off. No telling when they might need the offline app next. He tried a signal Desiree's way, but she had people to serve. He did some math to work out how old the woman would be in 2015, if she was still alive. She was, what, mid-twenties, running her own bar after the death of her father, hoarding her money somewhere nearby to use after the war. She might even be wealthy in the future. She'd be General Santarelli's age, at least.

Maybe he could set them up.

The door opened again, and four local men entered, huddled together. Or they *seemed* to be local, fashion wise. But Desiree stiffened. And as the men approached the bar, Dang noted their faces were close-shaven, their fingernails cleaner than others in here, their guns nearly-new. *German* guns. Kinda like a modern MP5, but clunkier and heavier, and Dang had an inkling that their own urban weapons back home were modeled on German designs.

To stay in character, Dang slouched off with his coffee and sat at Droopy Mustache's table, hoping his dark skin blended in with the Mediterranean hue of a handful of La Bastion's residents. It was situated close to the *south* of France, after all. He locked eyes with Monsieur Droopy Mustache, who gave him a familiar head-tilt—a friend greeting another—then returned to his book.

The new men reached the bar. Three of the four twisted to face outward, scanning the smattering of genuine locals. The one who remained in place was tall with a scarred face and milky eye. He addressed Desiree too quietly for Dang to hear. Desiree shook her head and shrugged the most innocent shrug in the world. The milky-eyed man gestured 'okay' and pointed to a spirit behind the bar and held up three fingers and a thumb. Dang could not remember where he heard it, but he thought that gesture marked him as German—using the thumb in signaling a number. Was it a Tarantino flick? How accurate was that? Not particularly, from what he remembered of the ending, although it never purported to be a true story. Perhaps that part of it was right, though. But it wasn't only the thumb that suggested this group was part of Eisenberg's guerrilla counter-insurgency. The local drinkers hunched tighter over tables, avoided looking their way. All knew instinctively who these newcomers were. And *what* they are.

Desiree selected four glasses and filled them with red liquor. Reuler paid and handed the drinks to his men.

Droopy Mustache took a discreet peek under the table. Dang pressed his SIG flat to the underside. The Frenchman tutted, and reached slowly behind himself. He kept on reading, but his hand rested on his gun.

The four newcomers sipped their drinks, guns in-hand, and stalked methodically around the locals, all of whom again ceased conversation. They remained in their seats.

Each newcomer finished his drink, then came to a halt, fanned out around the place so the covered every angle.

Earlier, as part of his protection detail, Dang examined the bar area, and approved of the shotgun Desiree kept there. Now he clocked her leaning on the surface, one hand wiping it down, the other moving something to within easier reach. No prizes for guessing what that was.

Under his own table, Dang steadied his grip on the SIG. Aside, Droopy Mustache held his rifle steady.

In English with a strong German accent, the Lieutenant said, 'I see you all know who we are. Good. If you do not speak English, you have no need to worry. I am *Untersturmführer* Max Reuler. You may think of me as *Lieutenant* Reuler.' He pronounced his rank as '*leff*-tenant,' like the Brits do. 'I have many men in the surrounding streets, but we do not want to hurt you if we do not have to.' He cocked his submachine gun, ranking the bolt on the side with a hard *clack*. 'We are seeking an American. Conceal him and there will be consequences.'

Each click of equipment, chink of a glass, every tiny creak sounded a thousand times louder than it should have.

Finally, watched closely by the newcomers, one of the locals stood shakily, placed his glass on the bar, and turned to leave. Reuler stood in his path and lifted the man's gun from his shoulder.

He said, 'You may believe this corner of France is liberated, but as you can see there is still some way to go. Once we have the American, and if I decide to let you live, you will leave your guns by the door.' Then he repeated the sentence in French, his hard consonants spitting from his throat, making his point more harshly.

As the newly-disarmed local man slunk past the newcomers, his friend reached shakily for a weapon.

Beside Dang, Droopy Mustache grasped his own gun.

The Germans did not raise their guns fully, but certainly held them tighter, fingers shifting to inside their trigger guards. Each time their gaze landed on a punter, that man tensed, and laid his hands flat on the table before him, proving he wasn't a threat.

One of the Nazis spotted Droopy Mustache, and when the old Frenchman did not release his weapon, the soldier trained his gun this way. The man's eyes narrowed. Dang had seen this before. Afghan-born men allied with the US, confronted by Taliban in public. Rules of engagement forbade troops from interfering unless life was directly threatened, but Dang always saw it in a squint, a downturn of the mouth, a shallow nod. A man, accepting his fate, expecting his death either now or very soon, and regretting nothing. Droopy Mustache was ready to die for a cause Dang knew ended well for the good guys.

'Okay!' Dang said. 'I'm here.'

Droopy Mustache returned his firearm to the floor. His

mouth twitched up at the corners, a show of appreciation to Dang.

Reuler strode over, the others remaining at their posts, but their machine guns were up. Their eyes twitching side-to-side, possibly more scared of the dozen men nursing their drinks.

Reuler said, 'You are who we want? What is your name?'

'My name is "kiss my ass."'

Reuler sighed like a teacher with an immature boy. A soldier stepped away from his angle momentarily, and clubbed Dang with the gun's stock.

At first, little happened, except a dull pain spreading from the back of his head. But then the world slowly spun. His vision darkened. He had enough time to watch Reuler signal to his men, and then his ears filled with cracks and bangs and screams. Through the fog, Dang saw the muzzle flashes, and within seconds, the gunfire eased, replaced by the whimpers and pleading of dying men.

And then all was black, and Dang again cursed Santa for leaving him behind.

31

The search of the airfield yielded little hope. In a way, Dr. Lear told them, the fact that their rad-pens registered a big fat zero was a problem in that they were not about to locate the lead and concrete-sealed vessels that Dr. Uhrmacher described, unless they somehow survived completely intact. So when, as the exercise moved from checking corpses for signs of life, and trying not to grow gills or mutate into some rampaging rage-mutant, they failed to locate any trace of the containers or the rods, they surmised that either the German scientist lied to them, or the rods were being stored underground. Therefore, they adjusted their search to doors and access hatches, but so far, like the rad-pens, they registered zilch.

The black smoke and choking pork-like stench of burning flesh made it hard-going, but Alpha Team and the GIs trudged through the wreckage separately, without registering their distaste. No matter how many bodies Santa saw, he always felt the same way: disconnected. The thing lying there was no longer human, but it had been once. It had laughed and cried, loved and hated, and it never would again. Whether a clean bullet wound, or a charred mass of twisted limbs, his revulsion level remained about the same. His sadness varied, though, depending on the victims. Children hit him the worst, of course, even more so now he'd gotten to know Lily, and each time he felt literally sick to imagine what future they may have had if not for the misfortune of being born in a country where war and conflict were an everyday occurrence. These men, though, *Nazis*, men whose actions caused more death and fear and loathing than any other war in the twentieth or twenty-first centuries, walking amongst their corpses made him proud. This is why he joined up. This is why he still did what he did. This is what was needed, day after day, to keep the good people of this world safe.

Most of the time.

When they won.

Before long, Santa crossed paths with Sergeant Brown, the ever-present cigar in his mouth, puffing away. Against regulations even back then, but Santa guessed it conveyed a certain gravitas to his men.

'So whadda ya think?' Brown asked, ducking through a column of smoke from a burning jeep.

'I think we told you we needed something from here, and you ignored us.'

'Yeah, but since you didn't give us a reason, haven't told us your unit, ranks, commanding officers, I couldn't verify anythin' you said. And since my boys were dyin' out there, I hadda make a decision. Now, if you told us what yer really lookin' for up here, we can maybe help you.'

Off to the side, the two docs convened two hundred yards away, deep in conversation near a fissure in the rock that rose sharply. Santa wondered briefly if he should be trusting Uhrmacher. He led them here to where he said the rods were, but an ambush waited instead. Perhaps that was the plan all along, and now he was stalling while Eisenberg armed the machine—something that same doc claimed would take at least twelve hours. Dr. Lear did confirm it, theoretically anyway, although he wouldn't commit until he'd examined the technology first hand.

Santa said, 'Anything that shouldn't be here.'

Understanding that these former human beings littering the ground had killed so many of Brown's men, he left Brown to his cigar, and hurried over to Thompson. He was the only voice he hadn't heard on the sub-vocal. He ordered everyone to take a break and get some water onboard. If they didn't find anything in the next half-hour, they would head straight over to the bunker and face Eisenberg before he could damage the allied war effort.

The team gathered, all but the two scientists, who continued their search of the mountainside. The GIs had the same idea, and hunkered down nearby.

Santa asked Thompson, 'You okay?'

'I'm sorry,' he said. 'How could I have known?'

'Save it. The only important thing is that the flashes have subsided.' That wasn't true, about it being the *only* important thing. One other important thing was that Thompson disobeyed orders in front of the team, but calling him on it now might have dragged him down further. Plus, the troops were fracturing into two camps already: *Team Santa* and *Team Thompson*. Not good. He said, 'The situation is unprecedented. But we're a part of history now. We probably always were. That's why doing nothing here generates the memory flashes.'

'So,' Chase said. 'What does all that mean? What if we do it wrong?'

'I don't know. Thinking back, though, I am positive that Nazi had his finger firmly on that trigger.'

'The fucker about to kill Anthony back at the bunker?'

'Yeah. I moved his arm to his head, but *he* pulled the trigger. I didn't do it.'

Mac said, 'So the angle changed the pressure when you moved him. So what?'

'So,' Hawks said, 'If we weren't present to stop him, his grandfather would certainly have died.'

'Wait a sec,' Chase said. 'If we weren't there, the guy wouldn't have taken him hostage. They faced a firing squad.'

Mac said, 'No, man, that Runner asshole might have saved 'em, or they mighta' saved 'emselves.'

Santa watched the two scientists approaching. 'No, not with those flashes, those future-memories, or whatever they were. Dang was right. We're meant to be here.'

Hawks said, 'Incoming.'

Brown finished his cigar and decided to amble over with his three surviving squad members. 'Private meeting?'

Chase lurched toward him, but Santa stepped in the way, his arm across Chase's torso. Chase said, 'You nearly fuckin' killed us.'

Hawks said, 'Why could you not have waited?'

Brown tightened his face. A 1940s man's man not accustomed to backtalk from a female. He said, 'B24s don't run on air, honey.'

The one called Martins looked her up and down. 'What's a nurse doing with a gun anyway?

Anthony made no secret of watching Thompson. He said, 'And why you got a Negro in your unit?'

'Hey,' Mac said, 'I don't care what hot stuff you become in the future, I told you already, we don't use that word no more.'

'Right, Private,' Brown said. 'I think they prefer "colored."'

'*They*,' Thompson said, 'don't like bein' talked about like *they* ain't in the room.' He glanced around. 'Or the smokin' crater.'

'Gee, sorry,' Simons said. 'Guess us following orders and being good at this is pissing you special boys off some.'

Chase said, 'What's pissing me off is—'

'Gentlemen … and lady.' Dr. Lear reached them. 'I believe we have found what we need.'

32

Everyone, GIs included, stood before a standard-sized door made of solid steel, constructed to open via a wheel mechanism, its surface dotted with rivets, all set into an iron frame molded into the mountain itself. It was concealed by an outcrop of rock and shrubbery. The solitary bunch of vegetation was actually what drew Dr. Uhrmacher's attention, or at least that's what he claimed. Dr. Lear wasn't as trusting as these chaps believed, and exercised that old adage of keeping one's enemies closer than one's friends. He could not deny that he quite liked the German doctor, and he admired the man's accomplishments, but the military men largely entrusted him to keep Dr. Uhrmacher in line, and he would not be the one to mess that up. That he'd been able to match them physically—at least from a cardio point of view—perhaps lent him more respect that he'd initially expected. It was certainly one reason his boss chose to send him out into the field ahead of Phil Mikkelson, who on the best of days resembled a tramp with an above-average IQ. But this mission—*wow, a real mission!*—took on a surreal quality from the moment he got shot.

Shot!

He couldn't wait to regale his colleagues at the Large Hadron Collider about that one. Not only shot, but *shot saving a life*. Diving in front of a bullet. Already, in his memory, he performed that feat in steely-cold focus, a slow motion heroic leap akin to Jason Statham or Bruce Willis. What he would not tell them was that his heroism was totally self-serving; if

Uhrmacher died, so died the man with the most knowledge about the machine that could send them home.

It still did not seem real. Although he was a physicist, he knew plenty about biology, and his only worry at the moment was that he was not afraid. He'd seen a squadron of Nazi soldiers lie dead at the hands of his new acquaintances, watched a man fatally shot on the floor of a bar in 1945, and sat behind the biggest rock he could find as a full-pitched *battle* raged around him. Amidst all of that, he made calculations in his head, referred back to Uhrmacher's notebook, jotted his own formulae based on the good doctor's workings: it took x amount of fuel to power up the crystal and link a tunnel to an existing spike, which required y amount of energy to push the subjects through the conduction chamber and guide them to the spike; moving forward, in linking to the original spike, x would be constant, but y would need some extra oomph to divert around the incoming tunnel or they would meet and, potentially, their particles would clash in a way that the LHC could only dream of. Dr. Uhrmacher felt the diversion needed a dog-leg route, but because of advances in humanity's knowledge of gravity, Dr. Lear explained they should use the Earth's gravitational pull to create an arc of sorts, which would use fifteen percent less power than the dog-leg, and therefore reduce the chances of an immediate meltdown.

It insinuated something of a squeaky-bum margin-of-error, though.

The biggest wave of fear for Dr. Lear came when the bombs dropped from on high. If the bombing raid destroyed the rods, all these calculations were for nothing. And now, facing this door, an entrance he would not dream of touching in his daily life, all that surged through him was impatience.

He wanted to get *in* there. He needed to *see* what awaited them.

'This structure,' he said in his calmest scientist-voice. 'It's still intact.'

'Could he be inside?' Santa said. 'Eisenberg?'

'He ducked out when the big shots started comin' in,' Brown said. 'But that was back there.'

'I cannot say,' Uhrmacher replied. 'I knew of this place, but I have never been. It is a cave system, tunnels everywhere. Maybe it is linked.'

They all stared hard at him, but Dr. Lear placed a bet with himself about Uhrmacher's reply.

'I swear,' Uhrmacher said. 'They do not share their secrets about the outside world. He listened to me when operating the machine, but nothing else. Well, except…'

'Except what?' Mac said.

'If this is a trap, I would tell you all is safe, yes?'

And Dr. Lear won his bet. He would reward himself with a slice of chocolate cake from Miss Pietre's bakery in Zurich. Perhaps he'd take a portion for Mikkelson—

'Gonna need some dynamite to get into that hatch,' Brown said. 'And we're fresh out.'

Santa gave a small smile. 'I think we can probably go one better.'

As Chase and Mac assessed the hunk of steel keeping them out of the cave system, Dr. Lear took the opportunity to ask Santa why the heck they carried so much C-4 explosive with them. The fellow who ran away and helped Eisenberg escape stole two blocks, while Hawks used one to destroy that tank, and now they squidged another into a crack between the rock and the frame.

'We brought six,' Santa said. 'Earthquake might've buried what we were looking for with rock fall. Problem was, we didn't know what we were facing. So we came prepared.'

Chase and Mac urged everyone back, to flatten themselves against the mountainside around the back of the outcrop. One of the GIs asked about a fuse and Chase flashed a device the size of a matchbox with a one-inch antenna and a switch. He grinned, flicked the switch, and the C-4 exploded, blowing shards of rock and metal across the already-devastated field.

Simons said, 'What the hell is that stuff?'

'It looks like RDX,' Brown said. '*Plastique.* But I ain't seen it work like that before.'

'C-four, baby,' Chase said, waving his switch box. 'Spec-i-al shit.'

Santa faced Sergeant Brown. 'Would you guys mind keeping watch out here while we head in to search?'

Brown nodded. 'Sure.'

'Oh, we could use a hand in there if you can spare someone.'

'Martins—'

'Actually, I was thinking your own Santa will do.'

'Keeping it in the family, huh?' Brown said. 'What're the chances of two Santarelli's, eh?'

'Guess it's fate.'

Dr. Lear almost chuckled. A day earlier they would never have made a joke like that. Maybe Lear wasn't the only one who needed a reality check.

Anthony never liked being talked about as if invisible, but in this case they were discussing the possibility of him going into that door with the special team, and that was fine by him. But as they prepped their weapons and voiced concern over their lack of ammo, the sarge draped an arm around his shoulder and said, 'Keep your eyes open, keep 'em on the specials. I wanna know what they're huntin' for.'

Anthony returned a vigorous nod. Sergeant Brown was his CO, after all, not the man with the similar name to him.

'Okay,' came the call from the other Santa. 'Time to go.'

33

As the special team prepped for the breach, Anthony could not take his eyes off their weaponry as they slid the mags out and back in with a smoothness he associated with Sarah's stockings. Even though they were together only once, on the night he deployed, he knew he would marry her. Apart from him having little choice what with the resulting pregnancy, and her parents being strict Irish-Catholics, but he would have proposed anyway.

Before the boating accident that claimed their lives, he was as close to his own parents as anyone of his upbringing— second generation immigrants and lapsed Catholics from the Old Country— could. When he decided he wanted to marry Sarah, he imagined his late ma scolding him that he was little more than a boy. But, in his imagination where his folks still lived, able to meet Sarah and the little girl he was certain would arrive shortly, when Anthony explained his feelings in more detail, his pop slapped his shoulder and expressed pride at Anthony doing his duty by the girl. The talk of love seemed alien in this fantasy version of his task-master father, but all Anthony could think about was snuggling up to Sarah, sniffing their baby's head for the first time, and opening a shop of some kind.

Yeah, a shop. A good business. People always needed shops.

And sticking close to these guys with their strange goggles and slick machine guns struck him as the best idea. It would also make a quite brilliant story for his family and closest friends.

But all of this paled in comparison to the letter in his pocket. They gave it to him shortly before this mission came in, and his fingers trembled when he held it. Sarah was due any day now, and if this contained the news he was waiting for—boy or girl—he wanted a beer in his hand. He was about to crack open a cold one and sit down to read it, when the sarge called them in for an intelligence briefing. Opening it then would have soured the experience, but he decided to keep it close.

It hung heavy in his pocket as he followed the special team—'Alpha Team,' they called themselves—along a well-lit corridor, sloping downward at a shallow angle. Most of them used their sidearms, having assessed their machine gun supplies and found them too low to be effective. Anthony carried his own Thompson submachine gun, the stock at his shoulder, finger on the trigger guard, barrel pointed down. Every so often he would turn three-hundred-and-sixty degrees to ensure nothing snuck up from behind, while Alpha Team swept along, clearing each nook and cranny as they went.

The two scientists pressed forward ahead of Anthony, with the one who looked like a circus strongman—Mac—urging them to keep up.

Santa and Chase led the team to a darkened entrance, a gap large enough to drive a bus through but, with no electrical lighting beyond, they faced nothing but darkness. They snatched those odd goggles from each other's packs and slipped them on, then stalked out into the space, guns ready and aimed, a tiny tube on top of each displaying a pinprick of light, like a miniature flashlight.

'How do they see?' Anthony asked no one in particular.

The woman, Hawks, replied, 'The spectrum we normally see by is enhanced by a low-level infrared filter.'

'Oh. Okay, that makes sense.' It meant nothing to him.

'Would you like to try?'

Hawks removed her goggles and placed them on Anthony. Everything turned green, but he saw inside a huge cavern, equipped with vehicles, boxes of supplies, and row upon row of shelving. Santa and Chase moved silently but swiftly, clearing each hiding place, those tiny flashlights now shooting a thin beam of light. He guessed you could only see the light when wearing the goggles.

He said, 'This is amaz—'

But he never finished as the lights bloomed to life with a series of cracks, illuminating the massive space. The glare hit him, a near-physical assault, and Anthony ripped off the goggles. Hawks took them back with a smile.

'Damn,' Mac said, blinking. 'I didn't realize how much that hurt.'

Anthony straightened himself up as if it didn't faze him at all.

As Santa and Chase returned to them, like action figures against the scale of the subterranean warehouse, passing among a treasure trove of ordinance: jeeps, bikes, airplane parts, all organized around a closed hanger door at the far end.

'Okay,' Santa said. Spread out. Find Eisenberg if he's still here. Eliminate him. And stay safe. Keep your rad-pens on, just in case.'

As they all moved out, Anthony wasn't sure if it was fear or a lack of hope, but Dr. Uhrmacher seemed unsure. Worried. He turned away from the team. Anthony couldn't worry about the German scientist's state of mind, though; his mission was to find out as much as possible about these strange people, and why they were here.

34

Alpha Team swept the warehouse in formation, pens on, their weapons out. Thompson was the only one with a full complement of ammo for his SCAR-M, while Mac switched to the monster Gatling gun during the airfield battle, so he was only down to half his initial allocation. Everyone else had less than one clip apiece. They could allocate the bullets evenly, but that would mean a whole team with fuck-all bullets. Better to have two with full clips, and let the others use their SIGs. Besides, this place was as dead as a mausoleum.

Despite his error in judgment during the firefight, Thompson focused fully on the task at hand. He and Mac pulled boxes off shelves, hoping for something useful, spilling crap all over as they went. At one point, he noticed Chase struggled with a padlocked door. He offered help, but Chase just shrugged, said, 'You wanna help *now*?' and then shot it off.

Santa told him to be careful.

'Seriously, Santa,' he said, 'no fucker's gonna hear. The place was in darkness when we arrived. It's abandoned. They're all at the time-bunker thing, sacrificing a Nazi goat or some shit. Now let's see...' He opened the door and found a refrigerator full of food. Closed it, and moved on.

Santa gave Thompson a look that was trying too hard for 'neutral,' then fell back to observe the search from the top of one of those mini tank things Thompson had seen on old movies. The new boss man sat there kind of like some general on a horse, like being right about one battle elevated him

172

above the others. The armored vehicle was missing its gun barrel, but other than that it appeared intact. Santa watched Anthony particularly closely.

Keeping the future general nearby, keeping him safe, made sure the future happens right. Thompson guessed it was the right call too, but couldn't find a way to say it without sounding patronizing.

Mac opened yet another door, body language suggesting he expected nothing. He was right. Sort of. A large crate of German guns greeted them. The pair poked through it for a few moments, about twelve in total, many different varieties, like they'd been placed here as an afterthought. A salvage mission, perhaps?

He selected a rifle with a telescopic sight. Heavier than Delilah, wood stock, but a nice balance. He racked the bolt, slapped in an old-time magazine. He learned to shoot with something akin to this, but nostalgia never beat progress, not when he had Delilah to take care of him. He placed the German weapon back in its box. 'Like Delilah's ugly Aunt,' he said.

They were about to move on to the next bunch of nothing, when he spotted a metal box within the crate. Something that might ingratiate him back with the rest of the team.

He grinned at Mac. 'Oh yeah. This'll do nicely.'

Santa watched over Anthony from atop the tank-like armored car. It made more sense using these over the terrain up here—huge wheels and an armored body meant it could maneuver well over the tracks and trails, uphill and down, and still be a lethal tool of war. The embossed plate declared the model an SdKfz 234/3. The gun turret was missing, and the engine had been gutted.

He was unsure if he should be mucking in his teammates or directing the operation. He defused the potential issue between Chase and Thompson, but didn't necessarily disagree with Chase's sentiment. From this perch, Santa caught glimpses of Thompson as he and Mac hustled between search points, and thought about making peace more forcefully in front of the others. But it was more important he kept Thompson in sight, made sure he didn't go his own way again, or attempt to organize a mutiny.

'You're all about to hear a big bang,' Thompson said over the sub-vocal. 'Try not to panic.'

Santa already asked Hawks how much juice was left on the sub-vocal net, and she replied that the earpieces would last another week, but her pack, where the comms intersected, would be out in half a day at most. But it could be powered up in daylight.

'It's solar?' Santa had said.

'Of course,' Hawks told him. 'We are a progressive country. And it is essential backup.'

Then came the gunshot. Then a second and a third. Anthony snapped his attention one way, then the other, but since no one else was panicking he calmed down straight away. Hawks had remained alongside him, curious about the old man he would become. Although she'd given off a hard-as-nails vibe from the moment they met her, she was clearly something of a fan of Santa's illustrious grandpa. A groupie.

Can't wait to introduce them, he thought.

Thompson and Mac returned with two metal boxes and opened them like a pair of knights presenting jewels to a king. Perhaps Santa should step down from the elevated position. He wasn't a leader; he was just the guy nominated for that role.

As Santa hopped down to crouch on the vehicle's hood, Thompson gave a grim, tight-lipped expression, somewhere between respect and apologetic, and Santa didn't quite know where to take the gesture. That aside, when Thompson opened the first lid, Santa did, for a moment, feel real warmth toward him.

The metal containers opened to smaller cardboard boxes. Full of bullets.

'Nine mil,' Thompson said. 'Finally found what looked like the right casings, 'least according to the markings, but test fired a couple in mine and Mac's guns to be sure. They're a fit.'

'Okay, folks.' Santa hopped down from the armored vehicle and ejected his SCAR-M's magazine. 'Fill your boots.'

As Chase also came back, that made up the whole team, and they dug into the bounty, replenishing their clips, securing them to their person, slapping them home.

Mac shone the biggest grin. 'No one'll fuck with us now.'

'Of course,' Chase said, 'we'll only need it if the docs continue turning up a big fat zero.'

'Right,' Santa said. 'Anyone see where they are?'

Drs. Lear and Uhrmacher wandered a corridor illuminated only by every second lightbulb.

'This place,' Dr. Lear said, 'it's … *awesome*.'

'Awesome?' Uhrmacher said.

In the olden days, the word 'awesome' was taken literally, as in 'full of awe,' but then, why not take it literally? It certainly fit. He said, 'If my mates and I found this place, we'd be abseiling, exploring every nook and cranny.'

'It is just a cave system. It links throughout this part of the mountain. Construction is less hard.'

They checked inside a door. Uniforms.

Uhrmacher said, 'In the future ... soldiers bring you on missions. You are respected?'

Dr. Lear's pen made a slow clicking noise. He said, 'Not exactly in the sense you mean. We can make okay money if we are at the top of our field. I even advised on a movie once. But we don't race around in Porsches.' He checked his pen. Still at only trace levels, but it meant they were closer to something that was, or had in the past, emitted radiation. He said, 'You, though, even without the time machine, you're the man who built the world's smallest nuclear reactor. Have you any idea how much this could help the world? It could power a nation like Haiti for a fraction of the cost of a full-sized one. You'd be famous. A Nobel Prize winner.'

'Me?'

'Yes. Heck, I've read a lot about the scientific discoveries of the second world war, about the awful things your government made scientists do, but I've never read about you.' Dr. Lear caught himself there. *Shit, maybe that wasn't so tactful.* 'Maybe you're meant to come back with us. Bring your knowledge.'

But Uhrmacher's gaze was already lowered, his shoulders slack. No need to say there could be another reason no one had heard of him.

Dr. Lear said, 'This way, I think.'

The pen clicked louder, becoming a beep, as Uhrmacher opened another metal door. The repetitive chirping remained steady. It was in keeping with the residue that would be left on the outer casing as Uhrmacher described. As Dr. Lear pawed at the wall for a light, he considered how hard it was going to be to lug such a vessel over the mountain, no matter how tough the Americans deemed themselves.

But, as the fluorescent bulbs flickered to life, with the exception of some poles and clothes, the room was empty.

Uhrmacher said, 'I need to speak to your soldiers. Quickly.'

35

Each clack of a bullet slotting into place echoed through the huge space, where Anthony wandered—*not too far*, as ordered—gazing around in wonder. Having been the one responsible for planting the flares, he still had a full mag in his Tommy, and proceeded to hold it in a way that suggested he was ready for anything. Although cheating on Sarah never crossed his mind, he couldn't help but hold himself taller around the one they called 'Hawks.' No, he would never do anything with her, and nor did he expect an advance from her—she was at least ten years older than him for starters—but still, the need to appear in control, to mask his fear and confusion, it remained front and center in his mind.

He called to them, 'You need me for anything?'

Santa said, 'Check the perimeter again.'

Anthony remembered to exude strength, and paced slowly toward the aisles of munitions and supplies. He loitered within earshot of the team, though, as Brown ordered.

Santa forced another bullet into his clip. He eyed Anthony, who piqued his suspicion in a way he could not quite articulate. The kid was taking too much of an interest in their work. If Anthony was single, maybe Santa would have written it off as him building up to hitting on Hawks. Or maybe his grandpa was more of a dog than he could have suspected.

'Use a hand?' Thompson asked.

'I'm okay.'

'Cos if you do, just ask. Okay?'

Although he appreciated Thompson's effort, Santa eyed Anthony instead. This wasn't like he'd caught the guy cheating at poker, or calling in sick when Santa knew it was a hangover. What he did back there, it cost lives. Lives that might already have blinked out long ago in 2015, but Santa watched it happen.

Thompson said, 'You know he'll be around for years to come, right? Thanks to you.'

'Thanks to us,' Santa said.

Thompson tensed, gave a nod. No arguing there. But holding such a grudge when they needed everyone on top of their game, was there any sense in this? Punishing him through the cold shoulder? Reminding him every time he opened his mouth?

'Not out of the woods yet,' Santa said. 'Not 'til we go home. He'll always be at risk. He'll need us all to be ready.' When Thompson didn't reply, Santa slapped the man's arm. 'All of us, okay?'

Thompson handed Chase a mag he'd loaded, and Chase accepted it with a solid, 'Thanks, man.'

Mac said, 'What about those flashy thingies?'

That pulled Santa out of the moment. He said, 'Flashy thingies?'

'Well, as long as we don't get 'em, we're good, right? Like a guide?'

Santa and Thompson glanced at each other in surprise that he actually said that.

'He sorta makes sense,' Thompson said.

'Yeah,' Santa said uncertainly. 'Trouble is it seems to be all about decisions. Stuff we can affect. If Eisenberg jumps out of a dark corner and shoots him, what happens? World War Three?'

179

Anthony tensed up and frowned. Either he heard them or he was concerned about something else.

Santa called him back over. 'Problem?'

'I've listened to you talking,' Anthony said. 'For a while now, I've listened. You're more than Special Forces. Like something out of a comic book.'

Now the whole team watched Santa and Anthony, face to face. In other circumstances, he would take Anthony to one side, but here, in this situation, the team needed transparency. Needed *clarity*.

'You *know* me,' Anthony said. 'Not just from when we met today. I can tell. You know something about me.'

Santa winced. An ache in his gut instead of pain in his head. 'Maybe a little,' he said.

Anthony fished an envelope out of his chest pocket. Santa tracked it. It was *the* envelope, the one he told the team about, one of the few details his grandpa gave him about his time here.

...he received a letter containing the tragic news...

'Got this before the sarge came in with our orders. My fiancée is due about now, so I know it tells me if I got a boy or a girl waiting for me back home. I can feel it.'

Santa said, 'You haven't opened it yet?'

Anthony clenched his jaw. 'You know what's in it?'

'No.' Santa's stomach turned. No one else let on that they were affected but, like him, they could have been masking it. It could also have been stress. A young man about to read the worst news he would ever receive. Santa said, 'What are you hoping for? Boy or girl?'

Anthony ripped up the corner of the envelope. 'Maybe I'll open it now.'

'No!' Santa said again. He regulated his tone, but with Anthony's thumb in the envelope his gut-ache strengthened. He said, 'You deserve to read that at a happy moment. Just … tell me, Private. What are you hoping for?'

'Girl,' Anthony said. 'She'll dress so pretty when I marry her mom.'

Sweat pricked on Santa's forehead. 'Sarah. Jesus, Sarah.'

'You know her *name*? How do you—'

But Dr. Lear and Dr. Uhrmacher arrived in a hurry. Anthony tried to continue, but Santa and the others stepped up to meet the scientists, their manner and gray faces making them all tense. As soon as Anthony gave up and folded the envelope and put it back in his pocket, Santa's breathed easier, nausea alleviated, just like that.

More help from the timeline, or the stress of knowing the situation could have blown up in their faces? Whatever, it was done with now.

To the docs, he said, 'You find them? The fuel rods?'

'Not exactly,' Dr. Lear said.

Uhrmacher looked first to the team, then Dr. Lear, who prompted him to speak. He said, 'We know what Project Return Fire is.'

36

Dang's vision cleared gradually. A dot of silver in a sea of black that expanded as if floating through a pipe, until he emerged out the other end. His head hurt even worse than that strange dream trip back at the bar, and when he rolled over, his stomach lurched, and he tasted Desiree's stew tinged with acid. His bullet wound parted and, with the morphine having worn off while he was unconscious, he hissed to stop himself from screaming. He managed to focus, to touch the scenery around him.

He was lying in the back of a flatbed truck, high up, so he guessed at military grade tires. They covered him in a blanket, but the biting cold still made him shiver. He was thankful for that, though, as it meant if the hole in his thigh tore any further, his blood flow would be slower. The truck parked in the clearing where the milky-eyed Reuler and his men disembarked a separate jeep. Reuler held Desiree by the arm; not roughly, but she would be in no doubt that struggling would mean pain.

The bunker door opened, and out strode Captain Eisenberg, in a fresh uniform, displaying the confident swagger of an overpaid football star. The two exchanged the requisite 'Heil Hitler' salutes with the appropriate level of sobriety, and Reuler's troops all did the same. When their arms lowered, Reuler and Eisenberg shook hands, hugged one another, then parted, and Reuler pointed at the truck.

Shit. They knew he was awake now. Reuler made some hand gestures and barked in German, and two of the men from the Bar du Pont slaughter rushed over and dragged Dang out onto the floor. For the first time, he realized dawn had crept up on them, the sun a speck of orange through the trees.

'I can walk,' he said.

When they released him, his head spun, his legs buckled, and he fell on his front, hands out to stop his face slamming into the ground. There was a fair-to-even possibility he suffered a concussion.

They picked him up again, and alongside Desiree he was manhandled inside the bunker, down the steel staircase and along the metal mesh of a walkway. Neither offered resistance, but Desiree's eyes glared daggers as someone clanged along at her rear. It was Eisenberg, in fact, marching right behind her, way too close. Dang bent his neck and tried to throw him a bastard of a look too, but instead he noticed his own bleeding leg leaving a trail.

He said, 'Don't suppose you want to tell me your plan before showing me the self-destruct button?'

'You are a strange little man,' Eisenberg said. 'But my "plan," as you call it, should be self-evident.'

Eisenberg overtook, and led the group into the laboratory, where squad of eight Brandenburgers stood to attention. All saluted, and gave the shout of, 'Zeig heil.' Reuler's men returned the greeting, and big smiles melted onto weathered faces, hands were shook, old pals coming home.

A nice moment. For them.

Dang noticed the scientists' bodies had been moved to where they would be found in 2015, and the sense of something clicking into place swam through him. Not in a fun way, either.

If those bodies will be there in 2015, then this is where it all ends. This is where it will finally play out. And it won't be long now.

Eisenberg said, 'What you find here, is a full complement of Brandenburger troops. We will not be taken by surprise again.'

Dang said, 'You still need the doc. Santa won't let—'

'He will not have a choice.' Reuler was pulling on a radiation suit. Easily. Expertly. Like he'd done it before.

Eisenberg said, 'You see, little future-man. This is not some science experiment. It never was. Even in the beginning. It is, and always was, a *military* operation. Our scientists are merely caretakers. Max Reuler is more than capable of pressing the right buttons.'

To Eisenberg, Germany's judgment day was approaching, and the dawn of a thousand-year Reich loomed ever nearer. The men he would select to lead him across Switzerland and help him into Great Britain would need language skills and strength. He would have liked his first choice complement to be there, especially Reitziger, but it was not to be. No matter. He had been isolated from the time stream long enough; it was time to suppress these notions of friendship and concentrate on the future. At least, the future as he would craft it.

He had not understood the concepts at first, but the long days in this little corner of the world left him plenty of time for contemplation, and because of the cast-iron procedures laid out and followed, he foresaw nothing but victory. Since he took over here, there had been only one lapse—the injured animal that got in somehow, and bled to death in the lab—but that was rectified by going on patrol each time a spike was created, locking the door behind them, and ensuring no one came or went in the meantime. The scientists were happy too, as they then had the cafeteria to themselves while the anchor point set, and they remained hidden, in case Eisenberg was required to use that spike. He dared not risk Dr. Uhrmacher or Dr. Gruber learning with one hundred-percent certainty that the machine would be used. As Uhrmacher said, if you know the future, you automatically change the future.

Here, in this place, he and his men were utterly sealed off from the world. They touched nothing and influenced nothing. They just existed. So if one of them needed to go back and alter the timeline for Germany, everyone here would remain untouched, and time itself would mold a new form around them.

The only problem with isolation was, well, isolation. Boredom. The town offered some respite, as isolated as the bunker, but when resistance started driving into the area, Eisenberg had to ship in others to fight them; they could not risk anyone having serious impact on the proceedings, or changes in the time stream may have been catastrophic.

That they stumbled upon the American saboteurs yesterday morning was nothing but luck. A standard patrol while Uhrmacher set the spike, and the Yankees ended up on the dangerous end of a firing squad. It was a risk, a potential contact with the world at large, but allowing them to live after discovering Germany's saviors was a far bigger problem.

Most of the time, they trained, they honed their bodies. Eisenberg even studied new hand-to-hand techniques, and became most adept at using a knife. He was a crack shot with a pistol, a rifle and the ever-trusty STG60 and MP40. He was in the best fighting shape of his life, and he would soon be a hero of the Third Reich. All because of that crystal.

Whenever he thought of the dull little object his chest bloomed within. Since he was the one who found it, the notion that he would be the one to utilize it gave things a sense of synchronicity that he couldn't help but enjoy.

The desert gifted it to him, on a day with nothing but sand in all directions, sun beating down. None of this freezing snow, blizzards, storms, landslides. The Giza Plateau, with the Sphinx and the Great Pyramids, were his expedition's starting point, but they left the famous monuments behind many days earlier, before their local guide announced their search was almost at an end.

'Just past this dune,' the dark-skinned man said in English.

Alongside Eisenberg, Reitziger mumbled, 'He said that two dunes ago.'

The guide did not speak German, but seemed to understand as he insisted he was correct this time.

The twenty men Eisenberg brought with them, a mix of German troops and Egyptian mercenaries, conducted the excavation. It took two days and one night for the first mercenary to try and abandon the operation, and Eisenberg rewarded him with a bullet in the back.

'The führer himself gave me this mission,' Eisenberg told the assembled workers. 'It may be nothing. It may be the key to our glory.'

It was 1935, a long while before war would be declared, but there were already rumblings that Herr Hitler was planning to destroy all his enemies. So everyone at officer class was keen to prove himself, to be an asset to their nation's rebirth.

Eisenberg's men uncovered a wall on the third day.

The Egyptian guide did not only know the desert; he was an authority in the ancient civilizations of his country, and once he worked out the dynamics of this miniature, scruffily-hewn pyramid, buried millennia ago, the doorway was dynamited, and Eisenberg followed the expert inside, with Reitziger bringing up the rear. They all moved quickly, deeper into the dark, speeding up each long, straight passage, until all that could be seen was the lights from their torches. Eventually, Eisenberg's flames reflected onto the wall that displayed drawings, dusty but clear.

The guide said, 'Yes, these are like the ones we found last year, the reason you are here. These ones...' he wiped dust away, reading excitedly. 'Like the other legend, but it is more detailed. Something has come from the sky ... fell to the earth ... a meteorite, we suspected, but...'

In German, Reitziger said, 'Maybe we should just find it.'

Eisenberg agreed, and they reached another entrance, the doorway edges decorated with faded gold. It was not locked, just a square stone that trundled sideways, scraping with some serious effort. When the gap was wide enough, they entered what turned out to be some sort of showroom. The guide lit as many of the torches along the wall as he could, the reeds still dry in this sealed environment.

A stone pedestal sat in the center as tall as a man, and held a crystal about the size of a fist. Eisenberg and Reitziger approached the plinth from either end, both extending on tiptoes to make a closer examination.

The guide said, 'I believe this is what you are searching for ... *El Kristall des Schicksals*.'

That Eisenberg presented it personally to Herr Hitler was a great honor, and when the great man himself chose Eisenberg to guard it once the scientists found a use, he could not say no. Over the years, to limit his exposure, he received little official news about the war, relying instead on radio reports, and rumors from the resistance. Not even those who shipped in supplies would speak or interact in any way. Their orders were to land, drop off, and take off again. There was still a chance that those supply runs could be affected by changes Eisenberg might make, but there had to be some limits to their paranoia. This was, after all, the ultimate last resort.

No, he had to work out for himself if he should return or not, and he had to work out the best plan too. Project Return Fire was his finest hour and, thanks to the Americans' arrive from the future, it was now in motion.

Dang said, 'Doesn't matter. We're US Army Rangers. We'll find a way.'

'For all your flashy boxes and special guns,' Eisenberg said, 'they are still only men. Mine survived the Russian front. Could yours?'

37

Alpha Team were growing impatient, although Dr. Uhrmacher needed only a moment to catch his breath.

He said, 'The cargo was here, but no longer. This is extremely bad.'

Although Santa was getting a feeling he knew the answer, he asked, 'Why's that?'

'Well, I am afraid it may be too late.'

Chase grabbed the German by the lapels and said, 'Spit it the fuck out.'

'Okay, okay.' As Santa eased Chase off him, Uhrmacher said, 'In the event of a catastrophic failure to win the war, Eisenberg is to use the machine to travel back to nineteen thirty nine and ... fix ... it.'

Mac said, 'We know this already.'

'Why is it worse now?' Hawks asked.

Uhrmacher took a breath and said, 'He only needs twelve rods to connect one spike to another. But he has taken three lead containers. Each contains twelve rods.'

'Thirty four rods?' Mac said.

'Thirty six,' Thompson said.

'Math Nazi.'

'Not funny, Mac—'

Santa coughed and nodded at the docs.

Lear said, 'I calculated we would need twenty-eight to burrow around our tunnel to the spike in 2015. That's with the gravitational flux.'

'Captain Eisenberg can only use the machine once,' Uhrmacher said. 'The risk of meeting his past self would be too great. He needs no spares.'

'So, chaps,' Dr. Lear said. 'Why would he need an additional twenty-four rods of uranium, each weighing thirty pounds?'

Chase said, 'Motherfuckers don't have the A-bomb though. Do they?'

Santa shook his head. 'The US only completed that a few years before Hiroshima.'

'What is Hiroshima?' Uhrmacher asked.

'You'll see,' Thompson said.

'Yeah,' Mac said, 'let's not ruin the surprise.'

Dr. Lear interrupted with a sigh. 'Don't you see? It doesn't matter if he has a device capable of splitting the atom upon detonation. If you blow up twenty-four uranium rods, the fallout still contaminates for miles.'

Santa's throat tightened. 'A dirty bomb.'

'He's going to set off a dirty bomb?' Chase said. 'Where?'

Uhrmacher said, 'There is only one place worthwhile.'

'London,' Santa said.

Hawks frowned, her mouth open. 'A dirty bomb, exploding on the day war gets declared...'

'Yeah,' Santa said. 'It *ends* the war.'

38

Alpha Team and the docs exited the bunker, with Anthony trailing last, the chill hitting Santa harder than expected. Each kept pace with the two scientists, hoping for more info, but it was proving difficult.

Dr. Lear had been silent for most of the journey, but told Santa, 'I'm not convinced.'

'About what?' Santa said.

'The bomb. Setting it off in London will be a breach of the truce that Hitler and Neville Chamberlain signed. The whole world will see the atrocity, and unite against Germany.'

'Or be too afraid to confront them at all. The American atomic bomb program wasn't complete in 1939. Might've made us think twice.'

'Or pulled the Americans in *sooner*.'

'Whatever,' Chase said. 'It's still settin' off a nuke when a nuke isn't meant to get set off. Time line is fucked whatever the result.'

'Chase is right,' Santa said. 'The outcome is irrelevant. We still have to stop him. Doc, I need to know everything about this machine. Our options.'

Although he was addressing Uhrmacher, Dr. Lear said, 'Well, to clarify, they set the spikes six months apart, and each spike can only be used once. If Eisenberg goes back, we ... *you* ... can't follow to stop him.'

'Correct,' Uhrmacher said. 'Setting them far apart was one of his conditions. So no one *could* follow him. And also ... uranium is very expensive. And difficult to make.'

'You'd be able to travel to six months after, but that will be too late.'

Thompson said, 'So we go back to six months before that spike, stake it out, and me an' Delilah'll plant a steel jacket between his eyes.'

Uhrmacher shook his head. 'Captain Eisenberg eradicated all those spikes. He sent men through, as training exercises. The earliest spike that exists is three months before the declaration of war. If you travel back, it will be three months after that, and Eisenberg will have carried out his plan.'

Sergeant Brown, Private Simons, and Private Martins approached them.

Brown asked, 'Find what you're needin'?'

'No,' Anthony said. 'They didn't.'

'Tough break. Now what?'

Santa considered the future, what the best move would be right now. He said, 'I appreciate the help. But you can all be on your way.'

The Rangers shifted their weight, eyes moving to one another, obviously wanting to question this course of action.

Brown said, 'Really? You're okay by yourselves?'

'You guys've been through enough.'

Brown wasn't buying it. He looked to his men and back at Santa with a side glance. 'I lost four boys back there. I think we deserve an explanation of what the hell you guys're doin'.'

Anthony said, 'You read HG Wells, Sarge?'

'When I was a kid. Why? They got a submarine or somethin'?'

'Okay, fine,' Santa said. 'Here you go ... and remember, you asked. We are more than Special Forces. We came a long way to secure the future of the United States.'

'Santa,' Thompson said.

Santa waved him off. 'Captain Eisenberg has obtained nuclear material and plans to travel back to 1939 where he will detonate a dirty bomb somewhere in the vicinity of the British government. The explosion will be big, but the atomic fallout will kill thousands, maybe more. The threat of further attacks will probably mean Britain surrenders on day one. No war.'

Brown blew cigar smoke. Narrowed his eyes.

Santa said, 'If he succeeds, Hitler will cement his base here. He will never split his forces during the invasion of Russia, and by the time the US gets involved, it'll be too late. You, and everyone you care for, will have to collaborate with the Nazis if you want to survive.'

'Okay,' Brown said. 'Anything else?'

'Still want to help?'

'Sure.' Brown threw his arms in the air. 'Simons! Saddle up the unicorns.'

Simons and Martins chuckled, but Anthony said, 'They're serious, sir. They really believe this.'

'You don't believe me?' Santa said.

Brown laughed. 'Would *you* believe *me*?'

Santa noted Thompson's clenched fists, his mouth holding in words that he'd probably regret. Especially since the pair were only just on speaking terms. Santa said, 'Then what are you still doing here? Get your men and go.'

Brown leveled his gaze at Santa, and drew it across the rest of Alpha Team. He said, 'I already got four real unpleasant letters to write. If you're gonna bullshit us, whatever your reasons, seriously, I wish you *all* the best.'

Although the sarcasm oozed bitterly, Santa said, 'Good luck to you guys. And a little advice. Lose the cigar. It gives away your position.'

Brown puffed away like a steam train as he headed back to

the forest, downhill toward his transport vehicles, followed by Anthony, Martins, and Simons. From here, they would return to their base and report a successful mission, and Anthony Santarelli would learn of his girl's demise, and resolve to raise his son in the best world he could build. He would fail, ultimately, but he would try.

Mac said, 'You're really lettin' them go—'

Santa held his hand up to pause Mac. He said, 'Faster that kid cracks opens a beer, faster he goes home and starts working on my gene pool.'

All remained silent. Santa was fully aware that he'd sent their best source of backup away, but there were more important things to consider. If they stopped Eisenberg, but Anthony died, there would be no General Santarelli to step in at Glasnost and cut off World War Three at the knees. Not to mention the moon landings. His grandfather trained Buzz Aldrin in his early years; he was fond of claiming to have *invented* 'the right stuff.' How many other things had he advised presidents for and against? How many great battles in Korea, Vietnam, the Middle East?

Santa said, 'Okay, let's stop pussying around with paradoxes and destiny and all that crap. We take the bunker, stop Eisenberg, and we go home. If we can't do that, we destroy the machine. Clear?'

All seemed uncertain.

'This is our job! 1945 or 2015, it's our job to stop him. I don't need to risk those guys' lives to do it.'

Nothing.

And I still have Lily, Santa thought. *I will blow the shit out of that machine, with me inside it, and all of you if it comes to it.*

He said, 'But we cannot sacrifice the general. Because if he dies, even if we stop Eisenberg, the world starts throwing nu-clear missiles at each other before most of us are even born.'

Even if it creates some kind of paradox, or we exist outside the time stream, or whatever bullshit head-fucking physics we might face, Lily won't ever exist. And I can't see a world like that making sense. I won't allow anything to happen to my baby girl.

Thompson stepped forward and shucked a fist into Santa's shoulder. The corner of his mouth turned up slightly. 'Well then, I guess that's the only plan left.'

'I'm ready,' Mac said.

'Fuck it,' Chase said, 'we gotta try.'

Hawks pointed the direction, a map in the other hand. 'Thirty minutes. That way.'

39

Alpha Team streamed uphill, over the snow-dusted forest floor, blades of dawn sunlight cutting through the trees to create a strobe-like effect in Santa's peripheral vision. They stopped every three minutes for the team to catch their breath, a stop-start rhythm that allowed maximum progress. After taking on water from the German supplies, Alpha Team would have been fine running all the way in optimum conditions, but having been awake now for coming up to twenty-four hours, their energy levels peaked at the airfield battle, and Santa was certain another firefight was approaching. Better to preserve energy for that than exert it all at once on arriving.

Interval running was key. It was how millions of joggers got started on fitness, how his grandpa got Santa into jogging at the age of thirteen. 'Run to that streetlight, then walk the next two,' he said. Santa obeyed, and repeated it for a half-mile. The second time out, he ran one phase, walked two again, but this time for a whole mile. The next day he swapped it, running two posts, walking one. They kept this third formula up for a week, with two rest days, and the following week they stepped up the training to two miles. The week after that, it was running four streetlights, walking one. Within two months, using this graded improvement, the young Jonathan Santarelli got a real buzz from his ten-mile runs, as well as a massive increase in appetite, and a growth spurt that shocked his parents and pleased his grandpa.

So that was the system here. Short bursts of energy followed by rest periods were better than slogging slowly through the woodland, especially now that they had descended from the pass on one side of the hill, and needed to pick their way upwards, back to the bunker. If they'd brought the scientists along, it would have been even harder. Civvie hyper-fitness, as Dr. Lear displayed, was impressive to other civvies, but when stamina is part of making your living, it exists within you on a whole different level.

Hawks paused forty-five seconds into the latest running phase. The team froze around her. She held up a small lens to sweep the landscape, and checked a handheld monitor. It flickered, the battery still active on good fortune alone, but with a shake and a slap, the screen cleared and showed the trees in hi-def black and white. Then it died completely. Like their iNavs had an hour earlier.

Hawks put it away. 'No more motion sensors. It has picked up zero for now. But we have some distance to cover yet.'

'How far?' Chase asked.

'Moving like this? Thirty minutes.'

All looked to Santa. He hesitated, then nodded. And they pressed on.

In a long woolen coat festooned with Nazi insignia, Eisenberg led two Brandenburgers from the bunker, who dragged Dang toward a tree. He twisted in their grasp, pulled free, and flopped to the ground. His sickness had subsided, and the dizziness eased, but if he moved his head too quickly, the world tilted and he lost his balance. With that in mind, trying to escape wasn't the best move. They punched him in the gut, then kicked his thigh-wound. His teeth gnashed to hold in the scream. His leg was virtually useless now, and he felt more blood leak. The dressing was keeping him from bleeding out, but he sensed he'd spilled enough to qualify for a transfusion when he got home.

Although 'when' was looking increasing like an 'if' right now.

Eisenberg checked the knot in a rope that now bound Dang's feet together. *When the fuck did they do that?*

Dang said, 'Santa ... will never agree ... to a prisoner ex-change.'

Eisenberg patted Dang's cheek, showing his teeth in a wide mouth. 'My boy. My brown mongrel. What makes you think I need a prisoner exchange?'

The two thugs who brought him out slid a meat hook into the rope between his feet, and in a second or two, Dang was dragged over the ground and into the air, upside-down. They had strung him up—a slab of beef in a butcher's window.

Eisenberg crouched at eye-level, turned his head sideways to try and meet Dang's eyes. He said, 'You, little boy, are nothing more than *bait*.'

40

In the supply depot, the two scientists wandered the racks that formed passages and nooks and crannies. Occasionally, they came upon a dead end, and had to double back, but more often they would think the end of an aisle was solid rock, then it would turn left or right and gift them a whole new set of shelves. Not that every shelf was full, or even close to it, but the Nazis racked it out with enough space for years of equipment and supplies. Dr. Lear voiced the possibility that this was to be used as a staging area, perhaps for sending more troops back to different spikes. Uhrmacher thought they were being efficient, as they did not know, when it was built, the purpose of the structure. Then conversation graduated to 'what-if' scenarios.

'If Eisenberg is successful,' Uhrmacher said, 'we will not feel a thing. We will be unaware of any changes. Maybe he already has been, but we are outside the chain of events that have been altered.'

'But our memories,' Dr. Lear countered, 'wouldn't they be changed? Yours may not, but I still recall that Germany loses the war.'

'But you are also displaced in time. The universe may exclude you as a paradoxical anomaly until you return to your own year.'

Dr. Lear conceded that was certainly a possibility. There was also the theory of fractured timelines, that one thing affecting him and the other 2015 travelers might not be the same events experienced by Eisenberg if he tunneled to 1939.

Therefore, Santa's worry about his little girl could well be unfounded; she would still exist, even if Anthony Santarelli died. It would open a new timeline and when Santa returned to his, all would be fine.

'Unless,' Uhrmacher said, 'when he goes forward, he is re-united with our timeline, the one in which the private dies. We have no way of knowing.'

The conversation took Dr. Lear back to his university days. They did not experiment a lot with drugs, but on those nights where a little herb made itself available, time travel paradoxes were a regular topic. Of course, those conversations were never put to practical use, and no one ever expected them to be.

'Not knowing,' Dr. Lear said. 'That's precisely why they will destroy the machine rather than allow Eisenberg to travel.'

'Yes, destroying it is the wise thing to do.'

They came to the end of another corridor, a rock wall.

Lear said, 'Guess we should turn around.'

'I am sorry,' Uhrmacher said.

'Why? We've hit a ton of dead ends already. We'll just—'

'That is not why I am sorry.' Uhrmacher knocked on the wall.

Dr. Lear stared at the rock for a moment, trying to work out why it sounded odd. The reason was that although it was clearly solid, it resonated a fraction of a second longer. As it was hollow.

The wall made a deep 'thoom' noise, and moved inward, creating a door. It slid open to reveal four winter-dressed Brandenburgers.

'As I told you,' Uhrmacher said, 'I am sorry. But I cannot allow your people to destroy my machine.'

'But...' Dr. Lear backed away from the highly-amused soldiers. He said, 'You're a scientist. You told us you don't want them to win the war. You ... ah, screw it.'

Dr. Lear threw a punch, impacting Uhrmacher's cheek. The German staggered, and the Brandenburgers were on Lear within seconds, pinning his arms. He writhed, his face hot and fists itching to pummel the man he had almost allowed himself to consider a new friend.

41

The journey through the cave system disoriented Dr. Lear in more ways than one. He could only think of a single moment when Uhrmacher might have gotten word to the other bunker, recalling him messing with a contraption that resembled a telephone, but had no speaker or receiver. Uhrmacher told him it was a radio from a jeep that had been cannibalized for parts.

The tunnels went on for miles, some of them obviously natural, but others had been blasted out of the rock, manufacturing a warren linking all the necessary parts of the mountain.

They emerged through a cave mouth, ostensibly hidden by foliage, two of the soldiers hustling the scientists roughly down an overgrown path to the bunker housing the time chamber. Dr. Lear was not wearing a coat and the bitterness surrounded him immediately. He spotted Dang moments later, his upside-down face swollen as his head filled with fluid.

The other two soldiers heaved the crate of guns that Thompson and Mac located, and placed it beside the bunker's entrance. Eisenberg was already waiting.

Uhrmacher raised his arm straight. 'Heil Hitler, *Hauptsturmführer*.'

'Heil Hitler, Herr Doctor.' Eisenberg returned the salute. 'It is good to see you back.'

Dr. Lear's teeth literally chattered, his arms hugging himself, breath misting. He spat the words, 'Treacherous snake.'

'How can I be a traitor?' Uhrmacher replied. 'I have remained loyal to the Fatherland all along.'

Thompson's view was not complicated: the new day cast long shadows, the longest of all being Dang, swinging upside-down from a tree. No chance of fancy scope settings right now. Just his sense of wind speed, distance, and air pressure. He could have killed that Nazi bastard, but Santa stopped him. Although it was possible the Brandenburger squad would crumble without their leader, the risk was that they would rally, activate the machine early, and still execute Project Return Fire. It made sense, especially in light of Dang being captured. No way did Eisenberg have time to snatch him, and do what he did up at the airfield. There were more players, and Alpha Team needed to learn all they could. So, lying on a bough behind a curtain of pine needles, he wrapped his legs around the wood, and watched.

Dang.

Eisenberg.

Soldiers ushering the scientists inside.

Further down the incline, others set booby traps—grenades, mines, and tripwires.

He said, 'I don't know how this happened, but as well as Dang, they got both our docs. Now they're booby trappin' the homestead.'

Thompson lowered the rifle.

'Bastards've strung him up like a lynching.'

'If we screw up,' Santa said, 'if we can't get that machine to work, saving Dang won't matter. He'll understand. Priority is either stopping Eisenberg or destroying this place.'

'I been thinking about that,' Chase said. 'If we blow it the fuck up, then how the fuck'll we travel back here?'

'I don't know. Nobody knows anything about this crap. We only destroy it if we have to. But it shouldn't be necessary.'

'Yeah,' Mac said. 'We got the edge in every department now. Training, equipment ... and surprise.'

Thompson again raised the scope to his eye. 'Speakin' of surprise...'

Max Reuler exited the bunker, followed by two men carrying a car battery wired to something in Reuler's hand. Eisenberg asked if he completed securing the additional fuel rods in the vessel that would become a bomb in a matter of months, and he confirmed he had. Reuler then presented Eisenberg with what the Nazi captain was sure was a more complex achievement than the device that would obliterate the UK government: the tiny screen Eisenberg liberated from the future team's leader, now jerry-rigged for power.

Ah, Max. Yes, Eisenberg had known Reitziger for longer— over ten years now—and he experienced a momentary pang of sadness when the man died, but Reuler was the one who led his men to and from the eastern front over the years. Reitziger was a brawler, a warrior, while the *untersturmführer* was a true soldier, one who fought with his head as much as his fists.

A dot flashed on the screen ... four dots ... *five* ... *moving...*

Eisenberg smiled. *It worked. Reuler was correct. The American fools are linked.*

Alpha Team crouched in a line close together. Thompson having no more intel to share, he joined them on the ground. The bunker was visible a couple hundred yards ahead. Santa would reposition him shortly.

Mac lowered his binoculars. 'They're chillin'.'

A pause while Santa thought about this.

Hawks said, 'This feels a little bit easy to you?'

'Yeah,' Santa said. 'A bit.'

Thompson said, 'Wanna come back when it's dark?'

'Ten hours?' Chase said. 'No fuckin' way, it's Dang up there.'

'Piece a' cake.' Mac pointed out the relevant features of the approach. 'I go right, circle round and wait near Dang. Santa, you take Chase up the left side and hit them from two angles. Hawksy sneaks up from the south east and Thompson lays it down from his nest.'

'Sounds easy,' Chase said.

'All the more reason to think it's a—'

A click sounded. No one needed to think twice; they'd all experienced it enough. That was a gun cocking nearby. And it was not one of Alpha team's. He should have known.

This group was a counter-insurgency, experts in their surroundings, and Eisenberg lived every moment of the past five years right here. Of course they would be waiting. Of course they would know the best way to conceal themselves. Of course, without the Rangers' technology, they would have the edge.

Santa bowed his head. 'A trap.'

As if morphing from the undergrowth, six men in heavy camouflage emerged, grass and leaves and sticks wrapped around them. Their guns pointed squarely at Alpha Team.

There was nothing left to do, but surrender.

42

Alpha Team marched, hands on their heads, stripped of equipment and body armor, surrounded by troops. Santa noted several booby-trapped grenades as they went. He tipped his head toward Chase, who picked up on what he meant, snagging Hawks' attention, then Thompson's and Mac's. All eyes roved over the ground, mentally assessing the minefield, hopeful there was a way out of this mess into which Santa led them.

As they arrived at the bunker entrance, Eisenberg and some grotesque freak with a white eye greeted them with barely-disguised smiles. Santa tried to get Dang to acknowledge their presence, but the kid's position had taken its toll. At Eisenberg's shout, two troopers brought Desiree and Dr. Lear out of the bunker, the woman furnished with a man's woolen coat, but the doc was only in his basic US blacks.

Once she saw Dang, Desiree's face dropped, and she rushed from the soldier's grasp to kneel beside him. He stirred at her touch and managed to say, 'It's okay ... don't worry. N'est pas ... worry. Okay?'

She couldn't possibly understand, but she wept for him all the same.

Uhrmacher also emerged from the bunker and allowed a guilty side glance at Santa, but arrowed toward Eisenberg. Santa hoped the doc didn't feel too badly about being caught. It wasn't his fault, after all.

They spoke in German. Santa recognized Eisenberg say, 'Good,' and then Uhrmacher returned inside. Presumably, they were forcing him to comply.

Eisenberg passed by Santa. Their eyes met. Santa's narrowed, hoping to convey 'fuck you' as they stood nose-to-nose. Eisenberg was still wearing General Santarelli's knife.

'One to one,' Santa said. 'Me and you. Rematch.'

Eisenberg tilted his head. 'Tempting. But sadly, I cannot afford such indulgences.'

'You know your plan probably won't work.'

'You do not think wiping out the British government will help Germany?'

'I think it will galvanize your other enemies, bring America into things faster. You'll kill thousands in England, but the war will end sooner. Fewer people will die. Your master race will go under before you murder millions more innocent Jews—'

'Innocent?'

'Yeah, innocent.'

Eisenberg smirked.

'Bottom line,' Santa continued, 'is hitting London with this bomb makes Germany's position weaker.'

Ten yards away, Nazis fiddled with the captured 2015 weaponry, figuring out the SCARs. A gun fired and the bullet hit the floor. The soldiers laughed at their friend's stunned face, and it was clear he was impressed with the lack of recoil, miming whilst explaining it. Then his friends wanted a go too.

Eisenberg said, 'Did you really think I would do nothing but set off a really big bomb? When Project Return Fire was first devised, I was already in isolation. By the time I jump back, our high command knows that if I arrive with a password, our country has fallen, and we must develop a new strategy.'

Santa's thoughts tumbled together. All along they assumed

he'd be a lone terrorist, attempting to wipe out Germany's enemies, a lone, mad wolf with his own agenda. 'They all know?'

'Herr Hitler, Goebbels, Goering, Himler, von Brauchitsch, Keitel, yes. I briefed them myself.'

'You're going to launch an invasion. Neville Chamberlain declares war, so he is the aggressor, you set off the nuke, and then swarm over the Channel. The UK is the perfect place to launch into France, and to defend Europe if the USA attacks.'

Eisenberg shoved Santa toward the rest of the group. 'An astute mind. A shame you are on the wrong side.'

The Nazis herded the Rangers into position beside the inverted Dang. Eisenberg's scheme tumbled through Santa's head, his history lessons sketchy, but World War Two remained relatively ingrained in him. With Germany still friendly with Russia, they might even honor their pact, deterring America even further. Italy, too, was still a German ally in 1939, and if they galvanized their positions in Britain and France, and up into the Netherlands, America would struggle to mount a feasible invasion. No base of operations. While America itself might not fall immediately, if the Nazis could infect everything east of France, that was a huge swath of land. He recalled African incursions, the Middle East, and with Japan's mighty forces not yet engaged with the US ... the possibilities were endless, the scenarios terrifying.

Men like Eisenberg would rule the world. Santa was low on ideas. Low, but not out entirely. This was still 1945, a man's world, where even those who did evil considered themselves either gentlemen, or masters of the female race. He saw one gamble left.

Santa said, 'I thought some honor still remained, even among you evil bastards. You gonna slaughter women like men? They don't deserve this.'

'You know,' the white-eyed asshole said, 'women can be useful in other ways.'

Eisenberg considered this for a moment.

From what Santa remembered, Eisenberg had no way of knowing Hawks was the one who fought and killed Reitziger. He said, 'Come on, she's only a nurse,' at which point Hawks threw him a frosty glare that thawed as soon as she realized why he said it.

Eisenberg nodded to a blond trooper who tied Hawks' and Desiree's hands in front of them. He said, 'Indeed. We are not animals. We will not execute your women like this.'

'Just Jews and gypsies, eh?'

'The führer's solution may be seen as a little … *extreme* to outsiders, but any blood spilled is on the hands of those who crippled the German nation after the Great War. Had they not made such unreasonable demands, our people would not have suffered so. Now Germany must rise again.'

Dang struggled to speak, his face so swollen he had transformed into a bloated caricature. 'What's … happening, Santa?'

Santa said, 'Firing squad.'

'I ain't smoked my cigar yet,' Mac said.

Santa pressed his lips together, admiring the big man's humor even now. He said, 'Don't work that way, Mac. No blindfolds, no last requests. Just bodies filled with lead.'

Hawks was led away along with Desiree.

Chase said, 'Well, color me fucked, Hawksy-poo. Looks like you're escaping this shit.'

'Give me a clue,' she said, 'and I will do something for you too.'

Santa and Eisenberg locked eyes. Eisenberg raised his hand. Now they understood how the equipment worked, the troops readied Alpha Team's 2015 weapons.

Saving on ammo? Efficient? Or a sense of irony?

Santa cast his gaze between his team: Mac stared hard at the gunmen; Thompson breathed steadily; Chase muttered a series of swear words under his breath, teeth clenched. Santa closed his eyes, and pictured Lily. If this was his final moment on Earth, he would not go out with his friend's dying bodies imprinted on his memory.

'Aw, shucks,' Chase said suddenly, 'we don't even have time for a farewell blowjob.'

Hawks flipped him the bird. 'A bit late for blowjobs. What time are you thinking of?'

Eisenberg said, 'Aim!'

The troopers aimed at the group as Santa snapped his eyes open to see Chase focusing on the land all around.

'I like what you're doing,' Santa said. 'Do it quicker.'

Hawks said, 'Be accurate.'

'Typical fuckin' Swiss,' Chase said. 'But okay. How about five o'clock, babe?'

Eisenberg whipped his attention to Hawks. Frowned. Then a look of surprised. But it was too late.

Hawks elbowed the blond trooper in the groin, and with her hands still tied, she swiped his knife, flipped it over so one hand held the blade, and launched it—at five o'clock from her position. The knife *thunked* into a booby trap down the hill, ten yards from the firing squad. The explosion ripped apart the closest two Nazis, and blew the rest of them over. It wasn't the most elegant escape ever, but Alpha Team leapt into action.

43

Hawks snatched the blond trooper's sidearm and pumped four shots into him, then fired on Eisenberg, who was already taking cover alongside Reuler. So, while Eisenberg scrambled to regroup his men and ready the weaponry, Alpha Team made a beeline for the nearest stash: the crate of German guns, grabbing what they could.

Mac selected an STG60 with a fixed stock, that classic Nazi firearm from a thousand war movies, and Thompson selected a Luger and the ugly rifle he noticed in the supply depot. Thompson said, 'Hello, Auntie.'

The German assault commenced, forcing Mac and Thompson toward the tree line, and Santa and Chase up the slope, but away from the bunker.

Santa and Chase came away with German MP40s, and Chase said, 'Okay, how hard can it be to make these fuckers work?' but before they figured it out, bullets peppered the wall around them. The shots came from Brandenburgers flying out of the bunker, joining their comrades, some with standard arms, others with 2015 weaponry.

As they ran for a semi-circle of boulders, Santa and Chase tried using the acquired firearms, but yanking at the stiff bolts they still couldn't get them cocked. They dove for cover, with gunfire all around. It came in from three angles, at least six Nazis shooting, coming closer.

Most guns worked pretty much the same, although each model and manufacturer has its own quirks. Secure the mag, cock the bolt, pull the trigger. And who hadn't seen war movies featuring these guns? So Santa racked the bolt back as he'd seen in various media, poked the barrel between where two rocks met, and squeezed the trigger to unleash Hell.

Nothing. The trigger didn't even click.

'Shit.'

I should be able to figure this out, Santa thought. *A gun is a gun. Just because these are clunky old things, it should make no difference.*

He ducked back down, and Chase tried too, moving a match-sized lever that appeared to be a safety catch, but Santa didn't even know if these guns *had* safeties. They had no time to check the guns over properly, and they were acting so quickly, with such hectic improvisation, that it was all guesswork right now.

Chase got the same result: *nada*.

No way to fight back.

The Nazis seemed to realize, and stopped shooting, instead speeding up, coming closer to finish them off.

'Okay,' Chase said. 'Fuck this shit.' He held the gun by the barrel.

Sadly, expecting they were done, Santa did the same. 'Batter up!'

Both men tensed, determined to take at least a couple of these bastards with them. The boots came closer, and someone even laughed.

They were ten yards away when something drifted on the wind. Something pungent, deep … *smoky*.

Santa said, 'Can you smell cigars?'

From behind the bunker, Sergeant Brown and the three GIs rose up and opened fire. Those troopers advancing on Santa and Chase blew apart as the Tommy guns did their job, spitting slugs through bodies, dropping most of the Branden-burgers in seconds. The others scattered.

Brown and Anthony dropped to Santa's position, while Simon and Martins retained the high ground.

'Hey,' Brown said. 'The kid felt bad about leaving. Even with that dumb-ass story.' Brown blew smoke at Santa, took the MP40s from him and Chase, and cocked them properly in turn, engaging a catch as he did so, before handing them back. 'There's a knack to it.'

Santa looked at Chase, eyes wide.

Chase shrugged. 'Fuck it. Let's go.'

Santa and Chase fired as the Germans regrouped. The guns bucked hard, the recoil levering the barrels high into the air. Santa fought the action to keep it steady, and noticed Chase was struggling the same way. The pair knew guns, though. They knew why they were acting that way, and forced them-selves to compensate. Santa aimed low and unleashed short volleys, not as accurate as he would like, but he gained enough control to lay effective covering fire for Thompson and Mac, who could now clamber up over the roots and snow, and charge for the remaining squad.

Using the crate as cover, the Nazi troops had no idea the American pair were upon them until Mac lifted one and crunched his fist through the guy's face. While Thompson stayed low, blowing three others away with the Luger, Mac yanked a second Nazi by the gun barrel, enveloped his head with his bear-like hands, and twisted so hard he detached the German's neck from its spinal cord.

With a momentary reprieve, Thompson struggled with the rifle's slide, but as a student of many firearms of this nature, he knew what he was doing. Just took a little longer than Delilah's smooth mechanism. He slotted the bolt home and fired. Twelve bullets in this mag, assuming it was full. He covered Mac so the big man could get to Dang.

Santa's group took cover in the bunker's entrance, Desiree and Dr. Lear now with them. That was right in the middle, with Dang to the right of them, and Eisenberg and the remaining bad guys to the left. No sign of Hawks. They exchanged fire with Eisenberg and two troopers who split from the firing squad, but Thompson clocked another German training on Mac as he ascended. He was about to reach Dang, but had to divert as bullets impacted too close.

Thompson shot the trooper, first in the hip, then square in the chest.

Two soldiers, bleeding from the grenade Hawks set off, recovered nearby and got to their feet. No one accounted for them, assuming them as dead as those with limbs scattered to the wind. Before Thompson drew a bead, both fired their guns toward Mac. He jerked but didn't fall, a round in his shoulder.

Between Eisenberg's angle on him, and these new players, Mac was stuck. He ran sideways, distracting the pair, meaning Thompson could take the less direct route to Dang.

Thompson zigzagged up the slope, and reached the youngster the same time as Hawks. She's been waiting for the chance of a clear run, which Mac now supplied. She shot the binding off and Thompson eased Dang down, but Eisenberg popped out of his hidey-hole. Thompson hadn't realized how far the ridge bent around, or how acutely. It allowed Eisenberg a vantage point Thompson would envy as a sniper, albeit far closer than Delilah would require. They noticed each other simultaneously, and while he could have shot either Thompson or Hawks, he took aim at Dang.

Three shots in quick succession.

Dang convulsed as two bullets hit. Hawks went down too, a round in her upper arm. Thompson's response via the rifle only gave Eisenberg and Reuler pause. They were dug in behind some conveniently-shaped rocks further along the ridge, beyond the bunker itself.

Mac saw what happened, swung his acquired gun, and fired at the two troopers attacking him. No clear line of sight, but it forced them to lie flat. He yelled Dang's name, ran in that direction, but Thompson shouted at him to stop, to wait. He didn't listen.

Santa's group watched on in horror as a second round hit Mac, this time high in the chest, and he dropped to his knees. Nor could they do anything to prevent Eisenberg and Reuler's assault on Dang, Hawks, and Thompson.

Brown said, 'Your colored boy's in trouble.'

'He'll be okay,' Chase said.

'Nah, we can take this. *Santa*, with me.'

Brown sprinted out from the cover of the doorway. Anthony moved to follow Brown, but Alpha Team's Santa leapt on him.

He said, 'No! I can't let you die, kid.'

'But he needs cover,' Anthony insisted.

Brown was already on the defensive from the two who split with Eisenberg. Covering fire came from Santa, Chase, and Anthony, but it simply wasn't enough.

With Anthony restrained, Martins and Simons dropped from the high ground to back up their CO. Their blanket spray allowed Brown to push on further, halfway to Eisenberg, forcing more Brandenburgers to cover.

But, it was all part of some pre-arranged tactic. This was

their territory, after all. What else would they do all day other than practice and drill? They identified every approach, every egress, so they would have devised a tactic for almost every conceivable attack.

Including this one.

The Brandenburgers' assault forced the GI down from the main path, and into the minefield. Before they even considered changing course, both Martins and Simons were right in the middle of it, and Santa could not even shout a warning. When a barrage of slugs raked the ground nearby, the pair darted to the side, and Santa foresaw their fate before they did.

A booby trap detonated beside them, blowing both men in two.

As their blood still rained down on the fresh snow, Eisenberg punched the air – *yes!*

Anthony cried out, and blasted blindly at Eisenberg until he clicked empty.

In confusion, Brown ducked behind a rock. Santa yelled to watch his back, having exposed it to the officers and their closest troops. The sarge didn't seem to hear anything, didn't even turn Santa's way. No one could help, no one could even try, as Eisenberg rounded on Brown, revealed nothing but his arm and a Luger through the boulders behind which he hid, and pumped six bullets into the GIs' sergeant.

The older man teetered. His cigar went limp in his mouth, and he keeled over.

Anthony cried out again, squirming to get free, but Santa would not let him go. *Could* not let him go. No matter how much he wailed and cried for his fallen friends.

Mac had never been shot before, but the two troopers laughing at him brought his focus back to why they were here. He saw them head toward Dang, where Thompson attempted to stem Dang's blood flow. Hawks held her own wound.

The two Nazis aimed, had them dead in their sights, when Mac emitted an almighty roar. The soldiers turned to see him rise.

'GO!' he yelled. 'GET 'EM INSIDE!'

Bleeding profusely, he barely felt the pain. He was a big guy, with a lot of blood and muscle. Even without the Kevlar, it took more than a 9mm slug to put him down permanently.

Mac fired the gun he picked up, the shot going wild. The troops fired back, striking him in the shoulder and chest. The first really painful wound came as his stomach opened, the mountain air rushing in as something slimy gushed out.

Santa and Chase laid down yet more covering fire. Chase kept Eisenberg pinned without any hope of actually hitting him, while Santa tried to snag the assholes currently turning Mac into a sieve. The gun, despite having a cushioned recoil thanks to its long bolt action, was still too unwieldy though. He knew to account for such recoil, but it was unpredictable after becoming so accustomed to the SCAR's virtually zero thrust. The best he could do was see how wide his shots flew, and adjust. But it wasn't an exact science, and with the only mode being full auto, he failed to drop a single body.

One thing it did accomplish was that it allowed Thompson and Hawks to drag Dang along the path, getting him stable being priority.

Once they reached the entrance, Mac advanced further on the Brandenburgers, blood pouring. That was okay, though.

Slip inside the machine, field dress his wounds, head home; they'd be in a hospital within the hour.

He took a bad one in the leg, made the mistake of checking it: obviously, it struck him at an angle, as the flesh hung ragged from his thigh. Hurt like a bitch, too. Must've lost a shitload of blood, as he struggled to lift the rifle. Something thumped his chest, and he could no longer take a breath. Glaring at the troopers, he guessed they could barely believe what they were seeing. What was that? Five bullets now? Six?

Never seen what a strapping farm-fed boy can do, eh?

Thompson made it to the entrance with Dang and Hawks.

Lungs rattling, Mac sank to his knees again. He dropped the gun, too heavy to wield in any meaningful way. And he was tired. So tired. The snowy ground came up and whacked him in the face, and he guessed someone would be along any moment now to shoot his tormentors in the head and drag him off on a stretcher.

He was lighter. He sensed it. Like he could float off on the breeze, should the fancy take him.

Something hard poked him. Then again, firmer, more of a jab this time.

Mac opened his eyes to a pair of shocked Nazis. A warm, growling burst of energy surged through him. He grabbed the gun barrel and sat up, dragged the man toward him, and wrapped his fingers around the scrawny neck. Mac's eyes bulged, throat raw through hollering, his whole body a knot of bloody rage. As he squeezed the life out of this trooper, the other fired round after round into Mac's back.

Eventually, the soldier in Mac's grip died, and Mac relented to the onslaught ... realizing finally that he was not going to make it after all. No one was coming for him; they were cut off, and they could not allow Eisenberg into the bunker.

That was okay, though. He'd done what he had to do, and now his friends were safe, and they would all finally return home.

He closed his eyes, lay down on the ground, and smiled, as he floated away into a deep, long sleep.

44

It was the worst moment of their lives. At least when Jacobs was killed back in La Bastion it was a surprise attack, an ambush over in seconds. Here, they watched it happen from the safety of their foxhole, helpless, stuck in the knowledge that they had to leave him where he lay. As if their limbs were made of Jell-O, Santa and Chase herded Thompson, Anthony, Desiree, Hawks, and Dr. Lear inside, then heaved the door closed, twisted the handle, and locked it with a heavy clunk. Santa firmed it up with a jagged stone, to prevent the mechanism from turning. He took a deep breath, and prepared himself to lose a third friend who appeared close to death.

Thompson and Santa carried Dang into the lab and lay him on the floor. Desiree tore open his clothes. Chase banged about, found a first aid kit, and rushed it over. Hawks pulled lab-coats from hooks, ripped them into strips, and wadded some against her arm wound, then passed the rest to help with Dang. Anthony helped her with the compress.

Santa stood back, literally no room for him there. It was because he was standing back that he noticed Dr. Lear seething in silence, glaring at Uhrmacher.

Dang screamed in pain. He said, 'Don't let me die ... Santa, please. I don't wanna.'

Santa knelt beside him. 'Then quit squirming.'

'Fucking right, yeah,' Chase said. 'Would Captain fuckin' Kirk behave like this?'

'Captain Kirk...' Dang said. 'Never had a ... bullet in him ... phasers...'

Santa said, 'Stop talking.'

Uhrmacher, sat on a metal box, pointed to a cupboard. 'There. There's morphine in—'

'I'll get it,' Dr. Lear said. 'You stay where you are.'

Dr. Lear retrieved several syringes from the cabinet and handed them to Thompson, who jabbed one straight into Dang's chest.

'Whoa,' Dang said. 'Haven't felt like that since... Fallujah.'

While Thompson and Chase worked on Dang, Santa heaved himself up and over to Hawks, and administered half a syringe an inch above the wound.

'That *is* good stuff,' she said.

As things calmed a little, they sat on the floor to catch their breath. Anthony stared at Santa.

'What?' Santa said.

'The sarge was a great guy. He led me and the boys on two missions before this one, and we didn't lose one man. Now we encounter you specials and ... we lose everyone. I could've backed the sarge up.'

'It was a dumb hallelujah run. You'd have been killed too.'

'Probably ... not,' Dang said. 'He can't die.'

Anthony pulled a sour face. 'What does that mean?

'Nothing,' Santa said. 'He's high. We need to get on with this. The machine—'

'And "hallelujah run"? What is that? What sort of person lets good people die like that?'

Santa saw no comeback. Well, maybe one: 'Calm down, soldier. I'm still a platoon CO. If I say you don't sacrifice yourself, it's an order.'

'Sir.'

Anthony slunk off to where Dr. Lear stood over Uhr-macher, who sat on an oblong box with poles down either side, perfect for four men to carry like a royal throne.

Chase held up his bloodied hands, searched around for a towel or something. No towel. He wiped them on his white coveralls, then unzipped at his neck to remove them. He flicked his head toward Dr. Lear. 'Uh-oh, looks like the doc-on-doc bromance has hit the rocks.'

Uhrmacher said, 'This ... is the bomb.' He meant the box on which he sat.

Everyone back away a little. Except Dr. Lear, who said, 'The bomb you helped him make.'

'Yes.' Uhrmacher's head dropped.

'And betrayed us to the Nazis. But wait, no, you didn't be-tray us. You were never loyal to us, so—'

'It is not like that, Nicolas.'

Dr. Lear turned his back on the German and spoke to the team. 'He grassed us up.' He held up his bruised hand. 'I al-ready—heh—softened him up, but if anyone else wants a shot...' He flexed the bruised fingers. 'By the way, how do you *do* that for a living?'

'Like this.' Anthony punched Uhrmacher in the face, spill-ing blood down his nose.

Uhrmacher tipped over backwards, his legs flipping comi-cally in the air.

Dr. Lear said, 'Nice.'

A soft *whoomph* sounded from outside, and the lab shook as if hit by a truck.

'What,' Chase said, 'the fuck ... was that?'

222

45

Eisenberg was growing more and more frustrated. For all the gifts the future might bestow in terms of ordinance and fire-power, why did they have to make it so damned complicated? This American plastic explosive resembled Hexogen, the Nitroamine derivative rumored to be used in R4M rockets. He had never received specific training in its use, just briefings, but in its crystalline form, Hexogen was extremely dangerous to handle. Hence why it required specialists. This version brought from the future was apparently more stable and, conversely, proved more stubborn to ignite.

He and Reuler examined the charred door. Both men agreed they did not possess enough dynamite to breach it, since it was designed specifically to repel such incursions, and besides, the force needed to dislodge it would bring the mountain itself crashing down. Eisenberg observed the Americans utilizing some sort of handheld radio transmitter to set off their own explosive, effective in much smaller quantities, but the contraption had no effect when he tried it. Instead, they smeared the gooey substance labeled 'C-4' on the bunker door, and attempted to set it off with a fuse and dynamite detonator instead. Rather than exploding, it simply flared, burning itself out too quickly. This 'C-4' appeared to be more powerful in a focused space, but was proving harder to master.

Reuler brought the radio transmitter switch to his face

again. 'Perhaps this is not so different from ours after all.'

'In what way?'

'Our detonators require a major shock to ignite the explosive. This box is electrical. I think, maybe, this C-4 is more chemical. Like our own plastic explosive, it needs something to set off a chain reaction. Maybe those small units…'

Eisenberg snapped his fingers and one of the four surviving Brandenburgers handed him the pack that contained the bits and pieces they had been unable to identify. Inside a plastic box, held together by a stiff clip, were a number of bullet-sized metal tubes. They assumed the objects were some sort of projectile to be fired from a gun not yet recovered, but when Reuler selected one and twisted it, a light on the radio transmitter flicked on.

Reuler smiled. 'Just a different method of delivery.'

To the side, the four Brandenburgers examined the Americans' guns. As ordered, they were trying to figure out what might be useful in the assault. If they could not, that was fine. Time was of the essence, after all. One of Eisenberg's men was wearing a Kevlar vest, pulling it tight to his chest.

Reuler focused on the task at hand, though. He molded the explosive around the door's handle, and poked the cylindrical metal object into it.

He said, 'And we stand back again.'

They retreated a safe distance. Near the trio of soldiers. A dark-haired Brandenburger aimed a snub-nose gun at his blond colleague in one of the heavy vests taken from the future-team, and pulled the trigger. The blonde fell. The other two held their breath. The blonde sat up, groaning, but alive.

He said, 'That hurts more than it looks.'

Reuler raised his eyebrows. 'It is lucky they are an elite fighting force, Captain.'

'Indeed.' Eisenberg pressed the remote switch. Nothing. 'There must be more to this.'

'I think I know,' Reuler said, and took the radio transmitter from him, and went back to work.

46

As Uhrmacher fussed around on the floor for his glasses, Santa pulled an acquired German handgun and, without checking the mechanism or even it was loaded, aimed it at the scientist. Uhrmacher held up his hands, one placed over the other as if that might stop a bullet. 'Wait! Please. Just … let me—'

'Explain?' Santa said. 'We can't trust you to send us home, and we sure as hell can't trust you to help stop Eisenberg.'

'I … thought you would defeat them easily. I wanted them to come for me. I could not risk you…' He located his glasses and dared move one bulletproof hand to fumble them on. 'I have nothing here. Nothing in my Germany. I thought of you leaving me behind, at the airfield. When you won, I…' He swallowed, shook his head, and appealed to Dr. Lear. 'Nicolas, you talk of respect for people like me, of fame, of wealth.'

Dr. Lear tutted, his face a pure sneer. 'You called ahead so you could come *with* us? So you could get *famous*?'

Uhrmacher dabbed his bloody nose with a handkerchief. 'Fame, no, that does not matter. But respect. Doing good for the world instead of … this.' He gestured to the huge flag dominating the lab. 'Did you know, there are colleagues of mine, whom I met in university, they experiment on people? Real people. To breed a pure race—'

'Yeah,' Thompson said. 'We mighta' heard somethin' about that.'

'With your guns, your devices—'

'All the technology in the world,' Santa said, 'doesn't make a bit of difference *when the enemy knows you are coming!*'

Chase said, 'Fuck it, Santa. Shoot him. Least if they get in, they can't use him to jump back.'

'They'll work it out,' Dr. Lear said. 'They have one man with them—Reuler. The one with the eye.'

'This is true,' Uhrmacher added. He lowered his hand shield and stood shakily. He dropped the stained handkerchief and slowly took a fresh one from his lab coat pocket, and squeezed it around his nose. 'No, killing me is useless, except for revenge. But I promise you ... I hate these people. Let me help. I'll do anything. Give me an order.'

Santa lowered the gun. 'Destroy it. Now. Stop him getting to 1939 once and for all.'

Anthony said, 'So this *is* some HG Wells stuff? It's all real?'

'No dinosaurs, though,' Chase said.

Santa said, 'Not now. We need to prepare.'

Anthony moved away and sat with Hawks. Desiree still sat beside Dang, the pair holding hands as if the previous night had been the finale of some rom-com rather than a pitched battle.

'It will be a mistake to destroy it,' Uhrmacher said. 'I can send you *back* to the—'

'And now you're *sure* you can do that?' Santa asked.

Thompson pointed at the control panel. 'Before, you said it's a risk. You said if we use the rods to go forward it would cause a meltdown.'

'Yes. But since I came back here, when I saw you might not ... overpower him, I was thinking about all the ways I might stop him, stop him from going back. Maybe I could send him back only a few months, but Reuler, he would check—'

'The point, fuckhead,' Chase said. 'Get to it.'

'Of course, of course. Yes. With Nicolas's additional calculations, taking into account the gravitational waves, I think I can overload the machine in such a way that it would send you back without melting down immediately. But it would need to be switched off a moment after you leave.'

They all waited on Santa. He pointed his gun at the controls. There were no flashes here, but still no one was entirely sure what they meant. It might have been okay to blast the controls, but the spike would remain. It would be an inconvenience to Eisenberg rather than a defeat.

Whatever the outcome, it would mean an end to *them* going home for sure, and the possibility of what Dr. Lear called an unresolvable paradox: if the machine is destroyed here, they cannot come back in time to destroy the machine. Perhaps Dang was right. No matter what they do now, things would happen as they happened. No control over fate. At least, no choice over their decisions. Anthony could not die, and the chamber could not be destroyed.

Santa checked the corridor. Unsure what to do.

Anthony stepped up to him. The youngster silently watched for a long moment, then said, 'You're supposed to be a *leader*.'

'I'm not a leader,' Santa said quietly. 'I didn't ask for this.'

'You're from the future, and I'm guessing we're related in some way. Yeah, I figured that out, I'm not dumb.'

And you'll recognize me when I hit my teens, Santa thought. No matter how far removed this kid was from the old man Santa knew, he held that thought, and it scared him. Scared him that he might disappoint his grandpa as a thirteen-year-old, how the general might look at him and know for certain that it was his own grandson he met on that mountain, who lost friends together and who fought together.

Anthony said, 'You wallow like a scared puppy. Giving up. Well, if that's the case, I need to meet my baby.'

Anthony took the letter from his pocket. Moved to open it, Alpha Team watching Santa. He met every team member's eye, all steeled, all ready, all needing him to be strong. Santa calmly but firmly folded his fingers around the envelope, and moved Anthony's hand back toward his pocket.

Santa said, 'We'll make a general outta you yet.'

Anthony mumbled, 'I don't really wanna be a general.'

Santa pointed at Uhrmacher. 'You sure you can make it go forward?'

Uhrmacher nodded rapidly.

Santa steadied his breathing, and faced the unit. 'They've got seventy years of weapons advancements. We got five ancient machine guns, half a mag each. One Luger and a rifle.' He cocked one of the German STGs. 'Anthony Santarelli, hand me your bag. This is siege warfare now.'

47

In the corridor leading to the entrance stairs, Chase and Thompson lay one metal cabinet across the width of the walkway. Santa and Anthony clanged another on top, with four helmets holding the second one up. It left a space of about nine inches. Chase aimed through the gap—perfect.

Returning to the lab, two more cabinets were lying on their sides, and Hawks tied something to the end of her radiation pen, using her teeth to hold the string, while Dr. Lear and Dr. Uhrmacher heaved the bomb toward the reactor.

Santa unpacked Anthony's bag on the fixed table in the center, Anthony watching with a frown.

He asked, 'You think they'll cut the power?'

'If they figure out our night-vis,' Santa said.

Hawks leaned behind the cabinet, checked the Luger one-handed.

'You okay to fight?' Santa asked.

'If this is the end,' she said, 'I would rather go with a gun in my hand.'

Chase slapped her good shoulder. 'Jeez, Hawksy, you are so fuckin' butch my balls are shriveling'.

'My butchness has nothing to do with your shriveled testes.'

Anthony said, 'Are you two married or something?'

Together, Chase and Hawks replied, 'Fuck you.'

With Eisenberg still unable to penetrate, Santa watched Lear and Uhrmacher operate the chamber controls, uranium room glowing with power to the side. He said, 'Doctors, repeat your orders, so I'm sure you understand them.'

'If Eisenberg or any of the others gets through,' Dr. Lear said.

'We flood the power room and overload the device,' Uhrmacher finished.

'No back door,' Santa said to the room. 'No backup. If we don't stop him, we don't go home. But either way, *he* doesn't get to win. Clear?'

Santa got no reply. Just the *click-clack* of firing bolts cocking. That was more than enough.

Eisenberg, Reuler, and the four Brandenburgers crouched behind a rock. Reuler showed Eisenberg the detonator switch.

'So, we try notching this smaller switch first.' He shifted a small nub of plastic that looked like nothing but a flaw in the design before. Now when he moved it, the transmitter device flashed rather than staying lit. 'So I press the larger switch here...'

The C-4 finally went up, the explosion firing dirt and smoke across the clearing. And when they peeked out, the bunker door stood ajar.

Smoke billowed down the corridor, enveloping the two-cabinet barricade, going straight up Chase's nose and stinging the back of his fucking throat.

Thompson didn't laugh so much as shrug, but as he couched on the steel walkway and aimed the German rifle through the gap, he definitely smiled while Chase coughed his lungs out. When he was done, Chase knelt beside Thompson, the MP40 in-hand, and waited.

48

In the lab, Nicolas Lear helped Uhrmacher into a radiation suit. Uhrmacher's gut still ached from his moment of weakness, of allowing his fear of never being anything more than a Nazi stooge to cloud his judgment. One message was all it took, and Eisenberg believed him. Now he had to hope the Americans repelled his former comrade—no, his former *jailer*—and allowed him to go home with them. What wonders awaited him? How long would it take him to catch up, to acclimatize? Did they have bases on the moon? Cars that flew, perhaps? There was no time for such conversations before.

Patience, he thought. *There will be plenty to discuss in 2015.*

The suit had holes cut into it. *Sabotage.* Short slits made by a knife.

Dr. Lear was currently distracted by the young one called Dang, whose wounds had been stemmed and continued to breathe, but for how long remained to be seen. The distraction was helpful, though. As Uhrmacher pulled on the rest of the suit, Nicolas did not notice the damage. He did not realize it would only offer the most arbitrary protection, and that if Uhrmacher survived the heat he would endure as he armed the uranium pool, he would die within hours from the radiation poisoning. Unless they developed a cure for such harm in the future.

Perhaps not as much time for discussion as he thought.

He could not ask about that now, though, or Nicolas might

233

get suspicious. Instead, Dr. Uhrmacher declined his offer of help, and dragged the sealed crate-cum-bomb to a spot outside the reactor's airlock.

Dang continued to speak in short bursts, the French woman stroking his hair as he lay slumped next to the copper chamber's door. He said, 'One ... One trip ...'

Yes, Dr. Uhrmacher thought. *If I can make amends for my actions today, you will go on one more trip.*

Chase heard the door screech open as the mangled thick hinges gave way. He and Thompson braced themselves.

Footsteps sounded on the stairs, at least four motherfuckers, but no one was yet visible between the cabinets. Just the end of the stairs and the wall.

A Nazi poked one of Alpha Team's SCARs around the wall and opened fire. The cupboards pinged and clunked, but they got nowhere near Chase. Thompson aimed calmly. The rifle roared and bucked, and the soldier fell, gurgling, a round splattered in his neck. His buddy dragged him to cover behind the staircase.

The other infiltrators held their position.

German words murmured back and forth in an unseen discussion. All was silent for a moment, then Eisenberg's head popped around the side of the stairs. He carried a chunk of plastique in one hand. Probably the last one. *Hopefully* the last one.

He said, 'This device is fascinating. I do like it.'

He flicked a switch and tossed it down the corridor. It arched through the air, spinning end over end, watched by Chase and Thompson, their mouths open slightly. The C-4 landed in front of the barricade.

'Well, fuck me with a bargepole.'

Santa heard them before he saw them, but Chase and Thompson came barreling in, and slammed the door.

Thompson said, 'Might wanna take cover now.'

They leapt behind the cabinet, joining Santa's group.

'Why?' Hawks asked.

The plastique exploded, debris blasting open the door.

'That's why,' Chase yelled through his ringing ears.

No one heard him. The explosion deafened them and would mask any clomping approach from outside. Before anyone's ears returned to normal, the lights died. The whole lab fell into blackness, the glowing reactor illuminating only one corner.

With a great deal of gesticulating to override the whistling and whining in Santa's ears, Anthony said, 'They got your see-in-the-dark goggles, don't they?'

'Yes,' Santa said with a deep, clear nod. 'They do.'

The eyeglasses were like magic. Neither Eisenberg nor Reuler would voice that, but it really did seem that way. *Seeing in the dark.* Once the smoke cleared, Eisenberg equipped two of the remaining three grunts, plus himself and Reuler, with the helmet accessories, figuring them out on the fly as they advanced down the steps. It was like watching a film with his eyes pressed up close to the screen. Reuler did point out, however, that there was a symbol on the viewfinder that looked like a little red battery, and he hypothesized that this meant the power was low. Eisenberg agreed, and sent the two privates ahead.

The lab door was open. One of the troopers' boots found glass, a crunch echoing through the bunker.

They all paused, listening for movement. Not even a whimper. If he had been successful in sending shards of metal ripping through the future team, there would be moans and begging. But there was none of that. Just silence.

They were waiting for him.

A quick glance around the door jamb, with the grunts in front of him, revealed the green-tinted lab, with its barricades and radioactive glow in one corner.

Someone yelled an English word: 'NOW!'

Eisenberg's vision turned white, shining so bright it was like staring at the sun. He jumped back, ripping the goggles from his face, while the two Nazis screamed and held their heads. He blinked hard, backing away, urging Reuler to remove his, telling him there was a serious flaw.

Two gunshots sounded, and the flaming light from within the lab was enough to see the men he sent ahead go down under enemy fire.

As the flares spat to life, Santa felt exceedingly smug, and as he and Hawks pounced on the Germans in the doorway, he thought for one fleeting second that they had done enough. Their hearing had resumed slowly, but once Hawks pointed out the metallic noise from outside wasn't an audio illusion, their counterattack fell into place.

Thompson fired twice and the two Brandenburgers went down, but they were in body armor.

'Chase,' he said, 'with me.'

He and Chase rushed to the door where the Nazis writhed in pain, and both threw off the helmets and goggles.

Chase said, 'That's our Kevlar, you fuck.'

The Nazis reached for their guns. Chase and Santa put a bullet in each head.

A quick glance up the corridor found Eisenberg, Reuler, and one more item of cannon fodder ducking behind the mangled cabinets. They unleashed the SCARs, forcing Santa and Chase back inside, although Eisenberg could be heard yelling in German.

'What'd he say?' Santa asked.

Dr. Lear translated, '*Bring me something to get these vermin out of my laboratory!*'

'Cute,' Chase said.

As Santa and Chase retreated, the lights came back on.

'Get ready!' said Santa.

Hawks dashed over to the door, holding her radiation pen with the appendage. It was a mirror. She used it to see around the corner. 'They like our guns.'

'One trip...' Dang slapped the floor in frustration. 'They got *one* trip...'

Uhrmacher looked curiously at Dang. Dr. Lear joined him, but Santa saw no time to interrogate their idea. Dang had lost a shit-ton of blood and sounded delusional. Besides, an uninvited guest approached. Hawks retreated to cover.

'Santa,' Dr. Lear said.

'Get down,' Santa hissed. 'Now!'

Dr. Lear crouched beside Dang, with Uhrmacher at his side, Desiree unsure what to do with herself.

The milky-eyed Brandenburger—Reuler—sprinted across the doorway.

'Takin' up positions,' Thompson said. 'Somethin's coming.'

And Reuler tossed a grenade in. A simple, German WWII grenade. No C-4 or detonators left. Another came from the other side. Everyone ducked behind whatever was at hand, Dang, Desiree, and the scientists protected by the angle of the wall, timing the countdown.

Both grenades exploded, the shockwave and noise slamming from all sides, shrapnel battering the walls and furniture. Again, their ears erupted in pain, numbing all incoming sound, including the gunfire that immediately followed; what should have been booming reports became a dull, thudding rattle. Reuler and the final trooper used the doorway to keep the room's occupants pinned. Eisenberg hung back.

Alpha Team squeezed off single shots only, unable to see through the billowing aftermath of the grenades, but then the Nazis had the same problem. Same problem, but more ammo. And better hearing.

It only took long minutes of exchanging shots for the thuds of machine gunfire to return to the familiar bangs of exploding gunpowder. Still difficult to communicate, but not impossible.

'One trip...' Dang managed to make himself heard over the gunfire. 'Use it...'

'Santa,' Dr. Lear said, gesturing as much as speaking. 'They only have *one* trip. If someone goes back, no one can follow.'

Santa shouted, '*What?*'

Dang grimaced as his pain fought back against the morphine shots. 'Send me back ... please.'

'No fuckin' way,' Chase said. 'I already lost too many pals here.'

Santa felt the exact same way as Chase, but dammit, Dang was right again. He said, 'What about the other end?'

Uhrmacher actually laughed amid all the chaos. He said, 'No, I remember. The protocol is in effect by nineteen thirty-nine. *No one is in the lab.*'

Bullets pinged off every surface, peppering the walls, the table, the massive flag.

Santa called back, 'So we send Dang back, what then?'

They were almost out. Every soldier this side of the barricade looking glum each time they checked.

Dang said, 'Please ... I go through, get to the woods ... just go to sleep. It'll close the spike. Santa, I'm sorry about what I said. You were right to leave me in the bar. But now ... gotta ... let me go.'

Reluctantly, Santa agreed. He was going to lose another friend for sure.

49

Thompson skidded toward Dang, and gave him as many morphine syringes as he could hold to his chest—upwards of ten. He injected Dang again. 'These'll help you go all fuzzy and cool and shit.'

Desiree seemed to understand what was about to happen and pushed Thompson, but she wasn't strong enough to budge him.

Dang said, 'I gotta go. Sorry. Woulda' liked to get to know you...'

Hawks eased Desiree away, comforting her, pulling her back behind the barricade that only Chase and Santa were able to man now. No additional ammo. Just what they preserved inside the weapons.

In a momentary lull, Eisenberg called, 'I offer you one chance.'

'Hurry,' Santa said.

The youngest member of the team could manage to crawl, but he was shaky. Thompson and Dr. Lear hooked the crooks of their elbows into his armpits and hauled him along, then helped him carefully into the chamber.

'Okay, doc,' Santa said. 'Don't screw with us.'

'Never again.' Uhrmacher pulled the lever.

'Surrender now,' Eisenberg said. 'And I spare your lives.'

The team craned to get one final view of their friend. Desiree's eyes widened in terror as the vault-like door whirred to life and moved on its hinge. Dang gripped the morphine in one hand, saluted with the other. All of them, including Anthony, returned the salute.

Santa's salute lowered first. Then he raised his hand as if waving goodbye, pressed his little finger to his ring finger, and his index finger to the next one, giving Dang a final send-off: a Vulcan hand sign.

Dang grinned sadly. The door made it halfway shut, and the group all mimicked Santa, Chase the last to do so, using his other hand to form the sign.

The door hissed shut.

Chase swung his gun over the top of the cabinets and fired his final three slugs into the lab's doorframe.

'That was very scary,' Eisenberg said. 'Final chance.'

Santa glanced around the remaining team members. They were all out of ammo.

The chamber sparked and hummed. Uhrmacher signaled 'okay.'

Santa checked his handgun. One bullet. He set his jaw and tossed the Luger over the cabinet. 'Okay! We're unarmed.'

Eisenberg entered, Reuler and the last grunt behind him, their weapons aimed into the room. Eisenberg's mouth formed an 'O' and his eyes bulged. Not looking at Santa or Alpha Team, but the chamber. 'Nein. Order the machine be switched *off*.'

Eisenberg trained a SCAR-M on Anthony.

'Wait!' Santa said. 'Not him. Point it at me.'

'Really?' Eisenberg said. 'This one is your favorite. I watched you. He is important to you, no? Then switch *off* the machine.'

A million reasons occurred to Santa to obey the *hauptsturmführer*, prime amongst them that his grandpa might die. Would that take him away too? Would it create a paradox? If it weren't for Anthony Sr. it was unlikely Santa would have enlisted, so if he died, no way Santa could be here to make this decision. But what of split timelines and parallel universes, of theories that they *might* somehow return to a time that was not their own? As Chase would say, *Fuck that shit.*

Now Santa *saw* why, understood that his grandpa knew him all along; he knew that young Jonnie would one day be required to lead his team to *this* point, to have the strength to say 'no' to a man who would inflict pure evil upon the world if given the chance. Anthony Santarelli would raise his son alone and—discouraged by Anthony's insistence that war was hell—his son would go into the banking industry, and Anthony would push on with his career, at least until one Christmas when visiting his son and daughter-in-law, and their thirteen-year-old boy, and noticed the striking resemblance to the grownup who saved his life in France...

Everything was exactly the way it was supposed to be.

'You're not going to kill him,' Santa said.

Eisenberg firmed his grip, eyes flicking to the machine. 'I can only guess your reasons for such affection, but I *will* do it.'

Not one of Santa's teammates gave a hint of concern. Just that same confidence that came with complete knowledge. Only Anthony could not pull away from the black eye of the gun barrel.

'Five seconds,' Eisenberg said. 'Shut it down.'

'Too late,' Santa said.

The chamber flared with brilliant white light. All Eisenberg could do was yell, 'Nein!' again, and rush toward the control panel, slamming his fist into it, turning random dials and shunting levers. The chamber's hum slowly drew to a close, revving down, to reveal an empty space of shining copper.

Dang was gone.

50

Eisenberg's teeth clenched, his hands balled into fists, and he pushed himself back from the panel. With the SCAR-M low at his waist, he stalked around them all, his two men flanking the exit route. He stopped at Uhrmacher. 'Idiotic sacrifice. Pointless. The next trip is six months later. The war is still young. It will be more difficult to enter England, but it is possible.'

He pointed the machine gun at Santa, who met the weapon the way he might meet the stare of a thug steeling for a fight.

'Whatever you do today,' Santa said, 'you lose.'

Santa closed his eyes. As always, it was Lily who came to him. She beamed her beautiful smile. He felt her arms around him, the light scent of apple shampoo as he held her as tightly as he dared; he held the drawing she made, of him and Alpha Team beating down some Arabs, the one that got her mom called into school for 'a brief chat.' The general knew this moment was coming, Santa realized, and made sure he inserted himself into Lily's life as much as little Jonnie's; because she would need all her remaining family around her.

In his mind, Lily's eyes sparkled. She said, 'I love you, daddy,' and Santa replied, 'I love you too, my baby girl,' and kissed her forehead, and—

Eisenberg pulled the trigger. A burst of three rattled out.

Santa opened his eyes. His chest was intact. A moment of

confusion. Then he saw Eisenberg had not shot him at all.

Private Anthony Santarelli stood there, pumping blood through three tight holes high on his chest. An expression of pure shock. His legs folded and Santa caught him.

Eisenberg said, 'I was curious about that.' He rested the gun on his shoulder, a casual pose. 'Now I know for certain the future can be changed, we shall bring glory to where it belongs.'

Anthony coughed blood, and Santa dispersed every image of Lily, of his grandpa, trying to hold onto them, expecting them all to slip away. He could barely form words.

'No one is immortal,' Eisenberg said. 'Say goodbye to your … grandfather, perhaps? You never did say how far in the future you traveled from.'

'Fuck you,' Santa said. 'Fuck you, fuck your führer, fuck *everything!*'

Eisenberg and Reuler laughed.

Anthony tried to talk. Santa leaned toward him. Anthony clawed at his wound as Santa applied pressure, the others gathering around too.

Anthony managed, 'Letter…' and pawed at his pocket.

Santa said, 'You don't need to read it.'

'Why not?'

Santa looked to his team. Every one of them stared open-mouthed, as shocked as he was, that everything they thought they worked out was for nothing. Not one thing made sense now, except a young soldier was dying in Santa's arms. As if reading his mind, Thompson and Chase both lowered their heads grimly.

'Because I know,' Santa told Anthony. 'I already know about your future. You got yourself a baby boy, Anthony. And Sarah, she's … so happy. Can't wait for you to meet him. Both are healthy, both love you so, so much. You hear me, grandpa? *You hear me?*'

Anthony sighed. His eyes closed.

'She'll be waiting for you, grandpa. She'll be waiting.'

Anthony exhaled, and died.

51

'Are you done?' Eisenberg said. 'Good. Everyone against the wall. All of them this time. The women too.'

The Nazis herded the sluggish bunch up against the Swastika flag, now fracked with debris but not, oddly enough, bullet holes. As he was pried away from Anthony's corpse, Santa guessed a firing squad would ventilate that flag just fine, so it would look the way he discovered it in the future. Only Uhrmacher was excused the line-up.

Confusion dominated Santa's mind, more-so than grief, even more than fear. If they were to die right now, and everything was as it should be, Anthony should not be dead. Unless this was punishment, their time to die, so they could not return to 2015 and see the damage their failure had wrought.

'There were no flashes,' Chase said. 'We did nothing to save the poor little bastard, but nothing flashed.'

'It's weird, alright,' Thompson said. 'Doc?'

Dr. Lear was finally too frightened to speak. For a civilian he had done himself proud but, for Santa, this felt like an ending, and he sensed Dr. Lear saw it too. If Anthony Santarelli could die, so could all of them.

The three Germans lined up. At Eisenberg's command of, 'Bereit,' they all held their weapons firmly pointed down.

In French, Desiree expressed a number of French insults that Santa didn't quite pick up. He worked out she called Eisenberg a 'coward.'

'He can't be dead,' Santa said, staring at Anthony's body.

Eisenberg said, '*Ziel.*'

The two Brandenburgers raised the guns.

Desiree inched up her skirt to her knee.

Women have other uses...

Santa said, 'My grandpa survived the war. Told me all about the conflicts he'd been in. About Ling Mai, the cold war, Buzz fucking Aldrin.'

Desiree's skirt passed her knee. *Come-to-bed* eyes lowered toward Eisenberg. She said, 'Bitte, herr *Hauptsturmführer.* Ich kann sehr sanft sein.'

'Please, my captain,' Dr. Lear translated. 'I can be very gentle.'

Hawks said, 'Burning bras is a long way away.'

'Try it,' Chase said. 'You got okay buns. No point in us all bitin' it here.'

Desiree showed thigh now. Eisenberg stepped forward. Smiled. Then slapped her so hard she spilled onto her side.

To the Americans, Eisenberg said, 'Harsh? Maybe. But I have more important things to deal with than some French whore.' He strode back to his firing position.

Desiree sat up sharply, her hair falling ragged over her face. In English, she said, 'No you don't, Herr *motherfucker.*'

Eisenberg whipped around.

Desiree hitched her skirt up fully, over her pale thigh. She unfastened a matchbox-sized item from her suspender: a remote detonator switch.

Eisenberg said, '*How?*'

She hit the button. A massive boom thundered overhead, and a section of ceiling caved in behind the firing squad. The Nazis dove together for cover, toward the wall and the flag, while Alpha Team scrambled away, approaching the generator room and control panel, shielding their faces. Everyone in the room took a moment to orientate themselves.

Smoke swirled.

The three Germans stood, peered at the hole in the roof.

A green laser dot drew down on Reuler. All gazed as it crept up to the man's head. Then a *bang*, and bullet ripped through his milky eye. Before anyone reacted further, machine gunfire erupted from within, impacting both remaining Nazis, blowing Eisenberg clean off his feet. The flag shredded, ricochets pinged into the floor and surrounding furniture. Wood splintered and rock plumed. Blood flew.

In a pause, Eisenberg croaked some German affirmation, and dragged himself across the floor, a thin red smear behind him, getting closer to Alpha Team, and Santa in particular. He actually managed to rise fully to his feet. He opened his mouth to speak, when another thunderous grouping of bullets slammed him forward, thumping him down on top of the nuclear casing. His final exhalation was the death-rattle Santa heard too many times before, but he welcomed this one.

The silence hung heavy in the air, punctuated by the ringing echo that always followed such volume in enclosed spaces.

A pair of feet dangled out of the ceiling.

Santa scrambled for Reuler's gun and aimed it up into the hole.

A man dressed in French civilian clothes dropped through, carrying the monstrous *Maschinengewehr 42* machine gun from Desiree's basement in one hand, a laser-sight-equipped SCAR-M in the other. His face was wrapped as tightly as the rest of his body, and revealed himself as the Runner who stole the C-4.

Santa held his aim. The man lay his weapons down slowly, and stood up, his hands to the side. Then he removed his mask. Bearded, more muscular, and five years older, yet all recognized him instantly.

Santa said, '*Dang?*'

'You crazy fuck,' Chase said.

Desiree swaggered forward, linked her arm into Dang's, and spoke in accented English. 'It worked, honey.'

And the pair kissed passionately.

'So,' Dang said as he broke away. 'I survived.'

'No shit,' Thompson said. 'Found a cool new accent too.'

Sure enough, Dang's American twang was now inflected. He said, 'I learned quickly, but ... sometimes I even forget English. Listen to me. It is actually difficult right now.'

Chase poked Dang's firm chest. 'Joined a decent fuckin' gym too?'

Dang said, 'The, err ... pain medicine...'

'Morphine,' Desiree said.

'Oui, the *morphine*, this healed me long enough to plant a dead animal in the machine. To cover for my blood. I lived off snow and bark for three days before Desiree found me. Nursed me back to health. Guessed I could help if we timed it right.'

Desiree stroked Dang's beard. 'It was so hard seeing you like that.'

'Bleeding, close to death?'

'No, that little whiny guy. He was extremely annoying.'

Uhrmacher and Lear seemed concerned with the machine, but Santa was still shaken from finding Dang again—or rather *him* finding *them*. 'You've been living here?'

Dang pointed to the hole. 'You know how long it takes to tunnel through a mountain?'

'About four and a half years?'

Two muffle beeps sounded.

Dang said, 'Three years, actually. Slowly, so we did not alert them. But I stopped when I heard voices. Then a case of waiting until you showed up so I could steal some C-4 and detonators.'

'My grandpa...'

'We had no idea,' Desiree said. 'Dang travelled before it happened, so—'

Beep ... beep ... beep...

'Gentlemen,' Dr. Lear said. 'I know the science bit can be boring, but do you remember the pens?'

Santa pulled the rad-pen from his pocket. It was beeping quickly.

Uhrmacher removed his glasses and cleaned them on his coat, facing the team with a grave expression. 'When your man was gone, you grandfather? I thought all was lost, so I started overloading the machine. Now, I cannot stop the re-action without shutting off the power permanently.'

52

Santa approached Uhrmacher. Worried Santa was going to hit him, he hastily donned his glasses. His jaw still ached from Nicolas's jab, and the little grandfather's punch made his nose throb. Even though they faced a massive nuclear eruption shortly, he was keen to avoid being hit again.

Santa said, 'So we can't go home after all?'

'You can go home,' Uhrmacher said. 'But you must leave immediately. One final journey. I must first load the rods from the bomb, but when you get back, you cannot activate the machine again. Ever.'

'A nuclear explosion,' Nicolas said. 'A tenth the size of Hiroshima, but still impressively deadly.'

'And I am sorry, but...' He braced for someone else to hit him. 'I have to be in the fuel room. I do not have time to load the rods *and* activate the chamber. One of you must stay to control it, and then switch it off.'

'I'm the one who trusted Dr. Uhrmacher,' Nicolas said. 'I volunteer.'

'Not you,' Dang said.

Thomson frowned at Dang. 'You've been back from the dead two whole minutes.'

'Dang,' Santa said, 'it's real brave of you, but I think I should be the one to stay. It's my responsibility.'

'No way,' Chase said. 'You are going home. You are not gonna break Lily's heart just to prove you got balls.'

Dang gently eased Lear from the panel. 'Sorry, folks. I

crawled out of the machine and into Desiree's life. I'm not leaving now.'

Desiree grinned shyly.

Uhrmacher pulled the radiation suit up, knowing full well it offered only minimal protection. He had to hope no one noticed or tried to stop him. Not that he expected they would. But he chuckled at one realization. 'I tell you about the animal, and you use it as a cover. A most useful paradox.'

Dang held Desiree's hand. 'I'm staying. Plus I'll get to be an early adopter for the greatest TV show of all time.'

Santa smiled. 'Star Trek, huh?'

'What else?'

With all that settled, Uhrmacher made for the case beside the airlock, ready to tip Eisenberg's corpse from it and drag the rods inside. Except…

'He's gone,' Uhrmacher said.

All heads turned to him. To the box where Eisenberg fell. Nothing but a bloody smear.

From behind the chamber's control panel, Eisenberg reared up, the remains of the futuristic body-armor hanging from his chest, and a swinging up a handgun toward Uhrmacher.

53

Santa flew across the lab and batted the gun aside. But he was off-balance. Eisenberg got in the first hit, a jab to the kidney that slammed a sharp pain up Santa's side. Chase was first to come in behind, but Santa pushed the mistake down, and kicked at Eisenberg's knee—a glancing blow, but it shoved him onto the back foot. The team seemed to sense Santa needed this, and the pair clashed hard.

The PS-930 body armor was predominantly made of Kevlar, which offered great protection for anything up to a standard 9mm, but when equipped with optional ceramic upgrade plates, it could withstand .45 caliber rounds at relatively close range. And since Alpha Team never skimped on protection—Dr. Lear's slight frame being an exception—Eisenberg faced down an MG42 with the most efficient combat defense money could buy. The MG42 was more powerful, though, and since those ceramic plates only offer maximum protection against a single bullet before cracking or even shattering, it would have drawn blood, breaking the skin enough to make Eisenberg bleed heavily, but insufficient to kill.

Santa went at him with modern fighting techniques, jujitsu and even a little taekwondo that he took up last year, while Eisenberg favored short jabs, ducking and diving, using his knees, his elbows. He didn't learn this in the regular infantry, or even as the Nazi equivalent of Special Forces; this was something else. A passion for it. A fluidity you only achieved with hours of practice, years of dedication. No wonder he'd taken Santa out back in La Bastion.

At least this time, Santa wasn't out of breath, his mind spinning with the realization of where he was. Now, it was all about getting home. And a little bit of revenge. Hence the one-on-one duel.

Chase acted like he was at a boxing match. 'Fuck him up, Santa!'

As Santa got in some firm hits to Eisenberg's head, the German locked up, practically embracing Santa, but bounced off the walls, Santa unwilling to break in case one of those knees came up again.

Out of the corner of one eye, he saw Uhrmacher shift to the side, and toss his notebook on the table. Then the scientist pulled up the suit's hood, and gripped the reactor's air-lock. It hissed open. He slowly dragged in the bomb. Even as everyone gawped at the Santa-vs-Eisenberg bout, Uhrmacher was still trying to make amends.

Eisenberg freed his own hand and punched Santa's ribs, wrenched him into a headlock.

Uhrmacher waited in the inside air-lock. Through the intercom, he said, 'You must hurry! I need to load these rods and stabilize the core.'

Chase said, 'Okay, I'll shoot this fucker.'

Santa's face felt ready to burst, but he said, 'I got this.'

Eisenberg laughed as the Kevlar absorbed Santa's sucker-punch. Laughed more as Santa grabbed Eisenberg's thigh. His fingers crept higher, toward the German's waist.

Eisenberg looked down. Too late.

Santa reached his grandpa's stolen knife, slid it out, and gouged it deep into Eisenberg's leg.

The Nazi captain released Santa, snarling in fury and pain, the blade still embedded in his flesh. He staggered, his back to the chamber controls. Seethed through blood-streaked teeth.

'You Americans,' he said, but his labored breathing meant he had nothing to add.

He tore the knife from his leg and lurched forward. Santa ducked and dove, keeping the knife at bay, but one attack sliced open Santa's shoulder, and another opened a gash on his arm. Santa kicked at Eisenberg's leg wound, causing the Nazi to howl in pain.

'Nice,' Chase said.

But it made Santa lazy. He thought he had Eisenberg right where he needed him, and went at his throat with a flat hand, the intent to slam the breath out of him, allowing Santa to move for the kill. Eisenberg was ready, though. He blocked the jab with one arm, and took the blade to Santa's neck with the other. Santa saw the move coming. Pitched sideways. The razor-sharp edge brushed the skin around his carotid artery, and he was thankful when it slashed a nick in his cheek.

Santa used the momentum to power more force for his kick to Eisenberg's gut. The captain doubled over. Santa struck an uppercut elbow to his opponent's chin, jerking the man's whole body upright. He snatched his grandpa's knife back, and launched a huge kick at Eisenberg's chest.

Eisenberg was propelled backwards, and hit the reactor air-lock.

It hissed open.

And, with Eisenberg still battered and reeling, Uhrmacher dragged him inside. Uhrmacher then opened the inner door, and hauled Eisenberg into the main reactor. He pushed the man up against the machine's core, and Eisenberg literally steamed, juddering as of being electrocuted.

As if registering the pain for the first time, he screamed so loud nobody needed the intercom to hear it.

54

Uhrmacher looked out through the window. Into a speaker, he said, 'Enter the chamber. I will load the fuel.'

'Load it,' Dr. Lear said, 'then get out here. I know the machine is gearing up for a big burst, but I don't see it will take that long. You could come with us.' He gave a wink to the team. 'Back to the future.'

'There is no future for me,' Uhrmacher said. 'God speed.'

'Wait. What—'

'The suit,' Santa said. 'It was damaged. He knew it when he went in. I didn't realize until I was toe-to-toe with Herr Blondie.'

The team gathered slowly at the observation window, gazing in. Uhrmacher opened the bomb and, using a pulley system set up inside the reactor, lifted all the rods in a bracket.

Silently, Dr. Lear manned the controls, demonstrating to Dang which buttons to press. When he did speak, his voice cracked. 'Then finally, this one. Pull it when the chamber goes dark, and we are no longer there.'

The reactor emitted a piercing screech. Uhrmacher allowed one of his chuckles as he lowered the rods into the core. His skin blistered through the face mask, his speech croaky. 'Everyone move faster please.'

The team all nodded to him as they filed into the chamber, a mix of emotions running over their faces. How do you thank the person who betrayed you, but then went on to save your life?

Santa had tied off lengths of cloth to the gash on his arm, and held a wadded bunch to his face wound, the remnants of a white coverall. He simply went with, 'Thank you, Dr. Uhrmacher,' and followed his friends into the machine.

Uhrmacher completed the fuel load. His face blistered under his helmet as he lowered the containment lid. 'Two minutes.'

Once Dr. Lear was satisfied Dang understood the controls, he pressed his hand against the reactor window's glass. As Uhrmacher waved him urgently away, he joined the others in the copper chamber.

Santa patted his shoulder. 'You did good, doc. I'm sorry about your friend.'

The doc's upper lip remained as stiff as the Brit stereotype, but his eyes filled with water.

Through the reactor window, Uhrmacher fell to one knee. The reactor bubbled. He said, 'It is time.'

Through the observation glass, Dang and Desiree readied the controls. A partial reflection ghosted back at Santa. The door started to close.

But then the whole world flashed white again, Santa dropping his improvised gauze. He staggered but did not fall.

Chase came to him. 'Santa...?'

No one else felt it; just him.

He looked up again, his image in the glass against the solid mass of Dang and Desiree.

His wound. He saw it clearly for the first time: it was vertical...

Right under his eye...

Extending down his face...

Santa removed the duplicate dog-tags from his pocket, those Jacobs gave him as he died. His eyes lingered on the dead Anthony through the doorway. He thought of his grandpa, the old general, smiling as Santa sent Dang into the house, but more specifically, his cheek, and his scar ... identical to Santa's wound.

And he pictured Lily again, and tears broke instantly down his face. His throat filled with bile and his stomach flipped inside-out. He knew, in that moment, he was not going home today.

Santa ran out the closing door, pushed Dang from the controls.

'It's not you,' he said. 'It's me. I have to stay.'

'But no,' Dang said. 'Your daughter.'

'I know. It's killing me, even now, it's really *fucking* killing me. But this is too important.' Santa pressed the spare dog tags into Dang's hand. 'Give these to Lily. She'll learn the truth one day, I promise. But right now I can't go with you.'

'I'm not leaving Desiree.'

'So take her with you.' Santa grabbed Desire's arm and sidled her over to Dang.

'Well,' she said. 'You *have* destroyed my bar.'

'You serious, Santa?'

'Yes,' Santa said. He addressed them all. 'It's *me*. Don't you see? All along. I gotta take Anthony's tags, his letter. His fiancée is *dead* and he's got a kid to raise. Only that's *my* job now.'

Dang looked around, his eyes sharp, taking it all in. 'You are right. You are so right.'

Not everyone was catching up as quickly as Dang, and their open mouths and deep frowns as he and Desiree join them in the chamber spoke to this. The door closed fully, but no one questioned it. It was too late for that.

Santa pressed his hand on the window, tears streaming. 'I'll miss Lily like hell, but I gotta do this. *For her.*'

A massive mechanical flare signaled the additional power pumping through the crystal. The room howled to life, and rotated. The crackle of power and sheer electrical energy ignited the copper, throwing the team between silhouette and fuzzy color. Each soldier, the shape of them, raised their hand to salute Santa—Chase, Dang, and finally—with real conviction—Thompson.

Through the smashing of atoms, the creation of a wormhole, the wrenching of space-time, Chase said to Santa, 'You're an asshole, you know that?'

The wall spun faster, and they all lowered their hands, sat on the floor, ready for the jolt this time. Within seconds, Santa could see nothing but shadows of his friends amid the whizz of copper. The room filled with lightening, the crystal in the roof glowed and pulsed.

Santa, too, saluted his teammates for the final time, and the window lit up in a brilliant square of white.

In the moments of silence that followed the machine revving down, Santa felt numb. It took Uhrmacher's croaky voice through the intercom to snap him back to reality. 'Now! Cut the voltage!'

Santa flicked off all the buttons on the controls, then grabbed a flashlight and raced into the power room, where he flicked the chunky master lever to 'Off.' Back in the lab, all the lights died. The glow from the uranium room faded. Santa's rad-pen beeped slower and slower, until it ceased entirely.

He used the flashlight to pick his way to the reactor window, where Uhrmacher lay in the final moments of his life.

Uhrmacher said, 'Thank you.'

'For what?' Santa asked.

'For stopping Eisenberg ... and his ilk ... from ruling our world.'

Uhrmacher died right there, lying next to Captain Eisenberg.

With nothing here left to do, Santa picked up his grandpa's combat knife, placed it in his belt, and made a mental note to obtain a replacement sheath. He removed own dog tags, and crouched beside Anthony's body. He detached Anthony's tags and hung them round his own neck, then placed those with Jonnie Santarelli's details on the table for Vince Jacobs to find in a few decades.

Finally, he carried Anthony toward the exit, using his flashlight to check the room once more. Satisfied, he tossed his radiation pen on the floor, leaving the scene exactly as he will find it in the twenty-first century.

55

A blinding flash. Static crackled all around. The light faded as suddenly as it bloomed, to reveal ... Alpha Team. Their hair stuck up every which way. Chase checked his head was intact, then his legs and, of course, his balls. All there. 'Motherfucker, that was trippy.'

The others' frazzled faces seemed to agree.

Dang checked Desiree, who was more shocked than the others. 'You okay?'

'Yes,' she said. 'This is the future?'

'Damn right it is.' Dang's French accent was easing already.

Desiree said, 'When do I buy an iPhone?'

A much-needed laugh rippled through the group. As the door opened, they all exited gingerly, the journey having been something of a blast. Each of them took a moment to observe different areas of the lab that still remained from the showdown in 1945.

Chase looked up at the ceiling to see Dang's hole. 'Dang's hole,' he said, sniggering.

Hawks noted the two scientists still in situ, then behind the metal cabinet at the four dead Brandenburgers.

Dang gazed into the glowing uranium room, where little more than skeletons remained of Uhrmacher and Eisenberg. He raised a single eyebrow, and beckoned them all over to see.

After a moment, Dr. Lear said, 'Okay, chaps?' A stutter, then, 'And ma'am, of course. As ever. Listen, um ... remember how Dr. Uhrmacher said not to activate the chamber or the reactor would explode?'

'Yeah?' Chase said.

'Well, how did we travel back in the first place if we didn't power up the core?'

Dang held Desiree's hand, peered into the uranium room. Water and steam reacted with the fully-immersed rods.

Hawks said, 'This looks bad.'

The team assembled, pens coming out, switched on. They beeped like mad, the ends flashing.

Chase shoved Dr. Lear. 'So stop the fuckin' thing.'

Dr. Lear shook his head, backing away. 'Even if we ceased the power, the reaction is too far gone.'

Thompson said, 'So you're sayin' we should probably run now.'

'How far do we need to be?' Hawks asked.

Dr. Lear rubbed his face, thinking. 'The initial explosion will cover at least four miles. The fallout after that? A ten, fifteen mile radius. We have less than twenty minutes.'

They needed no more chatter. All took off for the exit.

Chase said, 'Hawks, you got any juice left?'

'What?' she said. 'Everything is dead. And we left it in 1945.'

'Oh yeah.'

Thompson said, 'Choppers are at least thirty minutes on foot.'

'I do not know about you,' Desiree said, 'but I am going to try.'

All piled out of the lab behind Hawks, but she ducked into one of the doors.

Chase followed her into the radio room. 'What the fuck are you doing?'

She fiddled with the decrepit radio, squelch and static whooping on the analogue contraption. It *did* still work after all. And now everyone was waiting on her.

'Hawksy, come the fuck on,' Chase said. 'Only chance is if we—'

'I am calling evac,' she said.

'On that thing?' Thompson said. 'Get your ass out here—'

'Run if you want. Santa said this antique should still work.' She thumbed the button. 'Channel nine, channel nine, any friendlies out there?' Static replied. 'There must be an aerial. They would not have it here if they could not call out in emergencies.'

She tried again. Twice.

'Come on,' Dang said. 'It was a good try.'

Chase was worried. Not because of the imminent nuclear fallout, but because he was even more fucking turned on now than back at the airfield. He said, 'We can't make it on foot. Let her try. She's our only chance.'

Hawks held herself together long enough to suppress a smile. Then she continued. 'This is Alpha Team, requesting immediate evac.'

Chase entered the room fully. 'Go on, Hawks. One more try.'

She made a small adjustment to a dial. 'This is Alpha Team requesting immediate evac, copy?'

A long pause. All watched the radio.

Chase watched Hawks.

The radio crackled to life. 'Copy, Alpha Team. Co-ordinates?'

Chase whooped. 'Hawksy-girl, you are one beautiful human being!'

56

The team huddled at the tree line as the Black Hawk descended, rotors roaring, snow blasted by the down-draft. Dang sheltered the terrified Desiree. Thompson sprinted from cover, keeping low, and helped his friends in one at a time. Once he was inside with them, Thompson pulled on a headset.

The pilot asked, 'What the hell happened to you guys? World War Three break out in the half-hour you were gone?'

Half-hour...

All lost their whites, their packs, most carried an injury of some kind and, shit, Dang literally looked five years older. Plus, half the team was missing, which is never a good sign.

Thompson said, 'You got ten minutes to get us at least five miles away.'

'What happens in ten minutes?' said the pilot.

'Nuke,' Chase said simply into his own headset. 'Now can we get the proverbial fuck out of here?'

The chopper ascended, the full moon in a clear sky giving a panoramic view of the mountain range. The helicopter banked, dropped its nose, and the engines roared as it accelerated south.

They sped over flat mountain pass that served as both the chopper's staging area and the German airfield, the land upon which they did battle only hours ago, but a long-time forgotten about; a blip in a much wider conflict that would appear in no history books. Thompson mapped the lines and gullies over the terrain, contours he knew to be roads, and finally, as Desiree clearly recognized it too, the open land that was once La Bastion. A ghost town now, with a church spire the only clear structure. Trees had grown through much of the space, although a wide piazza was clearly delineated near the middle; the town square, where Bar du Pont lay empty for many, many years.

Thompson noticed Chase's gaze lingering on Hawks. Chase said, 'Good job back there, Hawkson.'

Thompson was about to add his thanks to her when a rush of air buffeted the Black Hawk. He shouted, '*Cover your eyes!*'

They all brought arms up to their faces, as a huge flash filled the chopper's belly. A terrific bang followed, and when the bright light subsided, the soldiers and civilians all risked a look.

The promised mushroom cloud roiled high into the sky, a thick billowing stem topped by clouds of radi-fuckin'-ation, spreading wider with every second, and would shortly blanket this pristine landscape. No one would set foot here again for about twenty years.

57

Oxford, United Kingdom, 2015

Alpha Team's Humvee pulled up General Santarelli's Oxford driveway, including Hawks—now officially on loan from the Swiss government—and Desiree, who was creating a Facebook account on her new iPhone. A newly-appointed guard flagged them down. Dang opened the door, wondering if anything at all had really changed over the years since they left 1945. He worried that maybe their memories were compromised, or that perhaps first time round, the Nazis *did* win the war, and their actions altered the natural order of things. He only worried about those matters occasionally, though; he lost no sleep about defeating the Third Reich, whether it was the original scenario or not.

It was five days since they got back, giving them plenty of time to chat this through, and although he still sometimes forgot the odd word of English, his French accent was gone. It occasionally sprang back to life, if he spent a few hours with Desiree conversing in French, but he banished it as best he could, especially during the interrogations that went round and round, back and forth, swapping out personnel to ask the same questions in a slightly different way. They grilled them all separately for another twelve hours after the initial reports, but in the end, Col. Johnson freed them. He didn't seem remotely fazed by the story, even if the other interrogators did, leading Dang to believe he and the general may have colluded all along.

Some viewed Desiree as some sort of alien creature and advised the colonel to keep her in isolation, but he said she was a French national, so they had no reason to hold her. Technically, she would be considered an illegal in America, but with the EU's open borders she was able to travel to the UK with ease. Her lack of a passport was a slight issue, but the French embassy issued her a temporary one in a name Col. Johnson researched on the computer, then vouched for her personally.

The whole affair was now classified above top secret, and the media was only aware of an accident involving nuclear material, one that sparked the usual wave of protests, but not something Alpha Team needed to worry about.

Dang said to the guard, 'We don't have an appointment, but we have to talk to—'

The guard, a Marine, cut him off. 'General Santarelli is expecting you.'

The team entered the cavernous drawing room en-masse, to find the man they thought of before as 'the general,' sat at the piano, coaching Lily as she played a tune Dang sort of recognized.

As they approached, all noted large photos of a youthful General/Santa—with Kennedy, Aldrin, Reagan, Gorbachev. The younger he was in the photo, the more he resembled 'their' Santa.

He is our Santa, Dang thought. *He always was.*

Chase in particular found that hard to accept, feeling duped by his best friend for all these years. But as Dang explained the concept of destiny, of fate, of Santa carrying the weight of the future of the world on his shoulders, he begrudgingly accepted it was the right thing to do. The *only* thing to do.

Old Santa remained focused on the piano, even though they'd made no secret of their presence.

Chase said, 'Santa?'

Lily stopped playing. 'Hi, Uncle Chase. Where's daddy?'

The general stood and positioned Lily on the seat. He said, 'One minute, angel.'

She continued playing, the naïveté of childhood keeping her ignorant for at least a few minutes longer. She believed her daddy was indestructible, after all.

As he led Alpha team away, the general, their old friend, said, 'I've been dreading this day for seventy years.'

'So you were Santa the whole time?' Chase said.

The general nodded. 'Sorry.' He gazed back at Lily. 'Waited sixty-four years to meet her again. Tried to make the world better for her, but... I couldn't. Some things really are... fixed.'

Hawks said, 'You just *became* Anthony?'

'I buried him and Mac, burned the other bodies, then destroyed every scrap of future technology you left behind, and made my way into France on foot. The military found me disoriented, and I faked what they called shell-shock for a while... PTSD... I assumed his identity, which was easier back then as long as I didn't meet anyone he knew. The scar helped. There was so much to deal with, no one cared that I grew six inches and looked six years older than my file said. Just wrote it off as an admin error. I spent my time building up knowledge of the era, and went home.'

'What about his folks?' Thompson said.

'Dead already.'

'His fiancée's parents?' Chase said.

'They disapproved of the relationship, and Anthony had never met Sarah's folks so that was the easiest part. Raising

Anthony's son with no grandparents? Not so easy.' The ninety-something-year-old Santa shrugged. 'But I dug in, powered through, and because I had a decent memory of the names of successful firms in the future, I ... lived long.' He addressed Dang directly. 'And prospered.'

Dang grinned. 'What did you mean by "dreading this moment"?'

General Santarelli regarded Lily. The team did too, and they all got it at once. The general held out his hand. Dang returned the dog tags Santa gave him in 1945. Then the old man walked away from them. His traipse back to the little girl almost lasted longer than any of them could bare, his advanced years now weighing on him. Out of earshot, he pulled up a chair and lowered himself close to his daughter/great-granddaughter.

Without anyone hearing, he conveyed the news that her father was not some indestructible superhero after all, and he would not be coming home this time. He fastened the dog tags around her neck. She burst into tears, and buried her face in her greatpa's shoulder, hugging him tight. Her body wracked with sobs.

And the old man embraced her, unable to keep from crying himself.

She'll know the truth one day, Dang thought. *I promise.*

Out in the sprawling gardens, the team strolled, drinking coffee and beer. The general joined them, having put Lily to bed with a children's medicine that calmed her down enough to sleep a little while. It would be unfair to stay away from her too long. Whiskey in hand, he said, 'Her mom's flying in today. She's upset. Terrified for Lily. She adored Santa so much.'

'You,' Dang said. 'She adored *you*.'

'Well, I gotta tell my son soon too. I'll do it face-to-face though.'

Chase said, 'Hang on, isn't that your dad?'

'Technically, yes,' the general said. 'Biologically. But you get a perspective over the years. I raised him, he's my son.' They walked a little more, the sunlight welcome relief after all that damn snow. The general asked, 'There a memorial for Jacobs and Mac? And me, I guess?'

'Thursday,' Thompson said.

'Thank you,' Desiree said. 'For all you did.'

The general patted her firmly on the arm, a real old-man gesture. It was still so weird thinking Santa got old so quick.

He said, 'So when are you heading back out there?'

'Where?' Chase said.

'Last couple of days will have been a tough debriefing, right?'

'Like getting ass-fucked by paperwork.'

Dang said, 'We had to sign stuff that puts us in jail if we go public with anything in our reports.'

The general's lack of expression suggested he already knew that. 'So you probably haven't had a chance to think about it yet. Nick. Dr. Lear. Where is he?'

'The doc?' Chase said. 'Dunno. Assumed he'd be out sky-diving or somethin'.'

'What made the crystal so weird? So fascinating to the Nazis?'

Blank looks for a moment, then Dang said, 'That they couldn't destroy it.'

Chase echoed him: 'Couldn't fuckin' destroy it.'

Hawks said, 'No matter how much energy passed through.'

'So it is still there?' Desiree said. 'Near my town?'

The general chugged back the last of his whiskey. 'I'm going back to my house now.'

'Wait,' Chase said. 'That's it?'

'You're leaving us?' Dang said.

'Don't worry,' Santa replied. 'I'll see you all again. Soon.'

And General Santarelli walked away, leaving them sipping their drinks, confused as hell.

Epilogue

The Juras Mountains – one month later

Instead of a summer alpine panorama, a nuclear landscape pervades. Mountains stand tall, many deformed and crooked, trees flattened and burned black. A gash rides through one section, before branching off into tributaries, reaching out like tendrils across the rocks and soil.

A military helicopter roars into view, armored and sealed, and no country willing to add its flag to the body. It lands, swirling the atomized dust and snow and ash.

A tall man climbs out of the chopper wrapped in a thermal radiation suit, a US flag on his arm. Two similarly-dressed men flank him, each with EU insignia, both equipped with heavy-duty machine guns, and large-caliber sidearms.

The tall man jogs to a tent, billowing in the downdraft, his granite-hard, no-nonsense face visible through the helmet's mask. This man is Colonel Johnson.

From within the tent, a shorter man in a radiation suit emerges, holding a metal box the size of a football.

Johnson says, 'You have it? You found it?'

The short man looks up. He opens the box, revealing a dull crystal. He says, 'Yes, Colonel. I have it. And as I predicted, it is completely intact.'

'Good. I want it in the lab ASAP. Dr. Lear, you've just been promoted.'

The four men jog back to the helicopter and climb in. It

takes off, snow and ash swirling, and roars away into the sky, leaving the ruined landscape in silence once again.

A note from the authors

Antony and Joe just want to say a huge thank you for buying this book. If you've made it this far, they hope they are not being too presumptuous in assuming you enjoyed it enough to not put it down. This also makes them hope you won't mind me asking you ever-so-nicely to leave a review.

Reviews are the lifeblood of up-and-coming authors, and positive feedback on Amazon, Kobo, Apple, B&N, or wherever you bought it, can mean the difference between an undecided reader hitting 'buy' and moving on to the next writer. If you have time, they would be truly grateful for an endorsement, no matter how brief.

Once again, thank you for buying this book – it really does make the authors happy to think they brought even a small amount of pleasure to a stranger through their words.

About the Authors

Antony Davies grew up in Leeds, West Yorkshire. In high school his ambition was to be a writer of horror novels, although in adult life he became an avid fan of crime fiction. After a long stint in an unsatisfying job, he attended the University of Leeds where he attained a degree in creative writing. He now writes novels under the name "A. D. Davies", and aspires to one day write for the silver screen as well. He lives in Staffordshire, UK, with his wife and two children.

Joe Dinicola is an aspiring screenwriter living in New Jersey with his wife and child. His interest in action and science fiction started at a young age. Some of his earliest memories are watching movies starring Arnold Schwarzenegger, and the *Star Wars* and the *Indiana Jones* franchises. He takes a lot of these influences and applies them to his writing with a modern day appeal. He has taken on a new venture into novel writing; which is equally rewarding and is looking forward to expanding his collection of work.

The Dead and the Missing

A missing girl…

   An international underworld…

      A PI who will not quit…

Two years ago, Adam Park was a private investigator at the top of his game, when a bitter ethical battle with his partners sent him into a semi-retirement of surfing and travel around his native Britain. But when his former mentor's niece goes missing, Adam's sabbatical comes to an abrupt end.

Returning to face his former colleagues, Adam learns that not only is the young woman dating a violent ex-con, but prior to disappearing, the pair ripped off a local criminal on the rise, and fled the country. Now this dangerous individual is demanding revenge.

Using cutting-edge technology, Adam tracks the couple through the Parisian underground and onward to dangerously exotic locales, where he will confront a ruthless international network that trades human lives like a business commodity.

To return the girl safely, protect the ones he loves, and save his own skin, Adam will need to burn down his concepts of right and wrong; the only path to survival is through the darkest recesses of his soul.

His First His Second

Meet Detective Sergeant Alicia Friend. She's nice. Too nice to be a police officer, if she's honest.

She is also one of the most respected criminal analysts in the country, and finds herself in a cold northern town assigned to Donald Murphy's team, investigating the kidnap-murders of two young women—both strikingly similar in appearance. Now a third has been taken, and they have less than a week to chip away the secrets of a high-society family, and uncover the killer's objective.

But Richard—the father of the latest victim—believes the police are not moving quickly enough, so launches a parallel investigation, utilising skills honed in a dark past that is about to catch up with him.

As Richard's secret actions hinder the police, Alicia remains in contact with him, and even starts to fall for his charms, forcing her into choices that will impact the rest of her life.

In Black In White

A. D. DAVIES

Meet Detective Sergeant Alicia Friend: cop, analyst, cutie-pie. She acknowledges she is an irritating person to have around at first but, when given a chance, all her colleagues fall in love with her. She can't explain it, but it's how she works, how she gets her best results.

And it is exactly how she must work when a British diplomat is murdered on US soil, and the UK Ambassador orders her to observe the FBI's investigation.

Soon, the murders expand to encompass a wider victim profile, each confessing their politically-motivated lies on camera, and Alicia shows why her superiors overlook her quirks, and consider her one of the best minds in her field.

Drafting in her old partner, Alicia imposes her personality on the investigation, and expands the focus from a politically-charged arena to the madness of a psychopath who cannot seem to stop.

Three Years Dead

When a good man…
Becomes a bad cop…
But can't remember why.

Following an attempt on his life, Detective Sergeant Martin Money wakes from a week-long coma with no memory of the previous three years. He quickly learns that corrupt practices got him demoted, violence caused his wife to divorce him, and his vices and anger drove his friends away one by one. On top of this, the West Yorkshire Police do not seem to care who tried to kill him, and he is offered a generous pay-out to retire.

But with a final lifeline offered by a former student of his, Martin takes up the case of a missing male prostitute, an investigation that skirts both their worlds, forcing him back into the run-down estates awash with narcotics, violence, and sex, temptations he must resist if he is to resume his life as the good man he remembers himself to be.

To stay out of jail, to punish whoever tried to kill him, and to earn his redemption, Martin attempts to unravel the circumstances of his assault, and—more importantly—establish why everyone from his past, his former friends, and his new acquaintances, appear to be lying at every turn.